Kay Coussens

COW DUST TIME

ONE

There's a blue scream slicing through the dark rain, and footsteps running up the stone steps. The door is open, wide as a mouth, no need for the men to waste time ringing.

A grim man and a grey-faced woman come out of the house and walk like stick people towards the ambulance, which waits throbbing and spewing out a blinking carousel of orange light onto the shining pavement. With arms that are stiff as wood, she is gripping a small girl to her breast. He is patting his pockets and checking his keys.

Doors bang and slam and the scream leaps up again without warning, scattering cats and bicycles and people coming home late, waking the baby sleeping inside the house and making him cry.

The sound fades and is gone in seconds, leaving space for a deep silence to roll back in.

TWO

Sophia crouches down and peers through one of the clear panes in the frosted glass front door.

"For God's Sake Soph, if you're looking for the taxi, just open the fucking door. You look like a spy."

She freezes, digging her nails into the carpet while a tingle runs down her back on spider legs. Uncurling slowly, she looks up, whispering hoarsely at his heaving chest.

"I'm *trying* not to make a noise, George. It's not even six o'clock yet. And I don't want anyone to see us leaving the house. Burglars look out for people going on holiday. They say so on *Crimewatch* all the time."

Sophia rarely looks George in the eye. Arguments lie in wait for them like feral cats.

"I don't know why you watch that bloody rubbish."

He makes a noise halfway between a snort and a grunt as he swings the bulging case out to the side and on to the hall floor.

"There's nowhere *near* as much crime going on as people think there is. It's all media sensationalism. It just a selling game."

"*George,* watch what you're doing. You've torn the wallpaper now."

"Oh God. Sorry. *Sorry*"

It has only just been decorated. The walls are sunflower yellow, and the woodwork a bold fuchsia, bright against the oatmeal carpet, and dark oak telephone table. She hasn't even had time to enjoy it properly yet. Sophia bites her bottom lip, and George looks at her in alarm while he fingers the deep scar, trying to press the paper back into the wall.

"I'll stick it down, don't worry Soph. You won't even be able to tell. I'll do it now before we go. Where's the glue?"

She doesn't reply.

The kettle begins to whistle and the microwave dings as he shouts from the kitchen;

"If your case wasn't so *bloody* heavy, that wouldn't have happened. British Airways still have a baggage limit, you know. And shouldn't Gabe be up? Isn't Lucian coming to stay while we're away?"

Damn. She had forgotten about Gabe's friend. George has equalised.

She runs back upstairs with her fists clenched, and crashes into Gabe's room. He turns over in bed and presses his face more firmly into the duvet, while she stands and watches him wake up.

His thick, dark brown hair, in need of washing, sprawls across the red and yellow pillow. She can smell it. Why had she never got around to replacing the Simpsons sheets he'd begged her for when he was ten years old? He's still curled up with Bart and Homer. How could she have ignored it? It was such a small thing for her to change.

The early sunlight is feathering his long eyelashes, making them quiver. At nineteen,
he is still beautiful in spite of the dark shadows under his eyes. When Gabe was small, women of all ages and races came cooing round his pushchair, offering him sweets or biscuits, as if he were an exotic baby animal. His face is as smooth as ice cream.

Without thinking, she snuggles her face into the warm dip between his shoulder and his neck, half expecting to hear the ghost of a baby laugh.

"*Fuck Off, Mum*! What do you think you're doing?"

He throws out an arm and jerks upright, wide-awake and staring, his blue eyes flat and hard as stones.

"Gabe!"

She takes a step backwards ,as if the power of his curse has propelled her out of his room and his glare melts into the anxious look she recognises.

"*Sorry,* Mum. I really didn't mean that. Sorry. Jesus."

"Oh. I shouldn't have surprised you. It's OK. But don't swear at me. That's not OK."

Her voice is shaking, and she clears her throat to cover it.

"I was half asleep, that's all."

Gabe holds out his arms and she hugs him to her, but George is on the stairs now and they break apart, like guilty lovers.

"Cheering your mother up, Gabe? Did she tell you about the wallpaper?"

"No?"

"Look, never mind about the bl…about the wallpaper. It's *OK.* I'm *not* upset."

George looks dubious. Sophia tries to look out of the window without moving her head, so he won't notice and make another sarcastic comment. The taxi might be waiting, but she is not going to open the door before they're ready to leave, no matter what he says. *Crimewatch* doesn't lie.

Across the road two pigeons are bobbing, necks entwined, on Amelia's roof. They are pecking at each other's beaks with soft clacking sounds as if they're kissing. Maybe they're only fighting over food.

"OK, so…" she claps her hands, and then regrets it. George mocks her for being a teacher. He calls her *Miss Jean Brody* in a high pitched Scottish accent. She could call him names too. Mussolini, or Pinochet. She's not as gentle as she used to be. She is developing hard skin, like a foot in a pinching shoe.

"Gabe, don't forget Lucian. You'll have to make up a bed for him. And please *don't* forget to water the garden before you and Lucian leave. It's dry as dust. All the plants will die if you do. George, will you lock the windows?"

She doesn't trust Gabe to do it. It'll be a miracle if he remembers to shut the front door. Oh God.

"Yes Miss."

"Shut *up* George."

Gabe sighs and swings his legs over the side of the bed, tossing

6

aside the cover with one fist wrapped around Marge's yellow neck, his knuckles white against his tanned skin. Sophia had cut out ads for temporary jobs at the beginning of the summer vacation and left them on his desk, but he'd spent three months sitting in the garden.

George says if he wants to be poor it's his funeral.

She runs a hand through her hair and looks around. It's hot already here and it'll be even hotter in Spain. She'd rather go somewhere cool, like Finland, or Alaska. She'd sit under freezing waterfalls and rub her face in snow and play with other women like her trying to keep cool. They'd roll around together like whales, she thinks, or eels. Middle- aged women are either stout or skinny, as if their true natures burst through finally, like bonsai trees reverting to their natural state. She's one of the skinny ones. It doesn't seem safe to eat much any more.

George is downstairs and she knows that in a minute he will ask her where the keys to the windows are, although they've been kept in the cutlery drawer for more than twenty years.

"*Kitchen. In with the spoons,*" she shouts, weary of the game, wanting to wrong foot him.

"*What are they doing in there?*"

She's looking in the bedroom, trying to find her paints, and she doesn't reply. She might start to paint again in Spain. She'd given up when Gabe was little, her days too full of mothering and confusion. When he'd asked to play with Mummy's pretty colours, she'd hissed: "*No you can't*", like one of his selfish little friends. He'd started to cry, and she made herself play his favourite game all afternoon, as a penance. There had to be two dogs snapping and snarling at each other until one cried and ran away. Gabe had called it the '*grrrrr* game'. It was a typical little boy's game he'd invented, dog eat dog. They're not the same as little girls, not at all.

She'd played different games with Grace. Games like tea parties, and cooking. She hadn't minded sharing her paints in those days. They used to sit together at the big pine table she and George had bought in the green spring days of their marriage, when they'd imagined a happy crowd of children waiting in the wings. There is still a fleck of yellow paint on one of the legs, left by Graces' fingers. Imagine paint – a spec of *paint* !- lasted longer than she did. The table will outlive all of them.

Fingering the memory like a dressed wound, it still hurts. Grace turned from a soft toddler into a crown of thorns after she died. Long, savage thorns. The kind that sprout from orange- berried bronze hedges, planted to keep burglars out.

Sophia gives up rummaging in the cupboard and sits down at her dressing- table. She frowns at the photograph which rises like a breakwater from a clutter of glass bottles, plastic pots, a pair of pearl earrings, a rhinestone bangle, three pens, two letters, sunglasses and a passport. It has a heavy silver frame with finely wrought leaves and flowers, tarnished now from lack of polish. Grace is there, nestled on Sophia's lap, sleepily holding her lamb and smiling at the camera, as if she has all the time in the world to grow up. Sophia snatches it up and shoves it deep into her handbag like a shop- lifter in a supermarket. She always takes it on holiday.

"Mum, I've taken the rubbish out. OK?"

Gabe still thinks he is the cherub lolling there, lord of the lap.

"OK, thank you darling. Well done."

She has a fierce and desperate love for Gabe, like a child's love for transient things, snowmen, or streamers, or bright balloons. At the time, she told people she thought it was cruel to burden their second child with the tragedy of a sister he hardly knew, and she'd decided it was kinder to never speak of her at all. Deep down, she knows that she was terrified to say their names in the same breath in case the bored and savage gods were listening, and snatched Gabe too, for their amusement.

"Buttering Mum up, are you Gabe?"

She hears George's mocking laugh from the hall.

"Shut up, Dad."

She knows Gabe's shoulders are drooping. He seems quieter than ever, these days. Sometimes she forgets he's in the house at all.

"He's being helpful actually George. If you remembered the rubbish occasionally, we wouldn't have to. We haven't forgotten last years plague of flies yet, have we Gabe?"

She peers over the banister, trying to see his face.

"Taxi's here. Hurry *up* Soph."

George isn't listening to her, and the door is wide open. She watches him wind milling his arms, trying to attract the attention of the surly driver who has overshot the house and doesn't care enough to reverse.

Across the road, Amelia is taking in her milk.

"Sophia! George! Have a lovely holiday. Bye- bye! See you in three weeks!"

Amelia's voice is husky and soft. George says talking to her is like having a cat wrap itself around your knees; she makes his skin creep.

"You'll have to do without me for a month, Amelia, I'm afraid. I'm going off to a conference as soon as we get back."

"What an action packed August for you George. And what will you be discussing this time? Installing a heated swimming pool for those precious gypsies of yours? Or landscaping the site at our expense?"

"We're considering a casino, Amelia. Possibly a Caesar's Palace where they can throw away all the money they get from defrauding the benefit system and robbing the houses of the gainfully employed."

"It wouldn't surprise me at all, George. You social workers are so *naive.*"

"Thank goodness there are people like you who are wiser than us, Amelia. Make sure you polish up your shotgun, ready for them while we're away. Careful though. If you kill one of our clients, we won't be running any campaigns to spring you from Holloway. You'll have to rely on the *Daily Mail*, Brown Owl."

She thinks he is flirting with her, and snorts with laughter, covering her mouth with one hand and reaching into the pocket of her magenta dressing gown with the other.

Amelia is a woman unable to spar. She keeps a nail file to hand on the grounds that any conversation that goes on for longer than five minutes is a manicure opportunity. George has timed her. Since her last divorce she has poured her passion into the Brownie pack, a pretty crowd of fresh-faced little girls, who do knots and semaphore and call themselves sprites and pixies. The last little girl who joined only stayed two weeks. Amelia said it was such a shame she didn't feel comfortable. She didn't hear one of the sprites tell her that black can't be brown, and she should fuck off back to Africa.

"George, if I had my way they'd *all* be moved right away from Heronmarsh. That place is an absolute disgrace."

She turns to the driver, who has reluctantly left his cab. He is nodding, his mouth turned down like a thin piece of wire.

"Oh come on, Amelia. You just want the site for camping, don't you? Marshmallows and Kumbaya? That *place* is home to a lot of people. They have nowhere else to live."

She looks up at him from under her Maybelline curtains and her swags of glossed auburn hair.

"Well, they're not *supposed* to have a home, are they? Gypsies are supposed to ramble and rove. I thought that was the whole point."

Sophia opens her mouth to speak, but George cuts across her with an impatient

"Let's just go," and opens the cab door as if he were her parent. Amelia looks satisfied. As far as she is concerned, the last word always wins the argument.

The driver heaves the cases into the boot, grimacing at the weight of Sophia's.

"Not guilty," says George, and the men exchange a look but Sophia doesn't notice. She is looking back at Gabe, who is standing in the doorway, gazing down the road, not quite seeing them off. When she tries to talk to him these days, he maintains a cerebral distance, like a doctor, or a post office clerk. She runs back to give him an awkward hug, holding her body away from him this time, but he grabs her and squeezes so hard, she nearly squeals.

As the cab pulls away, she glances at the house again, but Gabe has gone in now and closed the door. Will he remember to water the garden? Her heart shivers suddenly, as if it is scared, and she re-arranges her redundant hands on her lap, sliding them between her thighs in a downward prayer.

"All set Soph?" George turns round and grins. "We'll be there by about four with a bit of luck."

He'll lie in the sun and roast for three weeks. She doesn't do that any more. It isn't safe. Not even with factor thirty.

They drive quickly through the redbrick town, with its good end and bad end, and new shopping mall, whose concrete and iron structure is already turning green and brown, as if no one realised it would be left out in the rain. The grubby station is busy, early commuters already hurrying to breakfast meetings in the City. Just before the motorway, they pass the semi-rural scrubby ground where the caravans are.

"*Oh no!*"

"*What?*" George is alarmed, and the driver slows.

"Just my paints. I thought I'd do some painting. Oh damn." No one replies and the driver puts his foot down as he heads for the M25. Sophia closes her eyes in the indifferent silence and tells herself it doesn't matter. Not really.

THREE

"I'm tired of being an adult," says Sophia, reaching for the lemon linen shirt that is waving from the rusted hook of a blue and white striped sun umbrella.

"What?"

George is lying on a slatted wooden sun bed, legs and arms splayed like a pinned frog, his hands and feet touching the chopped coarse grass. George isn't a standard size.

Sophia is watching a little girl in a frilly white bikini, swimming in small circles and singing to herself under the bright sky. Her song is just words strung together like beads - *...roses... yellow flowers... black cat...splash... roses...yellow flowers...black cat...splosh....*

"It's just - well, look at her. The way she's trickling water through her fingers while she's swimming and kicking her legs. She's not worried about doing proper strokes or singing a proper song. She's so – together, and peaceful. Look."

"Meaning *what* exactly, Soph? That you're not happy?"

George looks away and shuts his eyes against the boiling sun. His face has a closed sign up.

Sophia has buttoned her sleeves, and is rubbing thick white lotion on her legs.

"You should cover up at midday. *No*, I just meant...George, don't you ever wish you could go back? To when everything was simple?"

"No."

She puts on her sunglasses.

"End of conversation?"

George mutters through taut lips, "I'm on holiday, Soph. Don't *start*. You've got the whole school holidays off like all your jammy mates."

12

The little girl is pulling herself out of the pool on thin brown arms, and shaking her hair. Glittering drops fly out and are gone, as she runs across the grass like a baby gazelle, and hurdles an over stuffed red and yellow flowerbed.

"Jammy? Teachers? You must be…oh, never mind, she's gone now. Everyone's going in. Lunch?"

"Good. Be more peaceful. You go on."

Sophia pulls on her shorts, and wanders towards the pink and white tiled steps that lead to their apartment.

It's light and airy, and she'd woken that morning with a light and airy feeling herself, as if the Spanish breeze were blowing right through her, parting her bones and cells and ruffling up her blood. She'd pushed back the shutters, and stepped out on to the wooden balcony while George was still asleep. The sun was hovering behind the mountains, and everywhere the light was pale blue. Her nose was filled with the scent of damp earth and rosemary and pine, and she'd stretched out a hand and picked a flower from among the glossy dark green leaves of a tall hibiscus, patched all over with scarlet. She'd smiled at the darker red tongue with its hard round tip poking priapically from the hidden centre of the bloom. She'd stuck it into her hair, and raised an arm above her head, turning slowly on one foot, while she pointed the other. Her bare feet stamped silently on the warm wood.

"Ole, Senora! Que elegancia!"

The gardener had started work and laughed up at her, his dark eyes coating her legs and hips and she stopped, thrown off.

She'd gone inside to put on coffee, and then she made the mistake, the effects of which are still apparent in George's surly attitude by the pool. She should never have taken the flower from her hair and laid it on his belly while he was waking up. He'd taken it as a taunt.

"There's always hostility in your humour, Sophia."

She'd flared up then of course, and the day curdled before it was even opened and exposed to air.

When he comes up for lunch, he ignores the apologetic egg and tomato baguette she has set out with olives and crisps, and sits in front of the television with a bottle of San Miguel, and she knows she is not pardoned.

FOUR

The pardon was several silent days in coming, but by the time they got home the skirmish was forgotten, or so it seemed. Perhaps it was only filed away, under 'pending.' The house hadn't been ransacked, although when Sophia walked in and saw the mess that Gabe had left behind, for a few startled moments she wasn't quite sure. How could anybody leave a house without doing the washing up? George said that was how all students behave, and particularly Art students. He said it with a great deal of authority, in the same tone of voice he might have used to describe the migratory habits of the European stork. He left the next day for his conference in an important flurry of phone calls and photocopying, and Sophia had to tackle the red wine stains on the living room carpet and the patio thick with cigarette stubs by herself.

At ten, she rang her oldest friend Phyll, desperate for friendly conversation, and arranged to meet her in town for lunch.

'*Ex*-ercise, *ex*-orcise, *ex*-ercise, *ex*-orcise.' she is muttering to herself, as she searches for a pair of shoes from among the jumble under the bed. She has to do it by touch, feeling around in the dark. George bought her a shoe rack once, sick of the shoe chaos, the whole shoe performance. It hasn't helped though.; the shoes defy order. They jump down from the bars and flee back under the bed, like mice.

She pulls out a matching pair at last and smiles, a triumphant child at a lucky dip. Her spirits rise and she dances around the room, before collapsing back onto the bed. It's too damned hot to dance. There she sits, mistress of all her shoes, contemplating her feet.

Exercism! She could become a fitness guru and that could be her special angle. She'll make a video with a furious woman on the front in a leopard skin leotard, screaming as cartoon devils burst out of her head and vanish. On the back, there'll be an 'after' picture, the harpy now serene in a lilac lace dress. She'll make a million pounds, give up being an Art teacher, and retire somewhere by herself. She could leave George, he probably wouldn't mind, she could buy a bungalow and finally sort out her shoes.

These red leather sandals are hardly worn. She bought them years ago in Italy. She still believed they could be happy then, she and George, with Gabe to fill the Grace shaped hole in their life, if they didn't think too much, or talk to each other for too long. They'd rented in a farmhouse in Tuscany, a year after Grace had died. It over-looked flower filled fields that led down to the shining turquoise sea and she and George made gentle love there in the garden, underneath the warm dark star blanket, while Gabe slept innocently inside. It didn't last, that fragile peace, that tentative intimacy.

Sophia opens her eyes. Forgive me father for I have sinned. Finding happy thoughts, fingering them furtively. When she and George got home, liberated from the immediate tyranny of early grief, de-mob happy for a while, they still lost each other in the crowd.

She could paste mug shots of him on the fridge door and the bathroom mirror: *Do You Recognise This Man? Last seen in Italy in the mid- nineties. George Please Get In Touch With Your Wife.*

Sophia is pulling on the red shoes, and looking for her cream linen jacket. The shoes seem too big, and she glares at her feet. Have they shrunk as well, like the rest of her?

By the time she reaches the middle of the precinct, she is sweating, and her feet hurt.

Sophia slows and scuffs the last few yards, disheartened by the sight of Phyll relaxing on the old iron-armed bench, coolly watching passers by through her RayBans. Phyll is always first.

"Soph! Hi! Good holiday? You're not very brown. What's up?"

"Hi. No, not really. George was a pig. And I've got a blister. Bloody shoes. I think my feet are shrinking."

"Really? That's amazing. I didn't think feet did that. Let's have a look."

Sophia sinks down on the bench, and Phyll produces a plaster from her slim leather bag, and gently wraps it around Sophia's toe.

"Thanks, Mum." Sophia shields her face from the sun. "Take me somewhere close for lunch, Phyll. I can't walk another step."

"McDonalds it is then. Shake and fries madam?"

"Don't be stupid. I can make it to the Plough."

"Now you're talking. We can sit in the garden; the fountain's back on. Come on."

The streets are empty and stifling. Once through the pub doors, Phyll moves like an eel across the crowded lounge bar, so swiftly Sophia is left looking around, thinking for a moment that she's lost her.

Phyll always gets the best table. She is sitting next to the fountain, pleased with herself. Single people usually are pleased, thinks Sophia watching her light a cigarette. It's couples that drown in disappointment. She has ordered a bottle of Merlot to drink with the Greek salad and the pub's famous, warm bread.

"You're having wine?"

"Don't worry, Soph. I'm not in court this afternoon. In fact, I think I'll take the rest of the day off."

"Lucky you. I wish I were my own boss. I'm sick of clocks and bells and term times. School starts again next week."

"You could resign, you know."

"I'd have to discuss it with George. He acts as if I should have made an appointment when I try to talk to him about anything important. Do you think I'm a demanding type Phyll?"

Phyll pours the wine. "Actually, you're one of the least demanding people I know, Soph. Good job I'm a solicitor, or I'd never get anything out of you. You're more like one of my shifty little burglars, trying to say as little as possible in case he drops himself in it. Why? Do you think you're demanding?"

"No. Not really." Sophia takes a gulp of the smooth red wine. "Mm. Heaven. George does though. And my mother too."

Phyll gives a wry smile. "Has she been on the phone?"

"Well, I rang her, actually. I was feeling lonely. George is away this week, and Gabe has gone back to Uni. I asked her if she'd like to go shopping with me, and she acted as if I were a whining child."

Phyll is looking at her in mock horror. "*You* rang *her*?"

"Yes, I know. *I know*. It was a mistake."

They chant: '*If You're Feeling Low Give Mum A Bell, She'll Soon Make You Feel Like Fucking Hell*' and the waiter, who has appeared with a wooden bowl of glistening salad and crumbly goat's cheese, hovers disapprovingly. He can't bear this type of middle-aged woman. They remind him of his mother.

"Do you remember my wedding day, Phyll? Your mother was there, weeping in the church, and I was so touched because I hadn't realised she cared about me so much?"

"And she told me later she'd been crying because I was still single and childless and she was frightened she'd never be a grandmother! I was *twenty-four*. You know,
I think it was then I made up my mind not to give her what she wanted."

"Maybe she did you a favour then."

They both glare at the waiter who is making his irritation felt by banging down the plates, and reaching rudely across the table. He retreats swiftly, aware he is into tip-jeopardising country.

Sophia piles salad on to each of their plates, while Phyll cuts bread.

"Do you regret getting married, Soph? Or just getting married to George?"

"Yes. No. I don't know really," says Sophia, chewing baby spinach leaves and black olives, " he seems to have morphed into someone else, like a nephew you haven't seen for ages. Do you wish you had?"

"Yes. No. Don't know." Phyll shrugs.

"I think we should divorce, but I don't have any bones, any

more. I'm like weak tea, or blancmange or- ectoplasm!"

"God, how disgusting, Soph. Pull yourself together, woman."

"Doctor, doctor, I'm a pair of curtains…I've had no luck with men, Phyll, right from the beginning. Did I ever tell you about my very first boyfriend?"

"I thought George *was* the very first boyfriend.. You were so pure at University. I was the old slapper."

Sophia is laughing. That was true. "It was just before I left school. So embarrassing and awful, I probably repressed the whole thing. George thinks he was the first one as well. He was really. Just not technically."

"So who was this teeny Valentino?"

Phyll puts down her fork and picks up her glass of wine, her head on one side. She likes detail. Sophia blurs edges.

"Well, he was a couple of years older than me. His name was Jez. James, really, but everyone called him Jez. He worked as a painter and decorator with his Dad and his fingers always had paint round the sides, stuck in the cracks…"

"And you let those painty fingers wander further than anyone else's? Tell me more."

Sophia is watching the wine in her glass glow as the light catches it. Dark red fire.

"Mmm. I'm not sure why. There was something about him. He was good looking, in spite of the paint and the smell of turpentine. Long, curly dark hair and this really sensitive face…funny, I can see him so *clearly.*"

"You've probably got early onset Alzeimers, that's what happens. The past sneaks up on the present, and shoves it out of the way."

"Stop it. I'm only forty five."

"Well go on then. Stop being coy."

"I'm not. I'm just trying to remember. Jez had this way of concentrating on whatever he was doing- he could be driving, or watching a film, or painting a wall and he'd be completely absorbed in it."

"Was he completely absorbed in you?"

"I suppose he was, before…he didn't really want me to go away. He seemed quite happy staying at home. He didn't talk all that much, really."

"Who needs them flapping their gums, honey?" Phyll is cackling, re-filling their glasses. Sophia laughs more loudly than she intended, and claps a hand over her mouth and nose.

"Well I prattled on, I expect. Perhaps he couldn't get a word in edgeways."

She is never quite comfortable with attention to detail. Her mind soars and darts, making great leaps in a wide arc. George says she's a kite with no strings. She thinks he's a great big barrage balloon full of hot air.

"So he used to slip in lengthways Soph, instead, did he?"

Sophia snorts. Her eyes are watering now, and she grabs for her napkin.

"Shut *up*, Phyll. It was only once, anyway. We were at the pool. It was just before I left home…"

The Lido had been crowded. Every inch of the dry scratchy grass was taken that   afternoon. They lay side by side under a cornflower sky. Jez rubbed lotion on her back. He didn't miss an inch that might have been left exposed. She's probably got him to thank for escaping skin cancer, so far anyway. She can see him sitting cross- legged against a tree in his purple tie- dye T shirt, watching the scene; swimmers leaping like salmon, the beached bodies reddening in the hot August sun.

"You didn't do it at the pool! How brazen!"

"No, no. It was later. At my parents house."

The evening had been so warm they hadn't dressed and left the pool until the evening, and they strolled home holding hands.

"We called into the *Fox and Hounds* for a drink- maybe the cider inflamed his passion!"

"And not yours?"

"I was more curious than passionate, I think, at that age. I resented being the one who was always poked and prodded. It was a long time ago. Not like today."

She and Jez had sat down together on the fat purple sofa, their

20

thighs touching. She didn't get up to offer him a drink or move away, although he felt sticky and too hot so close to her. When he leaned over and kissed her, he slid his tongue right into her mouth and his hands petted and stroked her breasts as if they were kittens.

"Suddenly, I just stuffed my hand down the front of his jeans, and then I was so shocked I nearly screamed!"

Phyll is still laughing. "Sophia Hughes's first encounter with the great male phallus! It sounds like one of those kid's Halloween games- you know, feel the dead man's liver, feel the cooked eyeballs, and it's all cold jelly and hard boiled eggs…"

"Well, this thing felt like nothing on earth to me then, hard as stone, and soft as velvet at the same time…! It was such a shock."

"Like touching a snake when you expect it to be cold and slimy…?"

"Exactly. I couldn't put it down…"

"You were so *innocent* Soph! I was discovering blow jobs when I was eighteen…"

Her touch must have felt like a signal to him. Green light time, baby. Christmas Day. She let him pull up her skirt and lie on top of her, his knee parting her legs and burrowing like a determined mole between her own. She would have like to stop for a moment. Come up for air. She craned her neck forwards from the sofa and raised her head, fear prickling in her belly. She was about to tell him to stop but then there was sharpness inside her, and she gasped, jerking her hips backwards to get away from him. It felt like the iodine her mother dabbed on an open cut. He'd done it.

Phyll has stopped laughing. "You look terrible sweetheart. What happened with him?"

"Well, nothing much, just stupid teenage sex, but the worst thing was…Jez never got in touch with me again after that. Ever. Never phoned, or anything. I was so upset. I felt as if I wasn't supposed to have let him have what he wanted after all. I couldn't even feel generous. It all seemed so complicated. What was I supposed to do?"

"Men are very odd. They don't know what they want themselves, half the time. We're supposed to read their minds like Mummy did, and when we can't they punish us for it. I think we take them entirely too seriously myself."

Sophia drains her glass. "I think that was when I decided that all I really wanted was a baby."

"Someone less complicated to love?"

"Maybe that was it. Phyll, do you think I just used George? Was I being selfish when I had Grace?"

"Look, you couldn't have possibly known she... Just because that little creep Jez, or whatever his name was behaved like an arsehole, doesn't mean there's anything wrong with you. Grow up."

Phyll is using her professional tone. The one she uses with the dead-eyed women who sit in her office.

"*Thank* you, Ms Legal Eagle."

Phyll looks hurt, and Sophia is sorry. Her skin seems thinner than it used to be. Perhaps it's shrinking, like her feet. She makes an effort to lighten the atmosphere. Phyll likes to eat and she doesn't want to spoil her lunch.

"Come on, let's have another bottle of this, and some of that chocolate cake with the orange bits in. We can grow old and fat together. Eat, drink, be merry, my friend...."

Phyll raises her glass, her long, manicured fingers curled around the stem, "for tomorrow we get high blood pressure, and increased risk of stroke, osteoporosis and breast cancer."

"Well, let's hope it's not quite tomorrow. I haven't pruned the roses yet, and you promised you'd cook dinner for me sometime this week."

Phyll raises a hand to summon the cross waiter, who comes quickly, trying to regain lost ground. Sophia kicks off her shoes under the table, and the afternoon fades pleasantly into early evening, when the office workers begin to drift in for cocktails.

Sophia goes home in a black cab. Relaxing in the back seat, her eyes half closed, she registers the tall figure of an elderly woman with very long white hair, drifting along the verge towards

Heronmarsh. One of George's people, she supposes, the non-travelling travellers, the sort who give Amelia palpitations. She wonders briefly how George is before she dozes off, snoring gently in the hot and dusty air.

FIVE

George is dreaming and moaning in the unfamiliar hotel bed. He is climbing a smooth surface that reaches up for ever into a black star studded canopy. His fingers find spikes. *'It's the crown'* shrieks the Queen from inside the stone, *'don't let go or you'll fall for ever and a day...'*

George's eyes snap open, and he is suddenly wide awake in broad daylight. His chest and back are damp and his heart is racing. He looks over at the travel alarm winking on the bed -side table, letting the dream slide away into the unreachable place in his mind. George doesn't waste his time thinking about dreams, even when they scream at him. He calls them screen savers.

Eight thirty. Oh Christ, he'd meant to set the alarm. Why hasn't Sophia phoned him? She knows he always forgets the alarm. He wants to ring her to tell her he's going to miss breakfast. He knows she's standing there in the kitchen in her long red dressing gown gazing out of the window as she waits for the kettle to boil. She's probably brooding about the state of the broken down fence and blaming him. She's been nagging him about it for long enough.

In the worst of early morning moods, he throws aside the shiny pink duvet. Dare he go into the meeting unshaven? Management don't approve of the unshaven, these days. They reward smooth upturned chins and pleasantly smiling lips. They like Coca-cola faces and like positive plans. They banned grey areas in social services when ideas were turned into packages. Philosophy's too long a word to fit in a box you can tick. It's all Pot Noodle planning now, he complained to Sophia, when they told him he wasn't a team player. He nearly resigned there and then, but she stopped him, as usual. She's such a mouse; no guts at all.

George steps into the shower and turns on the water full-pelt, enjoying the steaming rain pounding his body, easing the aches of the night. It reminds him of his rugby playing days, when Saturday afternoons were spent in a glorious liquid mash of rain and mud and scummy warm water and beer after beer after beer.

Stepping out reluctantly into the unpleasantly coral bathroom, he begins to shave in the speckled rectangular mirror, his impatient fingers pulling and pushing the flesh of his cheeks from left to right, then up, then down.

Sophia used to be there on the sidelines, cheering him on. His mother turned up too, now and again. She liked him better as a man. When he was a small boy, she was always scrubbing at his face with a stiff forefinger shrouded in a white handkerchief. He used to imagine she was rubbing him out, and he'd look in the mirror one day and part of his face would be missing.

Christ! Blood spurts between his fingers. The razor has dug deeply into his skin, just below the silver scar that remembers an old contact with boot studs. He pours a handful of shaving lotion to punish the wound. Eight fifty fucking five now.

He dresses swiftly, scrabbling in his bag for socks, dragging his suit from the plastic hangar in the wardrobe that smells of other men's suits. Suits make a fool out of George, he thinks. Always too short at the wrists and too tight at the waist, he appears to be growing out of them, like Tommy Cooper. He wore hand me downs as a child.

'When are you going to stop growing, Georgie, for goodness sake?'

He always thought he must have been the wrong size, not his clothes. Finding his tie at last he knots it crossly, turning it into a noose. As he picks up his briefcase, he sees that he's ten minutes late already. They can hardly sack him for that, can they? Maybe they can. Everything feels temporary to George these days.

He clicks the room door shut behind him and strides off down the corridor, the echoes of bacon and coffee and toast from the restaurant making his stomach growl. A thin brown woman wearing a green overall, scurries past carrying an enormous bundle of dirty bed linen over her child sized shoulder. George smiles at her, but she doesn't respond. She might disagree with

25

his definition of himself as a socialist, forged in the old days when he and Brendan McFall and the local Socialist Workers Party held meetings in the pub, analysing everything from the beams and the beer to the landlord and the fucking scampi and chips from a Marxist perspective.

He glances through the glass porthole in the door of the conference room, one hand on the handle. They've started without him and Leena is covering. They'll give her his job one day. She's the one with the sexy Roma credibility and the fabulous legs.

She glances towards the door, sensing his presence, like a cat. Leena always unnerves him. She looks without blinking, as if she might spring across the room any minute, and lick you. He wonders briefly what her tongue might feel like and is frowning as he enters the long grey-green room, throwing open the door with an unintended violence that sends it crashing back against the wall. Heads turn and now all the eyes are on him, some anxious, some irritated, some perplexed.

"It's the man himself." Leena laughs. Her laugh is catching, and ripples round the room like a light breeze.

"Afternoon George..."

"It's the Incredible Hulk..."

"Ta da!"

George walks up to the front of the conference room, stooping and apologising, keeping an eye on Leena, who has one foot up on the chair like a principal boy. Her thick hair is caught up in a jewelled comb, and as he gets closer he can see some silver around her temples. He'd like to know how old she is. She moves like a girl, but her strong brown hands are showing blue veins. He decides to look in her file when he gets back to the office. Knowing might bring back a sense of having some authority over her. It irks him that anyone watching would assume she was the manager, and not vice versa, and he almost shouts, "Thanks for starting off, Leena. I'll carry on now, shall I?"

She is balancing lightly on the balls of her feet and her smile mocks him, as if she's read his thoughts.

"Certainly, George. Carry on regardless."

She gestures towards the chair with a wide sweep of her arm, and bows slightly.

He looks at her suspiciously. Is this a shared joke, or a laugh at his expense?

He ruffles his notes and his audience look at him gloomily. They'd rather listen to Leena, if they are going to be forced to consider the gipsies problems for the next hour. George is too serious, and no one else really cares. Gipsies are too complicated to think about. They don't fit in anywhere.

George remembers magic words. *Cost effective…direct action…joined up thinking…education for all….respect agenda…* His talk goes on unchallenged, and largely not listened to and by the end the chiefs are nodding, and George can see the funding carrying on for another year. Sophia will be surprised. She has no faith in him; it still rankles.

"Soph has no faith in me," he complains to Leena over the coffee and biscuits.

Leena is sitting on the edge of a table, swinging her legs, while he stands awkwardly, trying to dip his biscuit into his cup and stop the spoon falling off the saucer at the same time. He is no good at this sort of thing. His hands are too big. Sophia is a cup and saucer person. He likes mugs.

Leena looks up at him, pulling her fingers through her hair, her silver rings glinting through the black waves.

"Why not?"

"What? I don't know. She just doesn't."

"Faith could move mountains I suppose."

"What? Oh shit!"

Now half his Bourbon has fallen into his coffee cup, and is floating there like a sugar coated turd. She laughs. He thinks he might really hate her.

"Don't laugh," he says pettishly, banging his coffee cup down on the table so hard that coffee splashes out of the cup and over her muscular thigh. She meets his eyes head on.

"You can't *control* everything George. Unreliable biscuits, rebellious teaspoons…"

"What are you talking about?"

At least she doesn't seem annoyed about her jeans. Sophia would have been furious.   Perhaps she didn't see. He squints at her thigh; there's a dark patch near the top of her leg.

"There's a particular look you get sometimes, George, like a kid whose building bricks have been knocked down. Do you remember the baked bean can?"

How could he forget? "I was trying to do something useful. That *bloody* site…Those *sodding* toilets..."

Rusting cans and bottles lie beside and around the bins at Heronmarsh. Old pieces of furniture, brown and lumpy, sit sullenly on the grass; debris is everywhere. George had begun his new job determined to create a smart ultra modern caravan site from the muddy, tumbledown shambles it had been for years. His first mistake was neglecting to consult with Leena before he decided to tackle the shit situation. He'd proposed, sweated blood to get the money for, and personally supervised the construction of a solid new toilet block of brick and gleaming porcelain and stainless steel.

"You didn't do your research. You should have asked me what was wanted."

"It was so hard to get money. Finance treated me as if I were crapping all over the site personally."

"Well that's what they're like."

"The toilets were taken to bits, practically overnight."

"You were furious because you couldn't force people to use them. You like authority. You're a bit anal actually."

"Me? Like authority? You must be bloody joking!"

But something had flipped inside him that morning when he'd seen it. They'd stolen the roof -the entire bloody roof- and the taps- and some bastard had sprayed: *Shit House: Keep Out* in red on the pristine white wash. When Leena strolled over, her eyes were twinkling in the chilly morning air.

"Oh dear, George. Collapse of stout toilet."

He'd rounded on her, his voice carrying across the open space.

"What is the matter with your *people*? Do they want to live like bloody *pigs*?"

He'd kicked out savagely at an empty baked bean can, lifting it with his toe. It had stuck on the end of his shoe and he had ended up hopping around trying to kick it away with his other foot. It wouldn't budge and in a blind rage he'd knelt down in the middle of a half-eaten prawn korma to pluck it off. The toe of his nubuck shoe was covered in shiny orange sauce and his trousers stank.

"You were hopping up and down, shouting your head off," Leena says through a mouthful of shortcake biscuit. Not to mention abusing our clients - and me - because somebody knocked over your sandcastle. A pig is a very bad name to call a Romany. You're talking serious insult. You sounded like one of the skinheads from the town."

George can see the gap in her top teeth. His mother used to say that having a gap like that was lucky. She was probably right. Look at Elton John. Leena takes a chocolate digestive and crunches down on it. It doesn't seem to stop her biting.

"Now you're calling me names."

Georges' nostrils are showing white against his skin. How dare she call him racist? He was in the SWP for years and in the Anti Nazi League before she was even born. Probably. He's got to find out how old she is. He needs to know. He is about to stalk away and talk to the men, when he feels her hand on his sleeve.

"I said you sounded like one, I didn't say you are one." Her voice is warm and soft and he hesitates.

"You dragged me off to your grandmother, for a dressing down."

"I dragged you off to clean your trousers."

Leena's grandmother Rose had glared at him, her pale eyes as cold as the day was. She looked like an ancient native chief. 'Geronimo' he thought, half in awe of her. It was in the brown skin and the white hair and the hook of her nose.

"She called me Gorgio George. Racism works both ways, you know."

"She's prejudiced; that's quite different. And you deserved it."

Leena has taken on the hawkish look of her grandmother.

George is silent. He hears a gale of laughter, and looks over his shoulder suspiciously.

One of his colleagues is telling a joke, he wishes he were standing with them.

He had crouched down that day going into Rose's caravan, as if he were entering a cave, expecting to find himself somewhere dirty and dank. He'd opened his mouth to let out the apology he'd already quickly framed, which included the words 'misunderstanding' and if he could get away with it 'misheard', when the light caught his eye taking him off guard. Bouncing and flashing from every wall, polished mirrors reflected bits of him like a multiplex jigsaw. Inside the caravan it was shining and spotlessly clean. It drove the set piece speech from his mind, and he sat down with a more modest sorry, aware of his stinking trousers and orange shoe. There was a smell of lavender in the air.

Leena is still watching him. There are biscuit crumbs by the side of her mouth, and she draws them in with a flick of her tongue. Her lips look glossy. Does she wear lipstick? Soph seems to have given it up. Her lips blend into her face these days, like pudding rice in milk.

"OK, Leena. You win."

"It's not a fight, George."

"I know. That was the day I realised all the crap is actually supposed to be outside at the site. We think we're cleaner people than your people, but then we keep all our shit inside, don't we?"

"Exactly. Tell that to your analyst."

"When hell freezes over. That's when you'll find me in therapy."

The coffee is being cleared away, and people are shuffling reluctantly back to the conference room, extinguishing cigarettes on the way. The laughter has died down, and George begins to shuffle too. A thought strikes him, and he looks back at Leena over his shoulder. She is still sitting on the table watching him.

"Are you into all this self-awareness stuff, Leena?"

That might explain her crackle and fizz. She goes on fire walking weekends. Maybe she's got a life-coach.

"No need." She yawns so widely he can see her back teeth. No fillings there. "I have my grandmother's second sight."

"Yeah, sure."

She laughs and George stretches out a hand to help her jump down from the table, but then takes it back. He doesn't want to touch her.

Rose had caught hold of his hand that day as he was holding it out to offer a humble goodbye. She'd deftly turned it palm upwards, and he'd seen an odd look in her eye as she traced the lines with a cracked forefinger. It could have been tenderness. It looked out of place there on her face, like a summer flower in a winter garden.

"You've had a hard time, Georgie boy," she'd said, and he'd snatched his hand back too quickly to be polite. No-body had called him Georgie since his mother died.

Thank God.

He walks off without waiting for Leena, and goes to sit with the men. Forty. She must be over forty. The thought cheers him up.

SIX

Sophia gets up early out of habit, rather than any keen desire to embrace the day.   She is dragging back the yellow curtains as if they are too heavy for her, and blinking at the sharp morning light spilling impatiently into the living room. She looks for a moment like an uncertain child waiting to cross a busy road without the benefit of stop, look, listen.

Coffee. She needs coffee to kick start her system. She's been dragging her body around this summer like a bag full of vegetables. She shuffles to the front door on flat feet, slippers sliding dispiritedly across the carpet, like the last one home in a ski marathon. Bending down to pick up the milk, she curses silently. She's forgotten to cancel the extra pint. Not that George drinks milk. She is living in a past when she made blancmange and bread and butter pudding and semolina.

There is a corresponding clink from Amelia's house, and Sophia waves. Amelia is wearing a lilac gown with a marabou hem that brushes her painted toes. She is staring at the two pints in her hands, as if they were something other than milk.

"Would you believe it Sophia? Just look at this!"

"What's the matter?"

"Three. I ordered three. It's Wednesday. I make custard on Wednesdays. Those wretched tinkers have stolen one again."

She throws an accusing look at Sophia, as if George might have organised a gypsy conspiracy to deprive her of pudding, before he left.

"Would you like one of mine? I ordered too many."

Sophia sounds dubious. She can't imagine why a grown woman has to make herself custard every Wednesday.

"No thank you, Sophia. I'll have yoghurt." Amelia will not be so easily appeased.

"I'm sick and tired of living cheek by jowl with these *awful* people."

"They're hardly that close. Heronmarsh is at least two miles from here."

"But they come into town, Sophia., and Cotton Park way is a very convenient short cut for them."

"Why shouldn't they come into town?"

"I should have thought that was quite obvious. They're dirty, they're violent and they steal. There! I've said it. I know I'm not supposed to, but it's the truth. I'm going to write to the Council to complain this time, as soon as I find out who's in charge."

"It's Brendan," says Sophia automatically, instantly wishing she hadn't told her. The teacher in her couldn't help it. "Brendan McFall. He's an old friend of George's," she adds, hoping to discourage her, and knowing it is too late.

"Really?" says Amelia. She has put down her milk, and is polishing her nails on the trumpet shaped sleeve of her gown. "Married?"

"Er…yes he is, though I don't see what…look Amelia, anybody could have taken your milk. Or the milkman might have made a mistake.; you know he's completely hopeless. George says he takes drugs. He forgot my cream last Christmas."

"I'm sorry, Sophia, but George is brainwashed. Your cream was probably spooned over an extra large, deluxe pudding that one of George's gypsy pals snitched from *Sainsburys* for the family, or the tribe or whatever they call themselves."

"Oh, I really don't think so, and they're certainly not all thieves. I've a girl in my class from the site actually. Brilliant artist. I even trust her with my *keys*, for goodness sake."

That's not completely true. Sophia has never trusted Keely with her keys, though she thinks she probably would. She's embellishing facts now, really wanting to discourage Amelia from contacting Brendan. There will be trouble and George will only blame her.

"Well, there's always an exception that proves the rule, isn't there?"

Sophia gives up. Amelia is like a donkey in make up.

"Must go. Sorry about your milk Amelia. Chin up. At least it's not raining."

"Yes. Well, that's true I suppose."

Sophia had intended to be ironic. Surely everyone in the country must be longing for rain except Amelia. This summer has gone on for far too long for most normal people. Amelia probably sees it in terms of a fortune saved on sun beds.

The two women turn away, each dissatisfied with the other, clutching their bottles of milk to their breasts like shields.

Back in her living room, Sophia collapses onto the sofa, pressing her back into its comforting squashy folds. She crosses her arms over her chest, one hand clasping each thin shoulder, making a corpse of herself.

This heat is leeching her energy. It seems an age ago since May, when the sun flared up like a new boil, refusing to die down even now the end of August is nearly here, and the new school term is beckoning with a crabbed and witchy finger. Every day begins with a clear sky, and the pavements are hot by nine. Dogs look worried, lolling their tongues and refusing walks. The grass has shrivelled and browned in the parks, all watering prohibited until further notice.

Sophia has taken to spending her evenings alone in the garden, drinking from tall glasses filled with wine and ice. George won't come out. He fusses with the remote control, hopping from sport to sport like a restless cricket.

She keeps a newspaper on her lap. It bubbles over with chilling stories, dismemberment and torture, terror and disease spill across her knees, making her shiver. Do people still eat fish and chips from newspaper? Sophia thinks she never will again. She sees that violence is gaining ground like a dark tide, inching its way across the world. She sees the restless eyes of the boys in her classes, waiting for the call, itching to join the grenade throwers and the village burners.

George says she's paranoid, and the world is safer than it's ever been, blah, blah, blah.

She gets up from the sofa, and he appears in her mind, as if to check she's not idling, He is standing there in the doorway, arms folded like a policeman who's seen it all before. An anxiety bubble floats upwards in her chest like the marker in an electric kettle, and when the doorbell rings, her skin prickles. Her first thought is that she might hide in the kitchen to avoid whoever it is, and she's only stopped from going to ground by a pervasive sense of George's disapproval. When did he become a part of her? At some point in their long association, she must have lost the lock on the inside of her mind, and now he wanders in whenever he wants to, like someone with a key.

She starts towards the door, trying to make a postman shape out of her mother, who is standing on the step and tapping her foot. Sophia's forgotten the shopping trip. She makes herself smile before she opens the door. Her mother stands importantly in hat and sunglasses, a wicker basket over her arm, her mouth already opening to speak, like a child out of school, overflowing.

"Hallo Mum."

"I *must* have a drink, Sophia."

"Would you rather not go? We don't have to."

There's no reply. Her mother is already at the sink, helping herself to a glass, holding it up to the light and tutting at the smears.

"Sit down Mum. I'm not ready yet."

"I can see that."

Her mother sighs. How those sighs echo down the years, a dismal paper chain of disappointment, of frustration, of things not turning out quite right. They live inside Sophia somewhere, like moles.

"Hang on a sec. I'll just shower. Sit down."

Sophia has showered once already this morning, but she's buying herself some time. She turns the water on, and sits down on the edge of the bath, biting at her nails.

When she comes down, her mother is clutching a cup of tea and a chocolate digestive and sitting in George's chair. She knows perfectly well she's not supposed to. George can't stand anyone

35

sitting in his chair.

The rising sun is touching the coloured glasses on the mantelpiece, making each one glow; yellow, pink, blue, orange, green. Sophia loves this room, with its pale cream carpet and white walls, its deep blue armchairs and sofa by the window. It feels like hers. She chose the large studded mirrors and the paper lamps and the delicate weeping plants standing gracefully in the corners.

"Am I alright here, dear? With George being away, I mean?"
Sophia nods.

"I know he doesn't like it."

"Yes, it's alright."

Not only does her mother have to make her point, she has to underline it too.
Sophia doesn't really want either of them in her room. When George is home he sprawls like a satisfied lion, books, newspapers, reports scattered around his chair, like bones. She skulks on the fringes, over by the window, or in the kitchen.

"How is he getting on at that gypsy place?"

"I don't know really. He doesn't say. "

"It must be dreadful. He's drawn the short straw this time."

"I think he likes it."

"Likes it? How can anyone like it up there? It's like Bombay."

"You've never been to Bombay. And its not called Bombay any more, it's Mumbai."

Her mother doesn't pay any attention. She yammers on like a jackdaw.

Sophia wonders how George is getting on. He doesn't really talk to her any more. He addresses her, as if she were a meeting and if she interrupts his flow, there's a fight. His words are nails hammered into her skull, bang, bang, bang, precise, logical, cutting. Her words come out treacly. Unable to form a recognisable shape, they coat everything with a sticky film, and enrage them both still further. George is a woodpecker, she is a jellyfish, floppy and stinging. She's become quiet so as not to add to it all, the discordance, the cacophony, a choppy sea of meaningless noise.

"Were you happy together Mum? You and Dad?"

Her mother has to stop and think

"Happy? We didn't worry about whether we were happy in my day. We just got on with it."

"Must have been simpler then."

"*You* were a happy little thing. Easily pleased."

"Was I?"

She'd felt more like a little ghost, wafting through the house alone, keeping quiet, waiting to be called for lunch, for tea, for cod liver oil, for school, for bed time.

"I will *never* forget taking you to *Peter Pa*n. You were about five I think…"

She does remember that. It's a colourful memory from the black and white album of her childhood. Mum was a dark and glossy bear in her fur coat, sparkling with raindrops like fizzy bubbles. Dad smelled of smoke and wet leaves. They'd seemed so tall.

"You were obsessed with the curtain, of all things. I thought your little eyes were going to pop out of your head…"

She can feel the scratchy plush under her bare legs, making her wriggle and squirm. Inside the darkened theatre, the curtain was shining in front of her, gathered into curls like a thousand mermaid tails, a brilliant shining blue delight. She drank it in, gulping down her disappointment when it rose and rose and nearly disappeared. Her mother turned and frowned at her, suspecting she had hiccups and was about to make a scene.

"You fell asleep, and Dad had to carry you out. Too much excitement…"

She'd watched spellbound until, drunk with colour and warmth, her head began to droop and she dozed against Dad's tweedy shoulder. Tinkerbell was scattering fairy dust in glittering arcs. She'd begged all the children in the world to shout : *I do believe in fairies*…Sophia had tried to stop her fading away for ever, but her eyes were heavy, and her mouth wouldn't open, and she wasn't allowed to shout.…

"You cried when you woke up in the car. You insisted that you had to go back and save Tinkerbell. We told you it was too late, but you cried all the way home."

"Did you mind?"

"Mind? What a funny question. You are in an odd mood today, Sophia. We didn't *encourage* you to cry. We didn't believe in crying in those days. We didn't think it was healthy. Not like now. People seem to cry at the drop of a hat.; even on television if you don't mind."

"Perhaps there's more to cry about."

Her mother thinks she's being contrary.

"It's nearly eleven o'clock, now, " she accuses.

"Already?"

"*Yes*. Already. We must go."

Her mother bustles about, and Sophia wants to run away.

She glances at Gabe's photograph on the wall. He is smiling proudly in a grey v- necked jumper. When he was little, she'd wanted to run away from him too, sometimes. Away from tears and tantrums and Mr Men and Thomas the bloody Tank. And later on, when the house crashed with heavy metal music and nothing she did was right according to George, and the house whispered to her that she was a failure, a failure, a failure.

Sophia takes a guilty step towards his picture and rubs it with a grubby tissue, as if she can erase the dishonourable backlog of unmotherly thoughts.

"Have you got your keys? I want to go to *Pricewise* first. You don't want anything do you, Sophia?

Her mother's voice gets fainter as she clip clops her way down the front path. It is bordered on each side by flame coloured nasturtiums, basking in the endless summer. They make Sophia feel even hotter and she kicks at one as she passes.

"No. Not really."

There are things she wants, but none of them are in *Pricewise*. Her mother turns and smiles at her fondly, holding out an arm. Sophia takes it, her eyes on the end of the road where the cats are playing in the dust.

SEVEN

"Post."

A fat bundle of letters held together by a dirty elastic band, plops down in front of Brendan who up until now, has been staring out of his grimy office window.

"Thank you so much," he snaps at the pink flowered back of his secretary, who is disappearing through the door before she can be called upon to fetch coffee. Celia should never wear sleeveless blouses. Her arms have gone to jelly.

"You're welcome."

Celia turns back. She is annoyed. She doesn't see why she should be spoken to rudely for doing her job. This summer is bringing out the worst in people.

"Celia, look at all these. I'll drown with them all."

"They're only letters, Brendan. Men. Honestly."

Celia goes a bit further than usual, such is the degree of her irritation with him.

"It's the contents of the letters, Celia. Not the letters in themselves. More specifically, it's the complaints in the letters, the stupid, petty, shitty little complaints from small minded people with nothing better to do. *'Dear Town Hall, My precious daughter got a splinter in her finger when she was running it down the fence in the park last week... Dear Council, My rubbish collection was two minutes early this week, and I had to keep back my teabag until the next one.'* God love us, I wasn't born for this Celia.....He tails off, and goes back to staring out of the window. A young woman is sitting on a bench, her feet slipped out of her shoes and her legs spread wide, teasing the sun. Other people have gorgeous sun kissed secretaries in short skirts.

Celia sighs. "Coffee help, would it?"

"It might. God may reward you Celia, local government never

will."

Brendan snaps off the elastic band from his letters, and flicks it across the room, as he does every morning. It pings against the window, and drops down behind the heavy cream radiator, covered in dusty cream blisters. There is a picture of Tony Blair hanging on the wall behind his desk, grinning down at him like a vampire, Brendan thinks, yearning to bite his neck. He flicks a backwards v sign at the picture. It's all Tony's fault that Brendan has become the town's aunt sally. Accountability, indeed. They might as well put him in the market place and let the public lob rotten fruit at him. Once Celia had come through the door in the middle of this ritual, and thought Brendan was making a rude gesture at her. He'd floundered in a mess of lame explanations, and she's not as friendly as she used to be.

He riffles through the letters with the dexterity of a Vegas croupier, tossing out the ones with handwriting he recognises. He has three piles: *'Get A Life', 'Bonkers' and 'Serious Reply'*. Some of the former, whose outpourings are Celia's responsibility, have become crafty and started typing their envelopes, having nothing better to do than cheap IT courses in the local library. If Brendan has his way, they'll all be cut in the next budget. Recession won't be all bad, by any means.

Celia trots back in, her backless shoes flapping untidily on the linoleum, and plonks a fat, steaming, jazzy blue tub in front of him.

"Starfucks?" Brendan smiles for the first time this morning, possibly for the first time in forty eight hours, thanks to a late night hostile skirmish with his wife the day before yesterday. "Thanks, Celia. How much...?"

"It's all right. Just pass me the pile of doom, and I'll one/two them for you."

They mount a two- letter attack on the crackpots and the wingers. The *'we are investigating...' followed by the 'we have investigated, no-one else has complained, sorry anyway...'*

Celia used to baulk at copying his signature, but he has persuaded her to send them out without showing them to him again. He's told her it's quite legal. Brendan believes in telling people what they want to hear, which makes him a successful Chief Executive, and an equally unsuccessful husband.

He pushes several letters across the desk to her, hesitating over a pale mauve envelope with unfamiliar writing. It seems to have a whiff of lavender about it and he grimaces. His hand hovers jerkily above the pile, waving backwards and forwards like a flimsy metal claw in a grab what you can arcade game. Celia snatches up her pile, and takes a step backwards, before the lavender surprise can be added to her daily burden.

Brendan gives a martyred sigh, and she feels as if she's won a small victory.

Alone in the unsatisfactory silence left by her smug exit, Brendan looks down at his watch and then back to the letters. He strokes his thumb along the edge of the pale invader, as if it were a knife. He observes it from all angles, a mighty connoisseur inspecting a humble family treasure. Exquisite writing. Beautifully formed letters in straight lines, no commas or full stops missing. He pictures an elderly lady, schooled in the days when children practised copperplate in copy- books. *'Cut Your Coat According to Your Cloth', 'One Swallow Does Not a Summer Make'* and other joyless admonishments. She had spent time on her envelope as if it mattered more than it does.

He shoves his thumb roughly under the flap and tears it open, unevenly. It'll be a posh old lady whinge about dog shit or travellers. He scans the page and nods his head, in self congratulation at his superior powers of assessment. Lives in Cotton Park…yep…stolen milk bottles…yep…ruin the town and have done for years…normal people…disgrace…yep, same old stuff, thank you very much Amelia Massie. Brendan glares at the letter. She has addressed it to him personally, and now he's going to have to answer it himself, and he doesn't have an answer. It was much more likely that her pint was pinched by some bug-eyed clubber, coming home parched in the early hours, but he can't say that or she'll start on about licensing hours.

In his mind's eye he sees a sour faced biddy, lipstick carefully applied to shrunken lips, pouring over the Daily Mail with her magnifying glass and solitary cup of mid-morning coffee. Black probably today, unless she's got some long-life. No, she probably wouldn't touch it; long life would be too common for her.

He takes a swig of his own coffee, and the sweet, chocolate froth mellows his hard-edged mood and makes him feel slightly sympathetic. A lot of complaints about Heronmarsh have been coming in lately probably because of the summer heat. A whiff of rotten rubbish and people think there'll be a plague of rats and a cholera epidemic. It's been more difficult to keep on ignoring the place this summer, which has been the unofficial council policy for some years now.

Brendan scratches the side of his nose with the edge of Amelia's envelope. He's beginning to wonder whether George is stirring up the travellers rather than keeping them quiet and tidy, which is what he's supposed to be doing up there. He was so keen to be seconded. George had said he was bored to death in housing, and Brendan hadn't bothered to interview anybody else; he'd forgotten George's wild side. Perhaps it's been lying dormant inside him, like a hibernating bear. Jesus. He takes a swig of his coffee, tossing it down as if it were Southern Comfort. George is supposed to be encouraging the tinkers to pick up after themselves, not roam round the town like normal people. Didn't he promise to do that at the interview? Though if he thinks back, George had waffled on about Equal Opportunities rather too much for his liking, and George had kept looking at him as if they were both on the same side.

Brendan has scalded the roof of his mouth and his throat, and is blaming George for the pain that is going to ruin his lunchtime crusty baguette with chicken and lemon mayonnaise. Fuck. Lunch is the only thing that makes the day bearable. He picks up a pencil and bounces the rubber end on his desk, wondering what to say to Amelia who is no doubt waiting for the Cotton Park postman to bring her a reply by special envoy. He aims the pencil at the window, startling a large magpie sitting on the outside ledge, waving its beak snootily at the car park.

42

Brendan decides to phone George, and re-frame all this as his problem.

George is washing his hands in the hotel cloakroom when his mobile rings. It makes him jump, and he drops it in the sink; he hates mobiles. The last time he'd tried to send a text, he'd ended up stamping on the thing. It lay there on the kitchen floor, its evil green eye blinking until Sophia had picked it up and given him a classroom look that said he was a complete fool.

Brendan hears a clattering and a *fuckit*.

"Hallo? Bloody thing. Just a minute."

"Good morning George. Or is it?"

"Brendan. God, how I hate these things! Talk about open all hours. I feel like a twenty four hour *Tesco*."

"You can turn them off, you know. They do have voice mail."

"I forget to tell you the truth. When I took Soph to Stratford for her birthday, it went off right in the middle of the dagger scene. Some clown shouted 'Call an ambulance will you, while you're on the phone.' I was actually hissed by the audience. Soph wouldn't go back in after the interval."

"Dear me. How is she now?"

"Fine. You know. She moans about teaching, she moans about being tired. How's Lisa?"

"Fine. Moans about the house. Moans about me. The kids call her moaner Lisa."

"That's not true. It's Brendan's name for his wife.

George laughs. "We must go out for a beer soon. Sounds as if you need a break. What did you want, anyway?"

"I need to talk to you about the site. There seem to be one or two problems George. Can I come up there today?"

"No," George sounds less certain, "no, I'm not there. I'm at the conference with Leena. Big annual team review thing."

"I'd forgotten. We'll meet as soon as you get back then. Leena too," he adds as an afterthought. Leena is a dazzling woman. Why should George have her all to himself?

"Look Brendan, let me just get out of here. I'm in the gents and it stinks. It's always the same in these hotels. They charge a fortune and employ two terrified asylum seekers to do ten peoples work."

Brendan doesn't reply and George frowns at the phone. Bloody Brendan. He always was a moody sod. George is beginning to suspect this isn't a friendly conversation after all. He changes his tone.

"Right, well, what are these problems, exactly?"

"Rubbish, at number one. At least three letters a week. Theft at number two. I've had a letter this morning from Cotton Park…"

George laughs, "Let me guess. Amelia Massie?"

"Yes it is. How did you know that?" Brendan looks at his letter hopefully. Perhaps George has sent him a spoof and he can forget all this.

"She's a neighbour of mine and obsessed with the site. She's also a Daily Mail reader, and a Brownie Pack leader. She's got a flag- pole, in her garden for God's Sake, with a Union Jack. You should make her take it down."

"Old biddy?"

"No. Rather gorgeous, actually. Looks like a cheap Doris Day."

"Shaggable?"

"Definitely not. She's between husbands and on the prowl. I think they lose the will to live. Come on Brendan, she's a *Bonkers.*

"I have to investigate all complaints," Brendan is stiff, "And I can't afford to have complaints from Cotton Park."

"Oh no, not Cotton Park. All white bloody Cotton Park. It doesn't matter if the travellers complain because they're harassed every time they step out of that shambolic site. It doesn't matter if they can't get a job, or a drink in a pub, or a doctor's appointment, does it? Well, I live in Cotton Park too, and I'm not upset."

George is almost shouting and in the corridor two thin women look up at him with worried eyes.

"No need to be defensive, George," says Brendan with the smug air of a man who has just seen check- mate. "Our Equal opportunities policy doesn't just cover your personal soul mates.

44

It embraces the middle class citizens of the Park, as well as our traveller comrades, does it not?"

George tries to smile reassuringly at the cleaners and glare into his phone at the same time, which makes him look insane. They hurry past.

"I'll be back next week Brendan. I could meet on Thursday? Friday?"

"Wednesday's best for me. 9.30. Here, I think. In the meantime, I'll have a wander round myself. I'll assess the situation."

"Well, just don't, you know, don't walk around looking official, Brendan. They wont like it."

Brendan laughs, and lapses deliberately into his native, musical Irish lilt, which has flattened out and hardened after years in the unmusical South-East of England. It's a tactic Lisa finds particularly irritating.

"Don't you be worryin' George. I'll have on me old stained slacks, and me grandaddy's vest. They'll think I'm one of their own."

"If you talk like that, they definitely won't. They're not Irish. Just don't *upset* them."

"What do you mean, *upset* them? They're not your children, George. We're all adults, aren't we?"

"I've got to go Brendan. I'm giving a lecture, and I'm late."

Neither is true, but George wants Brendan to think he has better things to do than talk to him. It works. He can hear from Brendan's voice that he is stung.

"Fine. I'll have my secretary confirm our meeting. Goodbye George."

"That's it Brendan. Have your people call my people. Say hallo to Amelia from me, won't you?"

The last thing Brendan hears is a chuckle. He thinks George might have scored in the final round, and makes an aeroplane of Amelia's letter, not quite daring to send it towards the window. He wishes he'd reminded George that it's not impossible to close down a site. There must be plenty of infringements up there that would give the council grounds. Perhaps he'll get on to Freeman

45

and Parker, have them check it out. They don't want to do anything illegal. He sips his coffee thoughtfully, tasting the cold fat.

EIGHT

Sophia looks as if she's washing up, but she isn't. She can't be bothered. She's standing at the sink, hands resting lightly on the warm stainless steel edge, watching the garden.

The roses are still budding and blossoming. A soft tapestry of pink and apricot, red and lemon yellow, clouds the broken fence. Petals have spilled on to the brown grass, blown off by this morning's warm breeze. She thinks of her water colours, and wonders where they are. She thinks of George's failure to mend the fence.

She shrugs off her dressing gown roughly, as if its Marks and Spencer's fault, and bends to the washing up in her t shirt and shorts, keeping her eyes on grease and crust and sticky residue, boiling her hands in suds and milky water.

She suspects George will not mend the fence, merely because she's asked him to. He likes to keep his hand on the tiller. Last week she shopped on Tuesday instead of Wednesday, and when she came in, three carrier bags in each hand, glad to be home, he looked at her as if she'd committed a crime, and she felt a corresponding shame.

Sophia shakes her hands dry, and turns on the television. A fresh- faced weather girl snaps on to the screen. Her voice is full of sugar and her hands move in slow circles over the orange and yellow map. She is pregnant, the buttons on her tangerine silk jacket tight across her hopeful belly.

Something in her still yearns for a perfect future where she and George smile at each other over breakfast, where all the floors are stripped and golden and where her children don't die in the night. That bloody weather girl has her future.

Sophia turns towards the garden door, soft words in a West country burr floating after her, *'still gorgeous in the South East,*

no sign of the weather breaking, good news for all you
holidaymakers down in Dorset...'

She pulls back the bolts and turns the key, opening the door
wide. When she breathes in deeply, her heart flutters; a little
something has altered. The air has changed overnight, and the
damp wood, bonfire smoke, ripe apple, earthy smell of Autumn
has come in under the skirts of the morning. It's a promise of
change, murmured to an impatient lover: ' soon things will be
different, soon, soon.'
The sky, still a deep summer blue, is preparing for the loss of the
sun. Sophia thinks of Gabe and misses him.
She is about to step out into the garden, when the phone rings,
shrilling in the quiet morning air. She turns back crossly, glancing
up at the kitchen clock on her way to the hall. Eight thirty. If it's
George, she'll tell him again about the fence.

"Hallo?"

"Mum."

"Are you all right darling?"

He makes his irritation known by silence. These are always her
first words to him. She can't seem to help it.

"It's lovely to hear you darling."

This doesn't work either.

"Dad's away this week. I'm all on my own."

"Oh."

"Are you relaxing darling? I'm trying to enjoy these last few
days before term starts again. Trying to make them last. I really
don't want to go back"

Sometimes he wishes he could just turn her on like a television
set without having to talk to her.

"No. Actually. Better go now. Bye Mum."

"Gabe, wai..."

He's hung up and Sophia stares at the phone in her hand.
What's the matter with him? Is he depressed? Fear wrings out
her gut. *'Oh please God, keep him safe, keep him safe,'* she
whispers in a mad sort of prayer. George says she smothers him.

George says she's made him irresponsible and afraid of hard

work.

There's a little tremor in her hands as she spoons coffee into a cup, and half of it spills across the counter. She knocks it onto the floor with a sweep of her hand, and the cat looks aggrieved and walks away, brown granules sticking to his ears.

The television blathers on in the anxious kitchen silence. The weather girl has gone home to the waiting nursery and the kind, good-humoured husband, and Roxanne, current hostess with attitude, has taken her place with her human interest stories.

'...and then he fainted clean away didn't he, knocked over the drip, and it all fell on the midwife. She's screaming, and the security come running in...it would have been comical if I hadn't of been in labour twelve hours by then...

There's a burst of laughter in the studio, and Sophia takes her coffee over to the kitchen table, wanting to calm her anxiety in the waters of other peoples' hopeless catastrophes. Gabe must have run out of credit, that's all.

Today is Birth: Fathers Who Can't Face It.' The women in the audience are looking smug, and the men uncomfortable. This woman's husband is squirming above a moving banner that proclaims his utter uselessness: 'disconnected wife's drip', it taunts. The microphone is nosing into his anxious face. 'But you see, Roxy, I hadn't had anything to eat for twelve hours...

George would never faint like that. He missed Grace's rapid birth, but he stood beside her while Gabe was disentangled and pulled out by strangers, never once flinching. She'd watched his face looming above her, his jaw tense, fear behind his eyes too. She saw him wipe away a tear when they took Gabe away to wash him; he denied it later, as angry as if she'd accused him of indifference.

Laughter bursts from the television as another husband is pilloried by his fat wife, her hour come round at last...and when the surgeon started to cut he had a panic attack! Started gasping that he couldn't breathe, and then he actually burst into tears! The nurses were wetting themselves, Roxy....'

Draped in green robes, Sophia had blinked at the overhead

lights as she was wheeled into the theatre. Someone had decided she should be conscious. There was the sting of an injection into her spine, and a blissful numbness seeped into her toes and crept slowly up her body, past her knees, past her belly, as far as her chest.

Gabe was a tiny face looking down at her, his dangling body held up like a trophy by two ghastly, gory hands. His eyes were wide open, and looking deep into hers. She reached out hands shackled by needles and tubes, and then he was gone, whisked away and dropped into the scales while the surgeon stitched the gash in her belly. He didn't talk to her either. She thought of Grace waiting anxiously for them to come home, and gritted her teeth, determined to get back to her with her new brother as soon as she could.

Roxanne is grinning at the camera, the close up paying homage to the whiteness of her teeth, the glory of her nose, the perfect swell of her breasts: *'well Dads, we've heard the Mums tell it like it is. So, if you can't stand the heat, please do us all a favour, and stay in the cafeteria until we call you!'*

She waves and turns on her heel, like an American president, and Sophia finds herself twisting the tea towel between her two fists. It's printed with brightly coloured fruit, a present from her mother, who thought it cheerful.

Sophia wants to talk to her about Gabe.

"Hallo? Hallo?"

"Just me Mum."

"Oh Sophia, you frightened me. I wasn't expecting the phone to ring. Are you all right?

Sophia hesitates, realising already this was a mistake. Phyll will be appalled.

"I'm fine. What are you up to?"

"I'm just going shopping dear. What did you want?"

"Nothing, nothing really. Just, you know…"

"Nothing wrong is there?"

She hears the tone in her mother's voice and shudders, recognising her own.

"Well, er, Gabe just phoned. He was a bit off-hand really, a bit rude. Not himself, you know?"

"Darling, I wish you wouldn't call that boy Gabe. You give him a lovely name like Gabriel, and then you make him sound like some cheap country and western singer. Honestly."

"I'm worried about him." Sophia hears herself sulking.

"Don't be silly Sophia. Young people are always like that. They think it's clever, or cool or something. You were just the same at that age. I remember when you were seventeen and you had that long haired boyfriend who broke your heart, another silly name he had, didn't he? It was James and you insisted on calling him Jez or something, and it was always…"

She goes on and on and Sophia presses the phone into her cheek until it makes a mark on her face. She huddles over, her teeth clenched against the flow of her mothers tide until she hears the usual finale… "anyway, that's only what *I* think."

Sophia sighs, for once not bothering to disguise it.

"OK, Mum. Got to go. Ring you next week, all right?"

"Thanks for ringing, dear. I'm so lucky to have you. Keep your chin up. We mustn't dwell on the past, must we?"

There's a click, and Sophia slams the phone into its cradle. Her mother means Grace, when she says 'the past' like that. It's the code for everything that can't be named. She gets to her feet, stretching her cramped and aching limbs. Perhaps she should take up yoga.

The television is still warbling in the kitchen. .'.*this Autumn think scarlet, think emerald green, think passionate, all you smouldering ladies out there. Gypsies are in with a vengeance!'*

She laughs. She must tell Amelia.

NINE

Sprinklers are playing over the smooth green lawns that sweep down to a lake fringed by willows. A sweet smell of summer grass drifts across the table where George and Leena are having lunch.

George has pushed back his chair, and is drumming his fingers on the table, Brendan's phone call still on his mind. Leena is looking out of the window, and he puts a hand on her arm to get her attention.

"Leena..."

Startled, she turns to face him quickly and he jumps too.

"Sorry, George. I was miles away. These gardens are magical, aren't they? Look at that little island in the middle of the lake. It looks as though it were made for lovers."

She is looking at him and he turns away. Her eyes are too blue.

"Probably full of old beer cans and rotting socks."

She laughs. "There is no romance in you George. If I were your soul I'd find a more congenial home."

"That's what Soph said on holiday. Well, she didn't put it quite like that."

"Two of us can't be wrong."

Leena smiles with her eyes. People hardly ever do that, George is thinking. Is it the times? Perhaps the past is full of people with smiling eyes. Soph doesn't smile at all much. Not at him, anyway. She smiles at Gabe and Phyll, but even then not with her eyes. Not like this.

"If I believed I had a soul, it wouldn't like romantic clutter. How do you think it went?"

"What?"

"The presentation and everything this morning"

"OK. You had the seal of approval from his royal highness this morning didn't you?"

"Sorry I was late. Soph didn't wake me up. She normally rings; she knows perfectly well I always forget to set the alarm."

Leena doesn't comment. She's gone back to looking out of the window at the shining water.

"Apart from that, how do you think the project's going?

She turns back again, her honey coloured skin puckering slightly between the sweep of dark brows. There are faint lines at the corners of her eyes, and George leans forward slightly, like a visitor at a portrait gallery, marvelling at how the fine brush strokes compose the whole. Soph doesn't have laughter lines.

Leena interrupts his gaze with a raised eyebrow, and he slumps back in his seat. The hot sun pouring through the window catches the blade of his fish knife, making it glint.

" Not bad all things considered. They accept us being there more or less, and some of them trust us. It's early days yet. What were you hoping for?"

"I don't want Brendan getting involved. He rang me this morning and said there'd been some complaints. Nothing really, but I got a bit shirty and he said he was going to go and have a nose around."

"Good. He'll collect a few more complaints to take back to the Town Hall with him. If someone collars him about Dr Lawrence's secret 'no gypsy scum bags on my list' policy, he'll wish he'd kept his nose to himself."

They both laugh, and George feels, fleetingly, as if they could be friends.

"Let me take you out for dinner tonight Leena, as a thank you. My treat. You were a real find."

She is not smiling back.

"Being half Romany isn't the only entry on my CV George, by the way. It's as long as yours. You're all the same you bloody gorgios. Couldn't see the middle of a glass onion."

"There's no need to be rude. You're beginning to sound like your grandmother."

"You don't need to *thank* me, George. I get paid for working. And you didn't *find* me, I applied for the job, unlike yourself."

George is regretting his invitation. Leena is the last woman on earth he wants to have dinner with. He glares at her, but she ignores it.

"But dinner would be lovely. Thank you. What time?"

Now he'll have to go through with it. And she mentioned time again. Is she being sarcastic?

"Eightish," he mumbles, committing himself to an encounter he's already beginning to dread. "In the lobby".

"Fine," she says, and leaves without drinking her coffee.

When George gets back to his room at six that evening, he's tired.

"I just cannot *stand* the bullshit," he complained to Jamie in the lift, "and I cannot *stand* hard chairs, flip charts, corded carpet, Columbian coffee or digestive sodding biscuits."

Jamie said he was a dinosaur.

The room is hot and smells of dust. George flicks on the air conditioning and curls up on the bedspread, knees bent like a child, his cheek resting on two hands in a sideways prayer. He drifts into a place where Leena is sitting on a soft blue picnic blanket by a slow running river, pouring him tea. It tastes sweet and he tries to hand it back to her saying he's given up sugar for the good of his heart, but she shakes her head smiling, saying what he can taste is honey, and he drinks the lot in one thirsty gulp.

The sound of the phone ringing beside his bed wakes him and he sits up in a panic. His first thought is that he has slept through the pre-arranged meeting time with Leena.

"Yes?" he snaps into the phone.

"It's me George," says a wounded-sounding female voice.

"God, Soph, what is it? You could have woken me up this morning, you know. I nearly missed my slot. Didn't get any bloody breakfast, either."

There is silence on the other end of the line, and George scratches his head. Soph is supposed to apologise.

"Leena covered for me," he says grudgingly. "We're funded again for next year, so you don't have to worry, " he adds, believing her to be far more worried about his job security, than she is. Sophia thinks it would be a good thing if George retired. He's so bad-tempered all the time.

"I'm *not* worried", she says and then stops short, sensing the beginning of another pointless argument, even at this distance. "I'm glad it went well for you. Leena's very good isn't she?"

The mention of Leena makes his stomach lurch horribly and he glances at the clock. Quarter to eight. He doesn't want to see the look on her face if he's not waiting in that damn lobby at eight.

"Mmm. I'm taking her out to dinner tonight. As a sort of thank you. Or something. Got to meet her at eight, I'm not even changed yet. I was asleep."

"Oh, OK," Sophia takes on his sense of urgency. She's very good with time.

"So what did you *want* Soph?"

"I just wanted to tell you Gabe rang this morning, and I felt, well, I felt a bit worried."

"What's happened?"

His tone is sharp. Why can't she just say what she means? With Soph there always has to be a preamble. She strolls up to the point as if she's afraid it will take off if she comes at it quickly. Obfuscation. Something else George can't bear.

"Well, not actually *worried*, as such, it was just the time and something about his voice."
"What?"
"I don't know really, can't put my finger on it. He sounded a bit…funny, then he hung up on me, I think. I suppose it could have been the phone…"

"Didn't you ring back?"

"No, I thought it might be a bit…"

"Oh for God's sake, Soph."

"Yes, ok, ok. Don't keep losing your temper. You're right, George, it was probably nothing."

George knows she wants to believe this, and she doesn't.

"Go up and see him, take him out for lunch or something and put your mind at rest. I've got to go, Soph. Bye."

He rings off.

The lobby is deserted when he arrives at ten past eight, out of breath, looking round wildly, baffled by the empty chairs. Through the window, he can see her sitting on the lawn with Jamie. Her hair is tossed over one shoulder, and her feet are bare.

There are daisies between her toes.

He strides over and Jamie stands up, smirking.

"Fancy keeping a beautiful lady waiting, George! A meeting's one thing, but nearly missing a date with Leena!"

Her laugh is like a butterfly shower. It makes the hairs on the back of his neck prickle.

"Leave it to the grown ups Jamie, there's a good lad. Haven't you got homework to do, or something?"

Jamie laughs generously and turns to leave. "Have a good evening folks!" he says over his shoulder, as he wanders off towards the bar with a deliberately casual gait, like a teenager aping an adult.

Leena pats the grass beside her and George sits down. The light is pinkish now, and the low sun is still warm. The shadows of the trees are fingering the lawn. Jamie was right; she does look beautiful. She's wearing a long red dress with thin straps across her brown shoulders. He never bothered to ask her where she went for her holiday. Her hair is standing out round her head and shoulders, thick and curly. She has just washed it, he can smell the shampoo. The sun is framing her in gold and she is looking at him from under her hand. It doesn't feel right that he isn't wearing socks. He frowns.

"We were supposed to meet in the lobby."

"You weren't there at eight."

"I'm sorry. Soph rang…"

"I thought I'd come outside and enjoy *go dhuli bhela*."

"What on earth's that?"

"*Go dhuli bhela.* It means cow dust time."

"Is that Romany?"

56

The shower again. Her teeth are very white against the palest of pink gums. He thinks of Neopolitan ice cream.

"No, it's Bengali. Nicer than plain old *sunset*. Makes me think of red earth and cow bells and going home to relax."

"You do have some odd thoughts."

"Do I? What were you thinking about?"

George stands up. "I was thinking about being late."

"Poor you."

She scrambles to her feet. "I do love this time of day. I can feel all my bones smiling. Shall we go?"

"Where?"

"Put yourself in my hands, George. I know somewhere."

George puts his hands in his pockets and sets the pace as they walk past the tall stone hotel buildings, down towards the river. He feels awkward beside her, aware of the sidelong glances she attracts. She barely comes up to his shoulder. He could carry her if she got tired, he thinks.

They walk along the slow green river ribbon for a while, in silence. Children are playing football on the grass and dog walkers are chatting companionably in the warm evening sun, like Europeans. Men, late back from work, hurry along, sleeves rolled up, eager to get home.

She stops in front of a pub and looks up at him. It's called the 'S*hip Aground'.

"This OK? They do nice food."

"Why not?"

George tries to sound casual, but he appears totally indifferent. They find a table and sit at high backed, cushioned benches. He feels like a child in a grown up's chair. It's unusual for him to feel small.

"How do you know this place?"

"It's my old University town. We came here a lot as students, when we could afford it." She is watching him intently. "You're looking surprised."

"No, well, these places are hard to get into. The standards are so high."

"Oh, I don't know. *The Ship's* not as fussy as all that, if you dress up nicely."

"No, I mean…" he realises she is laughing at him.

"I know what you mean George. I'm trying to save you from fatal rudeness. It's obvious you're amazed I was at a redbrick University when I really should have been selling pegs."

George is getting a headache. Perhaps he can cut the evening short.

"Well how did you do it?"

"I was a determined child. Head girl at school, in the orchestra, it all helped."

"What did you play?"

"The violin, of course. It came in handy round the campfire."

"I know perfectly well you lived in a house. Are you going to take the piss all night? Because if you are, I might as well…"

"I'm only teasing, George. Please don't get huffy."

The blue gems of her eyes twinkle. They really do. *'Twinkle, twinkle, little star, how I wonder what you are…'* The words come into George's head from long ago. The waiter is hovering with a pencil.

"Drink first Madam?"

"Yes please. I'd like a glass of champagne."

"You can't have champagne."

"I can't?"

"No."

Leena raises her chin. There's a cleft in it that lines up with the gap in her teeth and the parting of her hair as if there had been an upward flick of a paintbrush in the forming of her.

"Why's that George?"

The waiter looks anxious. He's dropped the hand holding the pencil to his side, so as not to draw attention to it.

"Because it's Tuesday, because it's expensive, because it's bloody obvious."

George's face says don't be stupid.

Leena beckons the waiter forward and smiles at him encouragingly.

"A champagne cocktail for me please, and a glass of milk for my father."

"Beer," George snaps, "a pint of draught bitter."

A thick red candle flickers in the middle of their table. The soft light makes the fine bones and hollows of her face gleam like a modern Caravaggio. *'The Social Workers'*, perhaps, or *'The Evening Meeting'*.

She speaks quietly into the twisting flame.

"Would champagne be all right on a Saturday?"

George wants to say sorry, but he can't.

She grins.

"Come on George, let's eat. I'm starving personally. I'll let you choose the food, if you like, it's all delicious. There's something about these conferences that makes me want to eat twice as much as usual. Must be all the empty words they dish out."

George laughs at last, and picks up the menu. His headache has gone. Perhaps they can be friends after all.

TEN

The mirror on Sophia's dressing table is dusty, and she is
squinting at her make up. She sighs in the dull evening light and
tosses down her hairbrush, which skitters across the glass surface,
knocking over a bottle of perfume. She leaves it laying there, in a
nest of fallen hair, tired of picking things up and putting them
back in order. Let mess and muddle confound the sterile
dormitory of their bedroom with its matching black and white
duvet and curtains, two white fluffy rugs, two Heals reading
lamps, her shelf of paperbacks with titles like *'No More Fears,
No More Tears', and 'Natural Highs Now!'* and George's row
which is all blue and black covers with silver flashes and
silhouettes of guns.
She pulls the photograph towards her, safely back after the
Spanish holiday. She'd been terrified customs officials would
deem it a weapon and take it away from her, and George would
look at her as if she were mad.
   Maybe she is a bit mad. Slowly turning into a mad old woman.
She'll end up wearing a thick coat in summer and living on a park
bench with a mouse in her pocket.
   The photograph is a studio portrait, perfectly posed and
lighted, with Sophia in the centre and George beside her, both of
them smiling broadly. She can still remember how proud she felt
to be married with her first baby. George's arm is resting along
the back of her chair, placed there by the photographer. It looks
slightly stiff and awkward, like a false limb. His boyish smile
touches her, even now.
   Her mother is there too, standing slightly apart, triumphant to
be included. George's mother had been overlooked, and she never
forgave them for it or spoke to George again. At her funeral,
Sophia reached for George's hand but he pulled it away and stuck
it deep in his pocket, preferring the comfort of wool and change.

There is a noise outside in the road and she jumps up and pulls back the corner of the curtain, peering down into the street. Her heart is pounding as if she has been running, although the sound is no more sinister than the slamming of a car door, and a shouted goodnight. It's ridiculous to start like this, at every little thing. She could talk to Doctor Lawrence, but he has her filed as pre-menopausal, so there's no point. If she breaks her leg he'll still offer her HRT.

She can hear Amelia laughing her flirty laugh. It's a pitch above her normal one, which stops just short of a cackle. She is posing between her gateposts, waving goodbye to someone with her hand raised, and fingers curled over like a child. A man's hairy hand is sticking out of a car window and involved in blowing her a kiss. Sophia assumes it's Amelia's latest prey. She lingers too long at the window, and Amelia spots her and waves. She blushes, and pretends to be fiddling with the edge of the curtain.

She sits down on the stool in front of the mirror and allows her eyes to rest on Grace for a moment. It's hard now to believe she ever existed.

After she died, Sophia used to sit here with the frame clutched to her face, the wrought silver leaves and flowers digging into her forehead, her lips pressed to the cold glass. George would come in holding Gabe sometimes, and watch her silently. Now he never mentions Grace at all. Lively, bubbling, beautiful, laughing Grace. Cold, silent, still, dead Grace.

The memory of that first morning without her in the world is scored on Sophia's heart. The emptiness blew through her like a tornado, and she became nothing but bone.

Sunlight had streamed into the house, pointing out sticky finger marks and dust left untouched during the brief weeks of sudden, unexplained illness. Grace's things were everywhere, left as if they'd gone to feed the ducks in the park thinking they would tidy up later before bedtime.

Sophia had prowled the house, picking up clothes and smelling them and putting them down again. George took over the telephone like a field marshal. He rang friends, family, anyone he thought of. People he hardly knew. People he didn't like. He couldn't seem to stop telling about her death, repeating the doctors' explanations. He needed it to make sense. She can't remember now who looked after Gabe that day.

When she got to the bathroom and saw their three toothbrushes together in the mug, Sophia snatched out the little yellow dinosaur and snapped it in half. Then she began to howl like an animal. George had found her sitting on the edge of the bath, sobbing and retching as she tried to fit the pieces back together. He had glued it for her.

Where is it now? Sophia thinks of it buried deep under the earth in a stinking land- fill, waiting to be found.

Doctor Lawrence arrived with Valium, without comfort. Her mother gave her the tablets crushed into warm milk and after a while, the pain began to throb one step behind her brain.

Grace slowly disappeared from the house in bags. Bin bags, carrier bags, small overnight bags. She was burned, buried, packaged up and re-directed elsewhere. How could her mother have destroyed the albums? *How could she*?

The evenings are drawing in now, and Sophia rummages in a drawer for a sweatshirt. Gabe was such a happy, sensitive little boy. She could never have talked to him about Grace as if she were only a story.

She pulls out one of George's and slips it on. Bounding down the stairs, she remembers he has the car and she needs to ring for a taxi.

When she finally arrives at Phyll's house, she stabs at the bell. She can't believe she's half an hour late for no reason. She is never late.

"Hi Soph. I was just going to ring you. What's up?"

"Sorry Phyll. George rang just before I left. I had to talk to him about Gabe. His birthday."

This isn't even true. Why is she lying to Phyll? She never lies to Phyll.

"It's soon isn't it? Shall I get him a decent watch? He doesn't have one, does he?"

"No, he doesn't. That's a good idea. Sometimes I wonder whether he can actually tell the time. It'll have to be designer though. You know how fussy he is."

The two women hug, enjoying each other's familiar scented softness, and Sophia heads towards the large and comfortable kitchen. The lights are on and she can hear a hum of voices and a clatter of cutlery. She turns back to Phyll, frowning, and Phyll grimaces back and wrinkles her nose. *Sorry*, she mouths.

Out loud she says, "Jennifer and her brother are here. She couldn't get her car started after work, so I brought her back here with me and he came to pick her up. They're both starving so I've invited them to stay for dinner as well."

"*Oh, OK,*" Sophia mouths back and carries on into the kitchen.

She likes this room. Gabe designed it, and they both helped Phyll furnish and decorate. The cupboards are mellowed old bare wood, found by combing salvage yards on Saturday afternoons. The floorboards are smooth and scrubbed and feel warm underfoot. Sophia takes off her shoes in Phyll's house. She never does at home. The walls are a deep red and rich cream, and now, in the gathering dark, throw up huge shadows of Phyll's giant plants, lit from beneath by silver lamps.

"Hi"

Disappointment clips Sophia's tone and thins her smile. Jennifer and the man sitting opposite her at Phyll's round table look up. He smiles; Jennifer smirks. Sophia dislikes Jennifer and is quite prepared to dislike her brother, and her whole family. She can see the family likeness in the large brown eyes and long lashes. He has the same slender build with broad shoulders, which makes Jennifer look like a swimmer, but suits him much better. He is balding, and wears small glasses with thin frames. The skin on top of his head is smooth and brown. Fleetingly, she wants to touch it as if it were a sculpture or a piece of wood.; she can't seem to draw her eyes away. His smile makes her think of chocolate in spite of herself.

He is already pulling out a chair for her.

"Hi, Sophia," Jennifer is drawling, in that annoying sing-song she seems to reserve especially for her, as if she is speaking to a child out of politeness to the mother.

"Bloody car wouldn't go, old heap."

"*Hallo* Jennifer," Sophia tries to sound pleased to see her.

"This is big brother James. He's staying with me at the moment. Gets in the way, but he has his uses, don't you darling?"

The man laughs good-naturedly, and half-rising, stretches out a hand across the table. Sophia glances down as she shakes it. There are wiry, black hairs on the back. Long, strong fingers flecked with white paint. No wedding ring. She seems to know this hand.

He pours wine for her and she raises her glass in salute.

"Pleased to meet you, James."

An old, blue van is driving through her mind's eye. There's a name on the side: '*Painters & Decorators: No Job Too Small: Freeman & Son'*. The van stops suddenly. It makes an emergency stop, because now she's put James with Freeman. Phyll's firm is *Freeman and Parker*, so he must be James Freeman. It's him. Jennifer's brother is Jez.

Sophia looks at Phyll suspiciously as if this might be an organised surprise, and snatches her hand back. She sits down heavily, scraping her chair and nearly knocking her wine over in the process. She steadies the quivering glass and glances across at his face. Is he playing along with this charade?

He is looking directly at her, his eyes alert, some puzzlement there. His head is cocked to one side, as still as a robin's. She remembers his ability to focus, and shivers.

She can feel the blush starting, rising slowly up her body to her face which is beginning to burn with what might seem to be girlish excitement. She pulls off George's sweatshirt, shaking out her hair and picks up her glass, looking over her shoulder at Phyll.

"And Brendan MacFall wants us to look into it," she's saying from the counter where she is chopping lettuce, "legally, there isn't much of a problem., unfortunately. Councils don't have to provide sites any more. They'd have to find a few licence infringements, which wouldn't be difficult, quite honestly. You'd better warn George, Soph, in confidence, of course. We don't want to lose the council contract, do we Jen? Looks like you're going to need a new car."

"Oh dear," murmurs Sophia. She's only half listening. Jez's eyes are still on her face, she can feel them, stuck like barnacles.

There are silver streaks in her hair now, and her face is lined and thin. The hand that clutches her glass is beginning to take on a gnarled look, like a tree. She should never have done all that sunbathing when she was young. She hears herself thinking like Amelia, and is suddenly defiant. Jez has his share of wrinkles and no doubt there's some middle aged spread beneath that jumper that looks like pale blue cashmere. Anyone over forty is falling to bits like Venice, all past splendour dulled by time and weather. At least she's not bald.

"I'm Sophia," she says in a rush and goes on recklessly, with what seems to her like excruciating innuendo, "I think we know each other?"

She is silently daring him to have forgotten, or worse to deny it, but he smiles back, the light of recognition dawning on his face.

"My God! Sophia! Soph it is you! What a marvellous coincidence!"

He looks at his sister and Phyll, gesturing towards Sophia. His smile goes on and on.

"Sophia was my very first girlfriend. We must have been, what, eighteen!"

He is a lot more outgoing than she remembers.

"Er, yes, we must have been. Amazing. Goodness me."

Jennifer doesn't seem to find this particularly amazing, but Phyll comes over to sit
at the table with them, giving Sophia's shoulder a squeeze as she passes the back of her chair.

"How absolutely incredible." She is grinning. "Soph was only talking about you the other day, weren't you Soph? This must be the hand of fate!"

Sophia doesn't dare to catch her eye. She knows that if she does, she will burst out laughing and Jez is still beaming at her with innocent delight. She grabs a fork and spoon and starts to serve spaghetti. As usual, Phyll has made enough for ten. A bright green pottery bowl splashed with pink daisies, holds a mound of buttery linguine dotted with black pepper, and a smaller matching one is filled to the brim with sweet smelling tomato sauce. A dish full of freshly shaved parmesan, and another of shiny black olives jostle for space with bottles of American beer and Italian wine.

"Always keep gallons in the freezer," Phyll is brushing away Jez's appreciative comments on her sauce, "I think it's these lovely bowls Soph brought me back from Spain, that give it a special flavour, actually."

"What an excellent combination of taste."

Sophia smiles at him in spite of her previous determination to keep him at a cool arm's length. Jennifer is rolling her eyes in sisterly contempt.

"Do you and Phyll always complement each other so well?"

Jez seems to have turned into a bit of a charmer. He used to be so shy. There is a pause that goes on and on until Sophia realises he is waiting for a proper answer.

"Oh, well, er, I suppose so." He seems to expect more, so she goes on: "Phyll's always calm and collected, and I just panic at the drop of a hat..."

"Really?"

He is leaning forward, interested.

"Have you always had a tendency towards anxiety? I seem to remember you as a very confident person."

"No, well, I can't really remember."

Sophia reaches for her glass again. There is something unnerving about this conversation. It's like wading out to sea and sliding down a sand shelf that takes you out of your depth without warning.

He is ladling sauce onto his pasta. He should watch his weight she thinks. He's already getting a double chin.

"I'm interested in the relationship between anxiety and excitement," he says between mouthfuls, "sometimes I think we confuse the two."

"How?" says Sophia with a sense of playing him at his own game.

"Well, it struck me last year. On my birthday."

Sophia is thinking that he is used to being listened to. Although the evidence on his hands suggests otherwise she can't believe he's spent years painting houses for a living.

"Here we go again", comments Jennifer, with the air of someone about to be bored.

"What happened?"

"Well, I'd promised myself I'd do a bungee jump," he says waving his fork in the air, "from this particular bridge in Germany that overlooks incredible white water rapids. It's a beautiful place. You should see it. I'd been there for a conference the year before, and a few of us said we'd do it." He laughs. "We stayed up all night talking about the nature of fear and living in the moment, and decided we should stop talking and start experiencing for a change. In the end I was the only idiot who did it, I must say."

So he goes to conferences, Sophia notes to herself, still trying to place him. Perhaps he's an academic, or a doctor? She glances across at Phyll who catches her eye.

"Anyway, to cut a long story short, I jumped, and as I hurtled through the air I realised I wasn't frightened at all. There was just this incredible excitement, and I remembered what it was like to jump for joy. I think perhaps we grow afraid of joy."

He stops, rather abruptly, Sophia thinks.

"Do you think we're still capable of everyday joy at our age? Knowing what we know about life, I mean?"

Jez looks at her. There's a question in his eyes, but he doesn't speak it.

"Does joy need innocence to flower? An interesting question. I think I'm usually too busy to find out."

"Too busy in the real world?" says Phyll, turning back to the papers she was looking at with Jennifer. She seems irritated.

"Dear old James doesn't know much about the real world," Jennifer says over her shoulder. Sophia frowns. Is he a poet? A dreamer? A bum? He reads her expression and laughs.

"By the real world, my sister means the external world. I'm a psychotherapist, now. Soph; I have my own practice in London. I'm staying with Jen while I take a break. I like decorating. It's relaxing."

Jez is chewing. He has a gold filling in a side tooth.

"Brings him back to earth, doing a bit of painting," Jennifer chips in.

Is he married? Hard to tell. Gay? Possibly. Could explain his coldness to her when they were young. The long hair. The sweet smile.

After the meal Jennifer decides Jez will drop her off first, and then drive Sophia home. Everyone agrees because Jennifer always gets her own way. In the general milling around, while Jez looks for his keys, and Jennifer packs away her lap top, and Sophia picks up her bag, Phyll grabs her arm and whispers in her ear: "Jez Two, Mind Fucker."

Sophia can't stop herself laughing and has to pretend she is having a coughing fit like a school girl.

He apologises as he pulls up outside her house. "I'm sorry we messed up your evening Soph, but I really am so pleased to meet you again."

She asks him in because she feels she should, though the meeting feels uncomfortable, and not altogether welcome. If he's so damned pleased to see her again why did he fuck her and dump her when they were both eighteen?

She brings coffee and opens the back door, letting in warm dark air. There is a faint fragrance of late roses in the sitting room. She catches him looking at her breasts and puts George's sweatshirt back on.

The grandfather clock is chiming eleven and she looks over and smiles at it as if it were a favourite pupil.

"You're fond of that clock."

"It reminds me of having coffee with my grandmother. She used to bob about like a friendly little bird. Her coffee was always really sweet. The milk was properly warmed and there were bubbles on top, like Cappuccino. Not that she'd ever heard of that!"

"Were you close to her?"

"Do you ever stop asking questions?"

"Sorry. Force of habit."

"I was, actually. She was the one person who was always pleased to see me. I used to sit there in her tiny little kitchen, and it felt like being in a big warm bubble."

"Bubbles have an unfortunate tendency to burst."

"Nothing lasts, does it? She wilted overnight when Grandad died, like a tulip in a vase. Suddenly, there was a grim old woman sitting there, as if she'd chased the cheerful one away. Even her coffee was nasty. Before she died, we didn't recognise one another any more. Depressing really."

She looks at Jez warily. He'd better not start trying to analyse her. He is nodding. He has thrown his jacket over the back of his chair and there is a faint smell of sweat and expensive aftershave. His shirt is a deep blue with a thin white stripe. It's nice.

"It sounds as if she nurtured you. You must have missed it."

"At home I felt like a weed in my mother's nice neat garden."

She stops herself. Why is she talking like this? He must be sparking off memories. He belongs to that time of her life; not now in her middle age. He should clear off back to the past where he belongs.

She picks up her coffee, and sits back in her chair, looking away from him towards the garden. The tick of the clock is loud in the silence.

He checks his watch.

"Well, it's been a long time Soph," he says shifting a little in his chair and looking around. His thighs are muscular, strong -looking under the cream linen trousers. "A lot of water under the bridge."

She doesn't reply, she doesn't want to talk to him any more.

George doesn't expect her to talk to him in the evenings. Now he's looking at the photograph of Gabe on the wall.

"Your son must be older now than we were then."

She nods.

"You must be proud of him. It's my greatest regret, not having a family."

"It's been a mixed blessing."

That was a mistake; he looks curious now. She had forgotten his friendly eyes. There is something canine about them. Not pleading like a Spaniel, but bright and open like a Jack Russell. Georges' are haughty. More Doberman.

"Are you worried about him?"

"No."

Perhaps she could pick his brains. After all he is a professional, and he has spoiled her evening. She could have confided in Phyll.

"Well, yes, but I've always worried about him too much. George says so. Phyll does too."

"Really?"

She puts down her cup too hard, sending it crashing into the saucer.

"If you must know I've been like this since Grace died."

"Grace? Your grandmother?"

"No. Grace was my daughter. She died when Gabe was a baby. It's all right. It was a long time ago."

People never know what to say next. '*How strong you are,*' they accuse gently, '*I couldn't cope if I lost any of my children,*' as if she should have done the decent thing and fallen on a sword, not hung around embarrassing ordinary people. She was glad when Gabe was out of primary school and she didn't have to socialise at the school gates any more. She didn't have much children small talk in her.

His eyes are soft on her face.

"I'm sorry Soph. How sad."

"Mm."

"Gabe must have been a blessing."

"I couldn't have gone on without him. George and

I…well…you know. And Mum didn't seem to…she'd lost Dad as well I suppose."

How did she get here from Gran? She reaches for a cushion and holds it on her lap, her hands picking at a lose thread.

"Actually, this is what I'm a bit worried about. We never told Gabe he had a sister. He was too young to really know her, but sometimes I wonder whether that was…right. You always get it wrong as a parent, don't you? Well, I suppose you don't, but you must see lots of people complaining about parents. Mothers probably. It always seems to be our fault."

Her laugh has no music in it any more. That's what he notices most.

"You've suffered, Soph. I'm sorry."

"Yes, well. I'm sorry to go on. I don't, usually; I know it's all in the past now. I seem to have done all the talking this evening. You're a very good listener Jez. Well, you would be, wouldn't you?"

She does her cabin crew smile. She wants him to go now. She's had enough listening. She's not used to it; it might make her ill. She stands up first. To hell with manners, she'll never see him again anyway.

"Shall we meet again Soph?"

She can hear an urgency in his tone. Does he think she's ill?

"Sure, why not? My number's in the book. Hughes. I'm Hughes now."

They edge towards the door with little steps and small gestures.

"Here's my card."

Oh God, a card. George would hate him. He'd call him a wanker.

He touches her shoulder as he leaves, and she shivers and hopes he thinks she's cold.

She leaves the coffee cups where they are and forgets to close and bolt the back door for the first time ever in her married life. Then she goes to bed as if already in a dream, and she sleeps badly.

71

ELEVEN

In the *Ship Aground*, George and Leena are half way through their meal. They have had fresh French Onion soup, the cheese still bubbling on top, and now they are eating wafer thin pancakes stuffed with prawns and covered with roasted garlic. It occurs to George that eating with Leena feels quite different from eating with Soph.

Leenas' eyes are shining in the yellow light. She waves her fork around as she eats and talks with her mouth full. She's enjoying it, he thinks; that's the difference. Soph is frightened of food, now. She's pegged a warning list, snipped from a Sunday supplement, to the fridge door, '*Food Watch*! - *chicken, lamb, eggs, soft cheese, sugar, root vegetables, butter, honey...,* ' that damn list goes on for ever. He's told her enough times that food is safer than it's ever been, that there are controls, legislation...' *'Don't be silly, George'* she says, in that prissy teacher's voice she has. He can never reassure her; it's a waste of his time trying.

"Enjoying it, Leena?"

"Mmm. Fabulous. Always great here."

He misses the innocent pleasure of eating; Sophia has spoiled it for him. Why did she have to ring earlier?

Leena is looking up at him expectantly. He hasn't heard what she said.

"Something the matter George?"

"No, not really. I was just...Soph rang before. She seemed a bit worried about Gabe or something."

He has fantasies that she will die, suddenly. She might be knifed by one of those louts in her school, or crash the car in early morning fog.

"Problem?"

"I don't think so. It sounded as if he was a bit rude to her, that's all. He's usually pretty considerate. They're very close."

72

Soph always leaks her worry into him.; she breaches his sea wall. His appetite is suddenly gone. Perhaps she's right about prawns being full of shit.

There's a silence and he passes his hand across his face, brushing off cobwebs. Over Leena's shoulder he can see a young couple. The man's knees are pressing against the girls and he is holding out a spoonful of cheesecake. Her mouth is open and her eyes are closed, like a child taking communion. George can see the tip of her tongue, pink and wet as a calf's nose. He pours himself some more wine.

"It must be really hard being a parent. People never seem to stop worrying about their kids, no matter how old the kids are."

He makes a noise somewhere between a snort and an angry laugh.

She laughs too. "Did you decide you couldn't face more than one worrying child? How sensible!"

His plate is almost empty. He won't pretend Grace never existed.

"No, no," he says too loudly, awakening the interest of the whole dining room.

People look across, and stop their conversation mid sentence. "She died, our first one, when Gabe was a baby. Our daughter Grace. Her name was Grace."

He doesn't usually name her; the hum resumes.

"Oh, I see."

"No you don't see. You haven't got any children."

Perhaps she has. Perhaps she's got ten children at home, twinkling, blue-eyed puppies running up and down the stairs and jumping on the beds.

The young couple are sipping coffee and gazing into each other's eyes. He murmurs something and she giggles and slaps the back of his hand, immediately picking it up to stroke it as if she's afraid she might have hurt him.

"No, I can only imagine."

"Don't even try. Have you ever been married, or…anything?"

"No. No, I haven't. I'm sorry for your loss George."

73

He brushes her away with his hand.

She looks across at the waiter, who comes to her immediately.

"How do you do that? They ignore me."

"Gipsy power. I'm going to order strawberry mousse. This place is famous for it. It's made with wild strawberries and Cornish cream. More wine?"

"OK. Why not?"

"That's the spirit George."

"I mean why no partners?"

He looks at her suspiciously. She eats like a man. Rarely wears a dress.

She shrugs. The waiter is setting down wine and a large crystal dish of moist pink mousse topped with flowers of cream and tiny strawberries.

"Really, why not?"

George persists, picking up his spoon, absolutely forbidding his tongue to add 'a beautiful woman like you' which it is trying to say of its own accord.

She licks at the corners of her mouth, her tongue flicking from side to side. George thinks of snakes in a pit. The wine is loosening his thoughts. He should stop drinking now, this minute. He knows he should.

"I've had a few offers."

She laughs and winks at him. She looks like a wave, he thinks. Her laugh begins in her belly. Soph laughs from her throat, barely disturbing the surface. Not that she laughs much; he can't even remember what Soph's laugh sounds like.

When he pours the next glass of wine, he sloshes some onto the tablecloth.

"You've missed out Leena."

"Have I?"

"Do you think you have?" George says, cleverly he thinks.

"Sometimes I wonder. Perhaps I've been too scared."

"What of?"

He can't imagine Leena being scared of anything. She's the sort of woman who would go on safari with you, or play ice hockey.

"You lot. Men, I mean. My father left very suddenly when I was eight. He said he'd had enough one night, and disappeared without a trace, actually; I had to watch my mother's poor heart sustain a nasty fracture. Her dazzling gypsy husband really was a rotten rover, and all the family hysterics over their relationship turned out to be for nothing. He broke his mother's heart too, when he went. Rose's only son and all that. All these poor hearts, broken to bits like chocolate eggs."

"Including yours."

"Indeed."

George shakes his head sadly.

"I remember when my father died. I felt as if I'd been turned into a man overnight. He left this big bag of responsibility behind, with my name on it : Property of George Hughes. My mother completely fell to bits. God knows why; she used to complain about him all the time when he was alive, poor sod."

"Poor little you."

The young couple are getting up to leave. He is putting his wallet back into his pocket; he has left a large tip. The waiter stands too close to the girl as he helps her on with her jacket, and George sees him murmur something in her ear. She is blushing.

"But there's still time, isn't there, Leena?"

"Time for what? I'm more interested in seeing the world than staring at the same face over dinner every night. I'm going to become nomadic; back to my roots sort of thing."

The waiter comes and goes and brings chocolates, and Irish coffee and they sit on at the table. George is pleasantly drunk, and enjoying it. He hasn't been drunk for years. He wags a finger at her.

"'Goin' to retire soon, Leena. Istanbul… I'll sit in the street cafes with the other old men. Drinkin' Raki and bullshitting and watching the Bosphorus… Sophia won't come there, will she? *Oh no.* She'll be in a rest home in Hove, watching out for burglars and worryin' about Gabe…"

"Each to their own George. I'm going to head for New York. I'll do Tai Chi in Central Park, and play my fiddle outside the

Lincoln Centre for dollars, and eat in Greenwich Village every night."

The restaurant is nearly empty now. The waiters are sitting at the bar, and smoking.

"The thing is, Leena, when you get to our age you got to have a fuckin' checklist. Start checkin' off all those things you got to do 'fore you die. Otherwise, you had it. Be too fuckin' late."

She asks for the bill, and pays half. As they walk back through the narrow streets, George puts his arm round her shoulders, like a blind man trusting his dog to lead him safely home. When she stumbles on the cobbles, he laughs uproariously, and she shushes him.

At the hotel, they wander down to the edge of the lake. The gardens are shrouded in soft darkness and the air is still warm. The water gleams with patchy light as clouds drift across a swollen Harvest moon.

Leena beckons him to stoop down. Her warm breath tickles the hairs inside his ear, and he shivers.

"I'm going to swim to the island," she whispers, "it's on my checklist."

George giggles and then stares as she strips off all her clothes, steps out of her shoes and wades into the water. Her skin is tanned all over. Swimming strongly, like a fox, she disappears from view.

An owl hoots somewhere in the trees, as he unbuckles his belt with clumsy fingers and takes off his shoes and jeans, walking in her footsteps. The bed of the lake is sandy under his bare feet. His extra height means he can wade all the way through the cool, dark water and as he gets nearer, he sees her sitting there, her wet shoulders gleaming in the moonlight and her knees drawn up to her chest. She silently applauds him, and then laughs with a hand over her mouth. He clambers up the reedy bank, disturbing a moorhen, which flaps away into the darkness, making him start. His heart is pumping hard.

He takes off his shirt, and lays it down next to her.

"Leena, what…?"

She puts a finger to her lips, warning him; George looks like a man who has just realised he is on the wrong train.

She reaches up and takes his face very gently between her two hands. Her eyes only half close as she kisses him. The tenderness of her lips calls up a long forgotten hunger in him, and in one rough movement he pushes her down to the earth and enters her, grunting at the effort and the sudden, silken, hot feeling. She wraps her legs around his waist and lifts her hips an inch or two pressing against him. In seconds, he shudders, then slumps against her warm body and rests there, in a moment empty of anything but the night and the air and the sound of water lapping.

A cool breeze blows across his back. He springs up on both elbows, and looks at Leena in alarm. She holds his gaze steadily, and then bursts out laughing again, burying her face against his shoulder, trying to stifle the sound. George gets onto his knees beside her, cold and dripping.

"Number one, checklist one," she whispers.

He stares at her; he's forgotten his theory. He wants to go to bed alone and sleep. This isn't sensible. He picks up his shirt and gestures towards the hotel. They walk the few paces to the bank and he picks her up in his arms without asking and carries her over to the other side. She feels solid. She is heavier than he would have imagined.

Leena dresses quickly, wrings out her hair and sprints off across the grass, blowing him a kiss. George dries himself with his shirt, and dresses slowly. He isn't drunk any more. The grass seems to have lost its spring as he trudges towards the hotel alone.

The night smells of earth and smoke and water.

TWELVE

Leena shakes out her hair before she crosses the dim reception. The hotel is dreaming, quiet as a library. A blonde girl behind the pale wooden counter is startled by the unexpected creak of floorboards and looks up from a thick paperback, frowning.

"Is it raining out there?"

"No, I wish it were. I went for a swim in the lake. Can I have my key please? Room 37."

The girl passes over the key without looking at her.

"Not supposed to," she mumbles, and is gone again, her eyes sucked back down to her book. Her knobbly fingers are twirling a thin strand of blonde hair and her teeth chew at her top lip.

Back in her room, Leena turns on the bath taps and pours in oil, then she lights a cigarette and switches on the television while the bath is filling. When her mobile rings, she turns down the sound and carries the phone into the bathroom. She reads the number before she answers, and smiles.

"Hallo...no, at a hotel. I'm away working...pity...mmm...very warm night...just getting into a bath actually Nick...you're right, I am a little bit tipsy, trying to undress and hold the phone...you're wicked...wish you were too...all right then..."

She stubs out the cigarette in the sink, and steps into the blue water still holding the phone to her ear. *"This water feels good...*She rests her head on the back of the bath...*"I'm thinking of you too, Nick... in here with me...you're touching my nipple..."*

The fingers of her right hand slowly pinch and circle her left nipple, making it swell. They flicker down then, across her belly. Nick is whispering in her ear. She's always loved his voice; it's as rich as a Christmas cake loaded with marzipan and cherries and nuts. He was always being asked to do food ads. Nick had been the voice of hot chocolate, gourmet soup and double cream in between his television work.

" ... now your hand's between my thighs Nick...you're stroking me, and stroking me...that feels nice... sweet and nice..."

She laughs out loud as the phone goes suddenly dead. "Goodnight to you too, Nicky" she murmurs into the silence, broken only by the whooshing of the warm water.

Her hand is still moving under the bubbles, pressing slow, deep circles into the pink curls of her flesh.

She closes her eyes and takes long deep breaths. She can see George's puzzled face in the moonlight, and taste his shoulder as he carried her back across the lake in the darkness. He was warm inside her. She's made love with men who've felt cold as a speculum. She'd felt his heart patter nervously against his chest as he lay on top of her on the warm, dry ground.

She wants to finish what George only started. Her fingers splay open and go deeper. They move faster and harder, in a tight whirl that makes her neck stretch backwards and both feet arch. The fingers of her left hand weaken and her phone falls into the water but it's too late to pick it up. The tingling wave has gathered momentum and is shivering there ready to break. She arches her back and spreads her legs wide, banging her knees against the sides of the bath. There is the sound of her phone clunking along the bottom, caught up in the rapid swoosh of water, and Leena's rapid breathing.

Seconds pass, and the sensation fades in the cooling air. She sits up slowly and plucks out the phone shaking it hard. "That was all your fault," she murmurs, and reaches for a towel.

In the bedroom, she brushes and plaits her hair and puts on the raspberry silk pyjamas she bought in Hong Kong, haggling with the tailor in a bright market full of ripe fruit and steaming bowls and bamboo cages stuffed with feathered birds. She'd felt at home there. Her brown skin and dark hair blended in with the buzzing boiling crowd.

She moves to the middle of the room, standing quietly, her bare feet slightly apart, and her eyes half closed. In one smooth, slow movement, she drops her hands to her sides and bends her elbows and wrists. She stands poised, her hands at her hips,

79

parallel to the floor.

As the television flickers out multi coloured images of people shoving and shouting somewhere in protest, she begins to make slow circles and moves and turns, gathering her spent energy back in. She moves silently, like a piece of ribbon.; she seems to have no bones.

If her evening had taken a different turn, if she hadn't gone out with George, if she hadn't drunk wine, if Nick hadn't rung at that precise moment, she might have paid attention to the late night news and registered that the man with the hate-filled eyes, a fleck of spittle at the corner of his dry looking, mean mouth, who is screaming at the camera: *"Gippos Out! Gippos Out! Gippos, Out! Out! Out!"* was one of a crowd standing in their local market place.

Long after the news has finished, she finishes her Tai Chi form and stands still, her hands together in front of her, palms touching. Her head is as clear as a Welsh spring.

If George had been watching television, he might have recognised Amelia's flaming hair on the fringes of the crowd, keeping well away from the police who have been forced to link arms to keep people in the square. Women with shopping bags are trying to push by, and grinning kids are leaping at the camera, loving the excitement in the usually dull, morose shopping centre, but George has been asleep for two hours. His clothes are in a damp pile on the bathroom floor, and he is snoring lightly with a gentle sound like a snickering animal.

Leena takes a cup of tea to bed, and reads for a while in the light of the pink-shaded bedside lamp, before she lies down and closes her eyes with a small sigh.

Outside in the middle of the lawn a vixen stands and barks at the moon. Her cry is harsh and strange; Leena smiles into sleep. The sound knits itself into George's dream about a baby lost in a desert, and the baby waves its hands and begins to cry.

THIRTEEN

Sophia hurries up the crumbling front steps to the sooty
Victorian house that
Gabe shares with Lucian and some girls, in a scruffy part of the
city. She is hoping they can cook; Gabe doesn't eat enough. He's
always been too thin.

Next door, three young men are leaning against the dull railings
that must have once been importantly black and glossy. Their
faces are turned upwards towards the sun like Russian statues,
their burnished skin gleaming in the midday light. The sweet
bonfire smell of cannabis drifts lazily up to greet her as she rings
the bell, and high- pitched laughter bursts from the men like
coloured ribbons.

This part of London frightens Sophia. It's too dirty and
unpredictable. Down and outs rub shoulders with actresses and
road sweepers and politicians; everywhere there's a muddle of
people. A siren shrieks in the distance, and sweat drips down the
back of her neck. The men are watching her and she is relieved to
hear the sound of a key turning behind the old scarred door.

"Hallo darling!"

"Hallo Mrs Hughes!"

Lucian holds out two hands to welcome her, and grins: "I'm
afraid you've got the wrong darling, darling"

He stands aside to let her come in and she glances nervously
over her shoulder, even though Lucian has shut the door and
locked it.

"Are your neighbours…you know, *all right* Lucian?"

He is still holding her arm and he gives it a reassuring squeeze.

"Ali and Steve and Harold. They're all perfectly charming, Mrs
H. Personal friends and fellow students. Well, Ali's a lecturer
actually."

"I just wondered…"

"Please don't worry. We're perfectly safe in our nest. Why don't you have a look around while I make some coffee?"

"Thank you, but where's…?"

"On his way, I think. He's expecting you. He's probably poking about in skips. Your talented son has been decorating again. What do you think of the colour scheme.. …"

Lucian's words tail off and he disappears into the kitchen.

Gabe could have made an effort to be here; she'd told him she'd arrive at one. There was a time when he would never leave her side. She can still see his big, anxious eyes scanning the throng outside the school gates. Her mother used to tell her it wasn't natural for him to need her so much.

He's painted the hall tangerine and gold and the wide high-ceilinged sitting room in the kind of blue you only find in Greece. Where the walls are cracked and the plaster crumbling, he's hung bold swathes of material. There are yellow embroidered silks and black velvet, and a piece of jagged scarlet linen above the fireplace. It feels like walking through a painting.

"It's amazing. It reminds me of Brighton Pavilion. Doesn't your landlord mind?"

"Charles? No, not as long as he gets the eight hundred quid a month in his greedy paw. Mind you, we don't invite him in if we can help it. Will you be comfortable on the floor Mrs H? Charles says he can't afford chairs. I bet he's got chairs in his own penthouse pad in Docklands, don't you? "

Sophia sits down on a large cushion with her coffee. She hasn't sat on the floor since she was a student herself. She can see her eighteen-year old legs in wide denims embroidered with daisies, her thighs young and tight and hopeful. She had happy legs, and happy little feet, in her flat Indian sandals. Is the smell of patchouli lingering in her memory, or a part of this room now? She begins to stroke her cushion. Perhaps she'll ask Lucian whether he thinks Gabe is all right. He'll be honest with her.

It's hard to find any space on the table for her cup. It's covered in books, newspapers, pens, filled ashtrays and an open packet of coconut Madeleine cakes, the sticky red cherries gleaming on their frosted thrones.

Lucian is making fussy piles.

"I swear I am the *only* one who lifts a finger in this place."

"Gabe's the same at home."

"You can't have trained him well I'm afraid, Mrs Hughes. I've never known anyone so completely oblivious to mess."

She reaches out a hand to help, and picks up an open book. Stevie Smith, it must belong to one of the girls. Before she closes it, she tucks the flap into the page where there is much heavy underlining in red ink. *'Much too far out all my life....'* She used to love those lines at their age.

She pushes the book to the edge of the table and puts the cakes on the top. A paper bag of multi coloured jellybeans spills out onto the floor and she begins to pick them up in handfuls. Lucian is pulling the curtains and opening the windows and fanning himself with a copy of *Time Out*.

"Shall I fetch the fan from the kitchen? I'm melting away. I can't believe this summer is ever going to come to an end."

"I want to talk to you for a minute, Lucian. Is Gabe...you know, *all right?*

Her eyes meet hers. She can see he is choosing his words carefully and her stomach lurches.

"I think" he says slowly, "Gabe is really...here!"

Sophia jumps at the sound of the front door slamming and feet on the stairs. She scrambles to her feet like a child caught in the act, and turns towards the door as Gabe comes into the room sideways, carrying a haberdasher's bolt of acid green shot silk.

"Bingo," he says, tossing it at Lucian who catches it and props it up in the corner next to an over full bookcase.

"More mess," he grumbles. Gabe ignores him.

"Hallo mother. Brought me some sweeties?"

He is not smiling and Sophia can feel her face tighten. She puts the jellybeans back into the paper bag on the table where they spill out again.

"Whoops," says Lucian.

"Hallo Gabe. Are you all right darling?"

She watches his fine features freeze into a glower.

"Only good boys get sweeties," says Lucian plucking up the bag. "You're late for your lovely Mum, and she's come all the way to see you in this terrible heat. You should be ashamed of yourself."

"Arsehole." Gabe picks up a cushion and throws it at him.

Lucian makes his mouth into a tight 'o' and pokes his tongue in and out, shutting the door before the cushion falls.

"He's a nice boy."

"Lucian's cool."

"We're late for lunch. I booked a table."

"Sorry."

He comes over to her and she hugs him, wishing she could press him back into her body like a piece of clay and start all over again.

The dusty streets have taken on the overripe smell of a Southern European town in August. Sophia has to walk faster than she would like. She always has to with Gabe. As soon as he was able to outstrip her, at eleven or twelve years old, he started to walk slightly ahead. She has been trotting behind all her life it seems to her, trying to keep up with her mother, and then with George and now with her son. Only friends and lovers stroll, she thinks, wanting the pleasure of matching their steps. She had strolled along with Jez in late summer, past newly creosoted fences and pebble dashed houses with clean windows and well kept front gardens.

"Come on Mum. I'll have to get you a shovel."

"What?"

"For the shit."

"What do you mean?"

He doesn't reply.

After a short tube ride in the clammy dark of the underground, they come out into a brighter, better part of London where Sophia feels at home. Girls with glossy hair and lean thighs flash glances at Gabe, but he doesn't look back. He walks like George, his eyes

84

fixed on the end of the road.

When they get to *Toni's*, he waits and lets her go in first. They've been coming here for celebrations ever since Gabe was a child. Toni has a rare collection of Maria Callas recordings which he plays on an old record player, housed in a solid walnut cabinet he polishes every day. *'Good for the food',* He says it to every customer, patting his tight round belly, *'makes for good digestion, no?'* Sophia smiles at him. The little café smells of sweet tomatoes and basil and beeswax and cheese as it always does. Her world pulls itself together again; everything is all right here.

Gabe orders linguine and clams and garlic bread and she has minestrone soup. She can see a smudgy darkness all around his eyes that gives his face a bruised look, but she knows she must not comment, and tells herself it is because he is going to parties at last.

Instead she chatters. He used to like hearing about her job, it used to make him laugh.

"And then, Gabe, the Head said to this very small boy in Year Seven who still had the lighted cigarette in his hand, and was showing no signs at all of putting the thing out, *'I shall make an appointment to see your father,'* and this boy stood there like Noel Coward and said *'In that case, mate, I shall try to do the same.'* Then he spat on his shoe. I think that was what finally finished the Head off. He went off sick the next day, and hasn't been seen since!"

Gabe's face has darkened again, and the atmosphere has changed; he isn't laughing.

"Can you believe the cheek? I swear they're getting worse every year."

Gabe is rubbing the scar on his neck.

"Yes I bloody well can believe it. Remember this?"

"That scar? Well, it was something you did when you were little, wasn't it? I can't quite remember…"

He is leaning across the table. The rims of his nostrils are white and his mouth is twisted. For the first time in her life, she sees he can be ugly.

85

"Well can you remember when I was eleven? When you kindly refused to let me go to the same school as Alan and Bradley?"

The music is too loud now, and a sudden trickle of sweat rolls down her ribs. The pasta in her minestrone glistens like lumps of fat, and she pushes her bowl away.

" But you were so clever Gabe. We couldn't have let you go just anywhere."

She can remember the conversation quite clearly. They were all having Sunday lunch together. She had said Elwood School would guarantee him a place at university. George had laughed and said Heron Park, on the other hand, would guarantee him a place at Parkhurst. It was all good humoured. No one was angry. There was no row.

"Oh no, of course not. It was only what I wanted."

Gabe had started to be sarcastic around that time. When he'd started walking in front of her, and stopped being her friend.

"But you did so well there. It was a lovely school. They really encouraged you with your art."

The music has stopped. Her voice is loud and plaintive in the gap.

"Do you remember that blazer with the purple and black stripes? Stood out, didn't it? Attracted attention of the negative kind."

"What are you saying? You were bullied? You never said you were bullied."

"Of course I was bullied. We used to come out at the same time as Heron Park. Those bastards got on the same bus."

It had started with name-calling. *'Got yer 'andbag Gabriel? Got yer lipstick wiv' yer? Aw, he looks tired today. Up late doin' homework, Gabby?'*

He sat downstairs on the bus. They followed him down. He sat upstairs. They pursued him up again. He got off the bus to walk home and they swarmed off at the next stop and stood waiting for him, an army of malevolent crows, jeering and cawing.

"Why *on earth* didn't you tell me Gabe?"

He says nothing. Just raises an eyebrow as if the very idea was far-fetched.

She did listen to him. She was always there for him.

When he had the nightmares that plagued him as a child, she used to lie down beside him and soothe him with colours while she stroked his head ' *Think about rainbows, Gabe, green and yellow and pink in a blue sky…big oranges in a red bowl…and…I know…a deep green sea for swimming in…just imagine…*

"When did it stop?"

"When I punched Bradley in the face, and knocked his front tooth out."

"*What?*"

Bradley had come bounding up the stairs first, his upper lip already showing the beginnings of a blonde moustache, bellowing in Gabe's face with the idiotic intensity of a future intransigent bigot: *'Yew sure Mummy lets you take this off, Gabby?'* He flung Gabe's blazer to the floor and wiped his feet on it. *'She'll have to giv it a little wash now, wont she?'*

"I aimed at his head and got him square on the nose" Gabe is laughing. "Pow! It started to bleed. Then I kicked him in the leg, and he smashed his teeth into the metal bar."

"How dreadful."

"Dreadful for whom?"

"I had no idea all that was going on Gabe."

"No you didn't, did you?"

When he went to bed that night, his shoulder and wrist were stiff and painful. In the dark he saw the blood dripping again from Bradley's nose, and heard the sound of his teeth crunching against metal. He was afraid he might have killed him.

"Were you hurt? Did he do that to you?"

Gabe is still rubbing his neck.

"The scar? No. I did that to myself."

He'd sat on the edge of his bed, feeling sick, the nausea rising and rising in his throat until he snatched up a plastic hangar that was lying on the floor, and broke it in half. In one sudden, jerky movement, he brought it up to his neck and cut in deeply. The sting of pain replaced the fear, and he was empty of thought or emotion.

"*What?*"

Sophia is pleating the green gingham tablecloth on her lap. She pleats it and drops it and pleats it again; she can't stop. She is biting the inside of her cheek very hard.

"Feeling sorry for yourself, Ma?"

Gabe reaches over and strokes her cheek lightly with one finger, like a husband.

"Don't. None of it matters now anyway. The world's only an illusion, didn't you know? I'm into Zen these days. I think I might go to India and become a sanyassin. Do you think saffron is my colour? With a touch of red?"

He is standing up and blowing her a kiss.

"Thanks for lunch, Mum."

"Must you go? I want to talk to you Gabe."

He doesn't reply, just waves to her through the window, before the street swallows him up.

She pushes crumbs around the tablecloth, filling in the white squares with piles of biscuit. The café gathers itself around her and she feels the comfort of the wax- covered bottles, the fat old tabby asleep on the window sill, the pictures of Sorrento and Capistrano. She orders brandy and strong dark coffee. If she could just stay here for the rest of her life, listening to Maria Callas and watching the bubbling crowd in the bright street full of department stores and busy taxis and laughing girls in shorts, everything would be all right.

Toni closes at five, and gently asks her to leave at five thirty. On her way back to the station, she hurries past a ragged man in the subway who is sitting on the steps holding out a plastic cup. There are cracks in his fingers, showing raw, red flesh through the grey skin. He shouts after her with a voice like a saw that echoes down the tunnel and bounces off the wall and beats at her ears, "*Thanks For Nothing You Tight Bastard!*"

Her train comes late. When it arrives, she locks herself in the toilet and cries. The whistle blows and the train lurches out of the station and someone raps impatiently on the door.

THIRTEEN

It's the first day of September, and outside the tempo has changed, although the weather is still as hot. The schools are open again, car doors are slamming an hour or two earlier than last week and the quiet summer streets are busy again. Sophia's cat jumps off the bed when the alarm rings. If George were home she wouldn't have been there in the first place, but she stalks away anyway, stiff-legged and ungrateful, swishing her tail.

Sophia showers reluctantly and puts on make-up and pulls her briefcase from the back of the wardrobe where she threw it, with a sigh of relief, in July. She leaves without any breakfast, her stomach already in knots.

She slides the car into the last space left in the staff car park under the tree where the birds sit; when she comes out, there'll be shit all over her roof.

Some of the members of her old form shamble into the Art Room and she sits down to take names. She does it by sight rather than asking for responses; she's given up trying to get their attention. Keely is absent as usual, and there's a note in the register from David, the acting Head, asking her to go to a meeting at lunchtime to discuss her truancy. Sophia curses under her breath; she was hoping the truancy issue had been forgotten over the summer holidays.

On her way, she walks into the first fight of term.

"Fuck off!"

"You fuck off!"

"Give that back you fucking bitch!"

Sophia looks at the two girls who are looking back at her with contempt. The slighter one sprints off down the corridor, cackling like a witch. The heavy girl throws Sophia a very dirty look, and balls her hands into fists before she thrusts them into blazer pockets made shiny with age and lack of proper care. She turns on her heel sucking her teeth, but Sophia ignores the challenge. She doesn't care any more. She might as well try to do something about global warming; they're all out of control. Their parents don't seem to care any more either. When summoned they come reluctantly, shrugging and sighing as if their children were strange countries half way across the world, trying to involve them in complex, international debate. Sometimes the parents come in fighting, overseas armies arriving to liberate captured hostages.

Sophia wishes she were at home with the cat.; this place will never change despite the ceaseless new government initiatives and target chasing and box ticking.

"Morning Mrs H!"

Sophia's heart jumps like a frog surprised in a hedge.

"Hallo Janet. Here we are again. Did you see those two?"

"It's hell out here quite honestly. The first day back and they're strutting around like the junior SS already. *Stop that Andrew! Now! Thank you!*"

Sophia looks at Andrew. She didn't recognise him; he's had his head shaved by some amateur and it's covered in scabs. Janet hasn't given up though. She still makes them pick up litter and clean off graffiti and stop fighting.

"How do you do it Janet? Last time I told Andrew to stop spitting he called me a fucking cunt and reported me to his parents as if I'd somehow violated his human right to spit."

"I've got natural authority Sophia. They smell it, like dogs. I see the school community as an extended pack myself. You have to show them you're dominant. Stop them jumping on the furniture, make them eat in a separate place, that sort of thing. You haven't got it I'm afraid."

"You're right. I think I must be a puppy. Or one of the old bitches no-one takes any notice of any more."

"Oh dear. Sounds like menopausal misery."

"And the cure is...?"

"Well, whisky and fags work for me, but I wouldn't recommend that to anyone still aiming for a healthy retirement."

"I'm more wine and crisps myself."

Janet swipes a magazine from a passing boy without breaking her stride. He says

"*Aw*".

Sophia looks at him. If she had tried the same trick there would have been pandemonium; she doesn't belong here any more.

Janet waves the front cover in front of Sophia's nose.

"Just look at the state of her! She's enormous. You don't seem to put on any weight Sophia in spite of all these crisps. You're still as slim as a sixteen year old. Where do all the snacks go?"

"It's all nervous tension; I burn the calories off just getting through registration every morning."

"You need to relax more. Have you thought of having an affair?"

A shaft of sunlight breaks through the grimy corridor window and makes her blink. She can hardly breathe in here; the smell of cabbage and chips mingles with a century of ground in dirt, unimpressed by cleaners' mops and buckets. Her mother used to think it was nervousness that made her vomit every Monday morning as a school girl, but it was the thought of that smell. It lurked in the corners, waiting to jump down her throat the moment she walked in through the doors.

They are passing the canteen, where children are shuffling past wry-faced women who frisk them with their small hard eyes waiting to pounce on those taking too much.

"Have you had affairs, Janet?"

"Oh God, yes. It was the only thing that got me through my forties."

"But what about…?"

"I…*what the*? Sorry, Sophia…"

There are raised voices and the sound of china smashing, and Janet has dived into the fray like the lead member of a crash team. Sophia walks on alone; there's no point in her going in as well, she'll only make things worse.

David prances by like a celebrity at a premiere, trailing a small boy behind him who is looking close to tears. She hopes he won't cry, the others will eat him alive. They don't like the stench of vulnerability, it attracts them like sharks around a bloody wound. You have to be tough to go to this school, it's one of the entrance requirements.

Did Gabe cry at school? She can't stop thinking about the bullying. Why didn't he tell her? Why did he keep it all a secret?

David's words are getting fainter as he turns the corner. "Meeting…Keely…ten minutes…you start…sorry…" That means he won't turn up at all. Now she'll have to sort out Keely and her mother and the snotty educational welfare man whom seems to think truants spend their time making explosives and sharpening the kitchen knives, rather than watching *Tricia* and *Home and Away*. They're probably better educated than the ones who do come to school. They can talk about near death experiences and transvestism and nuances of Australian culture.

Did Gabe ever truant? How would she know?

She slips on a crisp packet on the floor and nearly falls, earning herself a snigger from two girls strolling down the corridor arm in arm, discussing shoes. As she approaches the Head's office, she can hear a cough and the shuffling of feet from inside but no friendly conversation.

One of Keely's paintings is hanging on the wall outside, and Sophia glances over at it, one hand on the door. It is a glorious water colour of Autumn woods, yellow, gold, bronze and scarlet filling the frame with a cascade of whirling joy. Sophia had sat with Keely as she painted, long after the others had dismissed themselves and gone shrieking on their way to sizzling chip shops and warm damp buses. It was dark by the time she had finished.

"That is *fantastic*," Sophia had said, almost in a whisper.

"It's all right." Keely was indifferent. That's what they'd called I the painting: *'All Right'*.

Sophia had pinned it up on her classroom wall, where it beamed encouragement at her on bleak days when her head felt like a bag of marbles, but the Head took a fancy to it during one of his pre-inspection displays of guilty involvement. He came in to Sophia's classroom room without knocking and paced about for a while, glaring at the students as if they had no right to be there. He pointed to a boy, then up at Keely's painting and beckoned with a finger, giving the impression that he didn't speak much English.

"That is good Mrs Hughes. Very good indeed."

"Well…" She tried to dampen his enthusiasm but it was too late. He gathered up Keely's beautiful trees and they disappeared into the jaws of a new folder.

"But *I* want it."

She heard herself sound like a six year old. The Head smiled like Vincent Price, and left without saying goodbye.

'All Right' has been re-named *'Autumn Leaves'*. Sophia frowns, knowing it has been hung in the main corridor, not as testament to Keely's effort but as advertisement of the talent of the staff.

It is too hot and too dark in the Head's study with the blinds closed. Keely and her mother are huddled in one corner. The older woman has panda eyes and is trying to take up as little a space as she can. Dermott is spanning the other corner like a bridge, each elbow claiming the adjacent chair, his legs spread wide. He smells of sweat and leather. No one nice would wear a jacket like that in this weather, Sophia thinks.

She begins. "Hallo, everybody. David's asked me to start without him. Good morning, Keely, nice to see you back again, good morning Mrs…." Oh God, she's forgotten the name. It's odd; eastern European sounding, with 'c's' and 'z's' and an 'o'. No one tells her what it is.

Dermott grunts and shuffles his papers and Keely and her mother smile. Keely's smile is slow and sensual; her mother's is frightened. No wonder, Sophia thinks, after the latest vicious affair in the market place. She sits down next to Keely, to even up the balance of chairs claimed.

"Dermott, would you like…?"

No, that was wrong. She shouldn't have asked him first. It's Keely's mother who needs permission to speak.

"Non attendance…four out of forty…legal duty…major problem."

His voice is monotonous. It drips into Sophia's ear, hitting the same bone every time.

She sees him looking at Keely's tight, white satin shirt buttoned over fat breasts. It seems to make him angry; the smell in the room is getting worse.

"What do you have to say for yourself, Keely?"

He is glaring at her. Her mother is pressed so far back against the wall, she is barely there. Keely is smoothing her skirt down over her plump thighs. It stops a good six inches above her round, brown knees.

"I'm abused. When I'm here."

"What?" Dermotts' eyes have narrowed.

"They call me a gippo slag , they call me a gypsy whore, they call me a fucking pikey bastard and they do it all the time, every day, wherever I go. So I don't come. And I wont."

Sophia holds her breath. Why can't Keely just pretend she'll come? It's only a formality. No one really cares. She can't just say what she thinks, for God's Sake. Nobody tells the truth any more.

"*You...must...come. It's...the...law, girl.*"

Sophias' ears are hurting.

"I won't. Not until it's sorted out."

Sophia looks at her. It will never be sorted out. Doesn't she know? Not in a hundred years. Not in a thousand. As long as there are people alive like Dermott and Amelia.

"We can't have different laws for...*you people.*"

Dermott is spitting out his words.

"You tell that to the police and the social services mate. Tell that to the council."

Oh God; Keely is laughing at him now. She's hunched over, and peals of laughter are spilling out from between her fingers and her shoulders are shaking. Her mother pokes her in the ribs hard, but she won't stop; Dermott's fists are clenched.

Sophia stands up quickly.

"*Right,* well, thank you for coming in everybody. Obviously we need to address the bullying issue and come up with some

94

strategies to support Keely, and then talk again…"

Dermott stares as the women file out. Keely's mother presses Sophia's hand as she passes, but Sophia thinks that she doesn't deserve it. Dermott is left behind in the sweaty fug he created. She hears him mutter: *'stupid bitch'* and the cold snap of his briefcase. She knows he means her.

She can't even paint any more. Her watercolours had finally turned up in the shed and yesterday she went to buy sable brushes and some good paper, thinking that she'd forget about Gabe, and make something positive of the last day of the summer holiday.

She had snipped a rose from a one of the bushes in the garden, pink and gold and open as a baby's hand and then poured water into her favourite blue jug, put in the rose and set it on the kitchen table, taking care with the light and the shadows.

A warm breeze had blown in from the garden through the open door, ruffling her hair and kissing the back of her neck. Sophia was humming as she dipped her brush into the water and covered the paper.

She was still humming when she caught sight of the old paint flecks on the table leg, but then her fingers had stiffened and in the end her hand stopped and wouldn't move any more and she sat there for an hour before she got up and went to make herself tea.

 Some petals had fallen from the rose; it was overblown after all. Her paper was blank, except for one pink tear.

FOURTEEN

"These are bloody bone dry again, Rose, it's impossible to iron them. You wouldn't believe the fuss he makes over creased shirts."

The woman on Rose's right jerks her head towards the nearest caravan. The powerful black bitch asleep on the front step twitches her ears in sympathy, and a faint sound of snoring drifts through the open metal door.

"Why wouldn't I believe it? I had years of it myself when mine was alive. *Rose,* the dinner's cold, *Rose,* there's no beer, *Rose,* the boy's crying…"

"They're all the fucking same."

"My boy was turning the same way as his father before he went off with a local girl. He had a mean streak in him."

Rose kicks out at a chicken that squawks and flaps away, throwing up fine, dry, dirt.

"Their hearts grow hard as they get older."

"You don't realise until…oh!"

Rose claps a hand on her own heart and finds herself face to face with Brendan, who has come suddenly round the corner. His smile glitters at both of them; they could be his favourite aunts he is surprising with a visit. His sleeves are rolled up, showing off his smooth, tanned forearms and an expensive watch. He is wearing aftershave. There's some electricity crackling about Brendan that causes Rose to step back a pace; she senses a woman's influence on him.

Brendan had been singing in the bathroom this morning. His younger son stared at him as he crooned *Love Me Tender* to the showerhead. Brendan had winked, not caring that he would run straight down to the kitchen to tell his mother. His wife and daughter have fallen silent lately and are watching him resentfully, like cats on a window ledge looking in.

His first encounter with Amelia had been by telephone. He'd decided in the end to ring her personally, seeing all the signs in her letter of a classic long-term complainer. Thinking he would fob her off with a few conciliatory words and a dose of Irish charm, he jabbed at her number with an irritated finger, not looking forward to hearing more of the carping tones that dog his days at work. He has replayed that first conversation a dozen times since, like a teenager.

"Hallo?"

"Hallo Mrs Massie, it's Brendan McFall here, I'm the …"

"Brendan! Oh - *hallo it's you!"*

She greeted him with the unexpected intimacy offered by members of the public who believe themselves to be on first name terms with a celebrity, by dint of regular exposure to gossip magazines. Brendan faltered.

"Er…with regard to your complaint, Mrs Massie…"

"*Do* call me Amelia, Brendan. I hope you don't mind me calling you Brendan, it's just that I'm a neighbour of the Hughes, and Sophia told me to contact you with my little complaint. She was sure you'd be able to help. It's so decent of you to telephone me *personally."*

Her voice cracked in mid-syllable and Brendan swallowed. She made him feel like a decent man, though he can't imagine what Sophia thought she was playing at, encouraging her neighbours to complain to him personally. She's never liked him.

"I do try to be available to members of the public who have concerns."

Amelia giggled, and that was it. A cold tingle ran down his spine, spread itself out over his buttocks and lodged deep inside his testicles.

"I *hate* to trouble you Brendan. I know you must be a busy man."

"No, no," Brendan croaked himself, "please do carry on Amelia."

She told him about her disappearing milk and her Brownie pack and the rubbish from Heronmarsh that blows about the town, and how she fears for her safety coming home alone at night with no husband to meet her from the station. He made sympathetic noises as the sugar coated voice danced up and down his thighs, and by the time she had come to the end of her list, Brendan had an erection.

"Dear me, I have gone on, and there's probably nothing you can do. I expect your hands are tied? George is always reminding me that travelling people have rights and that's only fair isn't it?"

"Well… I think there are some options we could look at, Amelia. Definitely. Residents have rights too you know and we don't want anybody at all to be upset in our borough. Why don't you drop into the Town hall for a chat? I'll get my secretary to make you an appointment."

"Marvellous. I'll be there *totally* at your convenience, Brendan."

By this time Brendan knew two things clearly; one, that he had to go to bed with Amelia, and two, that he would do whatever it took to get her there.

The happy smile he is currently offering up to Rose and her neighbour follows a delightfully flirtatious meeting with Amelia and a lunchtime drink afterwards. He had given her a lift home and she'd looked at him as if he were a big bar of chocolate when she got out of his car. A brief flash of black lace suspenders made him grip the steering wheel tightly.

The women are waiting, not smiling back at him.

"Well, good afternoon, ladies. A woman's work is never done, eh? Don't mind me."

Rose is silent. The sound of hammers on steel is carrying in the still air as the men work on scrap cars. A curl of smoke rises from the far end of the field, and Brendan sniffs the air.

"Ah, the smell of bonfires. Makes me think of winter. Better be careful it doesn't get out of control; this grass is so dry."

Rose stares. He knows fires are banned.

"That was a bad business in the town the other day wasn't it? Very bad indeed. I'm going to take a walk around the place and make sure everything's all right for you. No sabotage, that sort of thing. You can't be too careful these days. Give me a ring if you see anything suspicious. Remember, we're all on the same side."

As he leaves, he takes a small black notebook and a pen out of the breast pocket in his shirt. The black dog looks up; she pulls back her ears and curls her lip showing long, white teeth.

"Is he the...?"

"He is. Big chief himself."

"What's he doing, sniffing round here? He's never come to hold our hands before."

"He's looking for trouble, that's what he's doing."

Rose looks around herself. She can feel a change of mood on site. The hammering has stopped, which means the men are listening to what's going on, toddlers are hiding their faces in their mother's skirts. Rose knows that all around people are taking in the chickens they are not supposed to keep, and the puppies they are not supposed to breed, gathering them up before Brendan appears with his little notebook.

She wipes her forehead with the back of her hand, and takes a deep breath. Last night she slept badly in the airless caravan, dreaming of a battlefield shrouded by fog. Voices kept calling to her out of the mist, but she couldn't move and the choking feeling of dread has followed her into the mid-morning.

Rose's neighbour picks up her washing and walks off towards her caravan, her cracked shoes crunching on the dried, brown grass. As she goes up the step her shoulders begin to droop and the snoring stops.

Rose looks worried for a moment, before she buttons up her face. She kicks her basket to one side, throwing the doorstep dog a threatening look, and follows Brendan, treading silently, keeping to the bare earth.

There is a smell of soft tar and petrol in the air. A cloud of flies buzz around a patch near the trees and that's where Brendan is, bending down, his lip curled like the dog's, his notebook in one hand and his pen in the other.

Rose stops and backs away into the shadow of the office, this week bolted and padlocked while George and Leena are away. Someone has drawn flowers on the wall with a marker pen. Someone else has vomited up the door.

Brendan's pen is moving swiftly and shining in the sun. Rose hears the superior snap of his book as he closes it and slots it back into his shirt pocket. In the glint of her eye, and the downturn of her mouth there is a lifetime of held in tears and swallowed angry words. Most of the pain has lodged in the joints of her hands and toes, which are twisted and bent as hazel twigs. She jumps at the sound of a noise coming through the trees from the main road.

"Coo-ee, Brendan! Coo-ee!"

It is a chocolate and central heating voice; a woman's magazine voice. It is a voice looking forward to dinner in a Chinese restaurant, with Chardonnay and Peking duck and fortune cookies. It doesn't belong near the site.

Brendan quivers and spins around, like a dog scenting a squirrel, and gallops off towards the road, waving his notebook and beaming; Rose screws up her eyes. She glimpses auburn curls and a small soft hand waving enthusiastically from the grass verge on the other side of the fence. Rose spits on the ground despising the dust which will be turning into mud in a month or two, making the van wheels spin and the little children fall over.

FIFTEEN

Sophia is in the garden shed, balanced on a coiled garden hose and the rusted tines of a fork.

She glances around, checking the corners for spiders. She hates the way spiders appear out of the shadows and pause, considering their next move. The way they speed towards another patch of darkness and disappear. Do you pursue a spider? Heave furniture out of the way and hunt down its hiding place? George might, and Jez certainly would, she thinks. Sophia usually turns away and tries to forget, hoping it won't turn up again in another corner in another room, another day.

She spots the shears and reaches for them. The fork shifts and stabs her in the ankle and she kicks an old packet of lawn fertilizer lying there, unopened and damp.

Other people have sheds where the tools are cleaned and oiled and hung up on racks. Jez would probably have a shed just like that, with gleaming tools and a shelf running the whole length of it. He'd have labelled boxes holding bulbs ready for planting at the right time of year. There'd be sunshine pouring in through clean windows. She wouldn't be risking tetanus if she went into Jez's shed, if he had one.

Even George's shears are rusty she notices as she strokes the blade edge with her thumb. Since Gabe left home there's been no spark in George. He's as flat as an old battery, crusty acid oozing out of his pores. If she touched him she'd burn herself.
She doesn't touch him anymore. He pushed her away once too often and that was the end of that. George's body is private land now, fenced off. When they first met they used to talk for hours in bed, lying close together, their eyes meeting, skin touching down the length of their bodies. It seems like another country now, the talking and the touching.

She heaves out the shears and slams the shed door shut before the mower falls over backwards and collapses onto the lawn.

George used to bring Grace up here. They spent hours playing postman, taking it in turns to stand outside the shed and post leaf letters to each other under the wooden door. She used to watch them from the kitchen window, her big man, young and energetic, his eyes dancing, and her little Grace with her serious expression, and tangled curls bobbing up and down.

"Post you, post you," she'd say over and over and over again. It sounded like 'poor you' in her two year old piping voice. Who could have imagined Grace was only a bubble, waiting to burst? That someone so sparkling and full of life was going to melt away like frost, and simply not exist?

Sophia thrusts the shears into the roses. The blooms that are left seem to glow with a richer colour in the late summer light, but the petals are falling and soon the hard hips will come.

After Grace died, all George could talk about was the news. He read to her from the papers when Gabe had been put to bed, and she used to stare at him, wondering why he hadn't realised her brain had been pulped along with her heart. She was all shredded, body, mind and soul.

She chops and slices savagely, thrusting her hands in and out of the sturdy branches. When she hears the front door bell, she drops the shears and runs down the garden, her hands scratched and bloody from the thorns.

"Coming!"

She knows it's Phyll. Sophia often doesn't answer the door, and Phyll, wise to her ways, always announces her presence by ringing a tune.

Riiiiiiig/ring /ring /ring/ring riiiing…

"Hi, Soph. Name That Tune in three."

"Song of Joy."

"God, Soph, you're rubbish lately. George is much better than you. Listen again. It's '*Are You Lonesome Tonight?*'"

"Well, don't tell him. He thinks I'm rubbish anyway."

"Oh, dear, having a low self-esteem day, are we? Go away and read one of your books. You know, '*The Sun Shines Out Of My Arse Day And Night*' sort of thing. '*I Am Wonderwoman.*' You buy them and you never read them. Waste of money."

"Very probably."

"Look at your hands, for Christ's Sake! Didn't you think to put gloves on?"

"Doesn't matter."

"Of course it matters. Remember that bit in *Carrie,* when her bloodstained hand shoots up out of the grave? Bloody frightening. Don't go shopping today. You'll have all the cashiers in *Sainsbury's* pressing their emergency buttons."

"I'm not that bad. Coffee?"

"Just a quick one, I'm going into the office today"

"On a Saturday?"

"'Fraid so. Your friend Brendan is calling the shots at the moment. He wants information, pronto. Look, I've brought back George's sweatshirt. You left it behind when old Sigmund Freeman-Freud whisked you off in his fancy car the other night. Wasn't that an amazing coincidence? You new age lot would say it was *synchronicity.*"

"Thanks. It wasn't that big a deal Phyll. It's probably more surprising I haven't bumped into him before when he's been staying with Jennifer. Anyway, he didn't whisk me off. Jennifer made him take me."

"Well, he was more than happy with the arrangements, I assure you. Don't look at me as if butter wouldn't melt, Sophia. Make the coffee and tell me what happened."

"OK. But nothing did. Nothing happened."

"He was certainly giving you deep and meaningful looks, my dear. Hasn't he got the most gorgeous eyes? Not at all like Jen, is he? He looked as happy as Lassie with his paws back under the kitchen table at one point, and it wasn't because of my linguine."

"Do you think he's got a shed?"

"A bed? Of course he's got a bed. King sized, probably, with one of those expensive furry covers."

"No, I said *shed.* I was just thinking, if he had a shed it would be really tidy and I bet you could find anything you wanted in there. And the shears wouldn't be blunt, probably."

"You really mean bed, Soph. Even I can work that out, and I'm not remotely interested in psychology. I like facts, as you know, facts and evidence. Now tell me again you're not interested in him?"

Sophia puts down two mugs of coffee and some rich tea biscuits.

"*Don't* tell me what I mean, Phyll. People have been doing that to me all my life and frankly, I'm sick of it."

"Keep calm. I'm sorry, I was only teasing. These taste of cardboard by the way Haven't you got any others?"

"They're organic. Sorry, Phyll. I didn't mean to snap at you. It's just that I've come to the conclusion that my whole life has had a direction of its own; I've never been able to make it go where I want."

"Like a rubbish supermarket trolley."

"Exactly. I've got wonky wheels. Perhaps I should tell Doctor Thing."

"Don't bother," says Phyll, standing up, "he'll only say it's a very common problem in menopause."

Sophia yawns. "That's true. Perhaps life's all a dream, anyway. My father used to ask me that when I was a little girl: "How do you know you're not a butterfly dreaming you're Sophia? Can you prove it?"

"Too philosophical for me, I'm afraid. My Dad never spoke to me at all except to tell me to keep quiet. Damn, I really must go. By the way, Soph, are you sure you've warned George about Brendan? He really wants to get the travellers off the site you know. He's got a very buzzy bee in his bonnet about it."

"No. I did ring, but he wasn't there, and then I forgot. He's coming home in a couple of days. I'll tell him then."

"OK, but tell him not to say it came from me. Hallo! What's all this in the hall? It looks like a shrine."

From the telephone table, Phyll picks up a small figure made from black polished wood. Behind it, is a black and white photograph propped up against a jar holding red dahlias.

"Well he sent it. This morning, actually."

"George? Wow."

"No, he never gives me anything. You know - *him*. Jez."

She feels awkward saying his name. He isn't a Jez any more.

"That's unusual. Most men send chocolates or flowers."

Phyll turns the figure over in her hand.

"It's someone all bent over, as if they're in pain. Or hiding their face like a child being invisible."

"Gabe used to do that. Sit under the kitchen table for hours with a tea towel over his head as still as a statue. He'd get really upset if I even spoke to him."

"It's nice to hold. Solid. Oh, just look at *this*. It's a photo of the two of you. I'd never have recognised Jez."

Sophia grimaces.

"He sent that with it."

"You were gorgeous, Soph. Look at your beautiful legs, and the length of that skirt! And Jez had hair to his shoulders for goodness sake! Not much left of it now, is there?"

Sophia takes back the figure, turning it over in her hand.

Phyll smiles.

"He still has that same sweet face, though. You're both blinking like little white owls in the sun. He looks proud though. Was it pre or post pool, would you say Soph?"

"Post. I told you, after the pool thing, I never saw him again."

She puts the figure down firmly, pushing it to the back of the table.

"He's not a sweet man, Phyll. Not at all."

"Sorry, I forgot. He's a complete bastard. A good looking one, though; I'm amazed he's not taken. People do change, you know Soph."

"Well, *I* haven't."

Sophia has folded her arms and is wearing what Phyll calls her fuck off face.

"Right on, sister," Phyll is stepping through the doorway, " a woman needs a man like..."

"...a fish needs a bicycle." Sophia finishes it off for her.

The phone starts to ring, and Phyll waves as Sophia turns back inside.

"Hallo?"

It's Gabe. Thank Goodness. Perhaps he's going to apologise for leaving her in the restaurant the other day, after she'd bought him lunch.

"Are you my mother?" he says.

She feels a cold prickle on her skin. That doesn't make sense. Is he being funny?

"Hallo darling. Are you all right?"

"Oh, for Christ's *Sake!"*

He crashes the phone down and the angry sound reverberates in her ear. What is playing at? How dare he treat her like this? She stabs at the re-dial number on the phone but it rings for too long. The ring becomes an unanswered ring, a different sound altogether. Where is he? She tries to retrieve the number, but he's withheld it.

He could be anywhere.

The familiar waters of panic lap at her edges, her heart's blood is crashing in her ears. Sophia is frozen in the hallway, on her knees, the phone pressed tightly into her head. She re-dials. At last there is a click, and he answers, sounding calm and normal.

"Gabe?"

She hears the quaver, and digs the nails of her right hand deep into her palm. She *must not* ask him if he's all right.

"Gabe. Um, something the matter?"

The words sound false. They both know that fear runs deep in her like a fault line.

There is silence.

"The matter," he repeats, copying her tone.

"Yes Gabe. The matter."

She is sharp in her fear. She uses her emergency classroom voice.

"You're being extremely rude lately, and I've just about had enough of it!"

She listens to him breathe in slowly, pause, and breathe out equally slowly and evenly. His breath sounds like a long,

106

whispered sigh.

"Sorry Mum. I know. Look, I'm under pressure a bit. The exhibition is in two weeks. Taking it out on you. Not fair. Sorry." She laughs in her relief. It's all right; she can understand that kind of stress. Work stuff. Exam stuff. Safe stuff.

"Oh darling, poor old you. Just try not to worry. You'll be fantastic as usual, just do your best."

He's her little Gabe again, worried about school. She can hear him breathing and realises she is holding her own breath, as if there is not enough air for the two of them.

Then he says *"Speak softly to your little boy and beat him when he sneezes, he only does it to annoy, because he knows it teases."*

Her brain is muddled and confused. She ignores the rhyme in the same way she used to ignore his teenage cursing.

"Good darling, OK. Don't overdo the work, will you?"

"I won't overdo the work, will I?"

His tone is a horrible parody. She knows she is on a completely different track to him; one with no meeting points.

"I must go, goodbye darling. I'll phone you tomorrow, shall I?"

He doesn't say yes or no. He just puts down the phone, but very quietly, this time.

She replaces the receiver and begins to cry, covering her face with her bloody hands.

Nothing much happens while she comes apart; the hall clock continues its steady, measured ticking.

Sunlight pours in through the glass window in the front door, bathing her in light and warmth, and after a while she lowers her hands from her face and fumbles in her pocket for a tissue. She blows her nose several times, and leans back against the wall. From here, her legs stretch almost to the opposite skirting board. She feels like the giant Alice, her face swollen and her legs heavy and clumsy. The torn wallpaper hangs down, a scar on her perfect yellow wall. The pain has gone. She can think; but she can't feel anything at all.

SIXTEEN

Gabe has painted his bedroom door in Sabbath Black. Across the glossy panels, obese pink cherubs are swilling from bottles, smoking enormous joints and fucking each other like animals. Lucian hangs coats over it when the landlord comes to collect the rent.

Gabe looks up as Lucian knocks and walks straight in to his room.

"What is the point of knocking, Lucy if you're going to walk in anyway?"

"Manners, Gabriel. Mother believed in showing courtesy. Your mother didn't teach you properly. You were horrible to her when she came to see you."

"That's none of your business. Fuck off."

"Charming."

"I'm not charming."

Lucian comes further in and leans against the wall, looking over at the desk where Gabe is sitting, chair tipped back, feet up against the edge. His room smells of unwashed socks, tobacco and stale cider.

"Bloody hell, it stinks in here."

Lucian wrinkles his nose and flaps a hand around in front of his face. He pushes up the window, letting in a tired drift of warm and humid air.

"Well get out then."

Gabe is rubbing his forehead with fast, irritated movements of his fingers. His thumbs are pressing deep into his temples.

"You look like a bad-tempered masseuse."

"What would you know about masseuses, you queer fucker?"

"Meow! Put your claws back in Gabe. I've been delegated by the girls to go out for
vino and take-away. Do you want to chip in?"

"No. I'm broke."

Gabe throws down his charcoal with such force, it splinters against the desk.

"You're always broke. Why don't you get a job like the rest of us?"

Gabe's pale eyes begin to glint.

"Ok, Ok, I'll treat you. *Again*. What on earth is that thing on your wall?"

Gabe shrugs. He has painted a skull with thick worms crawling in and through the empty eye sockets, which by some trick of the light or skill of Gabe's, follow the viewer's every move. A fleshy mouth is half hanging on to the bones and the lips are blowing a drooling kiss.

"That is *disgusting*. You need a shrink, Angel Gabriel. You need to exorcise your demons. And you should have grown out of drawing on the wall at your age. Charles will go mad if he sees that. It's worse than your pornographic door; at least he might think that's funny."

"Don't care. Get lost."

"You are *so* immature. I'm going anyway, before the off-licence shuts."

"Good. Get plenty."

"I just hope the local thugs are somewhere else tonight. Did you hear about the stabbing down there last week? Someone took exception to a student's hairdo and decided he shouldn't be allowed to live another day. I can't deny I've been pretty repulsed by some fashion statements myself from time to time, but all the same... "

Gabe reaches for a half-smoked joint, and lights it with a lighter shaped like a pistol.

"You can get arrested for having one of those, you know."

"Who gives a shit? I stole it in the first place."

"Dear me, such delinquency from a celestial creature. You're turning into your door, did you realise?"

"Fuck off, Lucy. You're turning into Julian Clary. *So* 1990's."

"Don't be mean. What are you smoking? It smells like Hell's

bonfire."

"Skunk. Finest Jamaican. Courtesy of Courtenay next door."

"I wouldn't trust *him*. He's probably mixed it with all kinds of crap."

"Who cares?"

Lucian turns to go, then stops. He spreads his arms wide and cups his hands to the ceiling.

"You're hard work lately, Gabe. What's wrong with you? You never come out any more, you lurk around in this pit like the troll under the bridge."

Gabe laughs and thrusts his tongue under his bottom lip, making his mouth bulge outwards.

"That's the spirit, Igor. Do you want me to tell you about the skirmishes in your lovely home town last week? You probably didn't see it, you never notice anything these days."

"No."

"Then I will."

Lucian comes back in and sits down on Gabe's bed.

"It was *horrible*, actually. There was a huge crowd of people up at the top end where the raving ranters stand, and they showed these two guys kicking seven kinds of shit out of each other. You couldn't see one of their faces for blood and people were actually watching and *cheering*. Can you believe that? Some woman with red hair was calling the police on her mobile. She had six-foot long nails with Union Jacks painted on them, and a voice like a cracked bell. It was too awful. I switched it off."

"I don't blame you. They should bring back bear baiting round there. People would queue up all night and pay a hundred quid for a ticket. What was it all about, anyway?"

"Travellers, apparently, your father's client group. There were hundreds of leaflets lying around that the camera crew helpfully zoomed right in on - *Heronmarsh Hell Hole! Unsanitary Site of Sin!* Your old man won't be too pleased."

"My old man thinks they're all misunderstood. My father would defend a rat's right to bite your baby."

Gabe exhales, and screws the smoking cardboard stub into the

110

desk top.

"And *your* right to destroy perfectly good furniture, I suppose."

"Yup. He's big on personal freedom."

"Come to the off-licence with me? I could do with a hand."

"No."

Gabe picks up his packet of tobacco and reaches for the plastic bag on his shelf.

"If I'm beaten by a mob, it'll be your fault, ex-best friend."

"I never had one in the first place. Anyway, you're not a gipsy are you?"

"The Nazis handed out pink stars as well as yellow ones, you know."

"Piss off and leave me alone."

"You're smoking too much of that stuff, you know."

"I don't care."

Lucian slams the door as he leaves, and Gabe listens to his boots echoing down the landing, as he treads heavily on the old wooden boards.

The squirming eye sockets of the white skull gaze at Gabe as tears fill his eyes and slide silently down his face. These sudden tears are one of the things keeping him in this room for hours on end; they arrive without warning and he doesn't know where they come from. One hangs for a moment in the cleft of his chin before it splashes onto the desk, gleaming dully in the late afternoon light. There is laughter from the sitting room below and the muffled sound of music.

Gabe's head feels hot, but his hands are shaking with cold; he is gripping the edge of his desk to fend off a sense that he is floating inches above his chair.

A sudden breeze rustles the leaves on the tree outside his window; the branches are reaching towards him like pleading, skinny arms.

SEVENTEEN

In the sitting room, the girls have taken over the cushions like pampered pets.

Lucian and Gabe are sprawled on the floor. The music has a heavy, rhythmic beat and Gabe can feel the floor vibrating under his fingertips. The beginning of an earthquake would be like this, he is thinking.

"Look at the Holbrook," Vicky is saying, "Robin Prynn has made so called art from a piece of aeroplane seat from that terrible air crash soaked in real blood. Can you believe it?"

"It isn't real blood."

"It *is* Lucian, I saw an interview with him last night. He said it's from the plane's cockpit. God only knows how he got hold of it; some ghoul must have sold it to him. He's rich enough now to buy anything and anyone I suppose. He was saying it's a comment on the fragility of life and the pointlessness of trusting others. Stupid prat. He just wants publicity."

Gabe is smiling.

"Those who I fight I do not hate, those who I guard I do not love."

"What?"

" '*An Irish Airman Foresees His Fate*'. Except our pilot didn't foresee his fate, or he'd have bailed out beforehand."

"What are you talking about now? That is not the fucking point, Gabe."

He turns towards her, raising his glass like a wine taster.

"And what, my dear professor, in your *esteemed* opinion is the fucking point, then?"

"Shut up Gabe, you patronising *git*."

Lou takes it up. "The point *is* Gabe, how's that poor man's wife feeling today? Or his kids? Knowing that part of someone they loved is being gawped at by a Sunday afternoon crowd?"

"Perhaps the public should be screened for sensitivity before they're allowed in to the gallery."

"The thing is Gabe, it's exploitation, that's not art." Frankie has joined in.

"*Here's* the thing," Gabe is stabbing the air with a finger, "nobody should feel anything about it; it's all just matter. It's a collection of molecules, like paint, like a canvas. Art can't pander to trashy sentiment, unearned emotion. This crash did happen. Poor old Pete the Pilot won't be visiting the Captain's bar any more. There's no need for all this self-righteous hysteria."

"Art reflecting life," says Lucian, realising his mistake too late.

"Thank you, cliché-man".

"So where do we stop?" says Vicky, fighting her way back into the conversation.

"The tumour that choked the life out of someone's granddad? A teenager's abortion? Scraps of brain from a road accident, by the way, so sorry about your mother?"

"I'm an existentialist, I wouldn't stop anywhere. It could all be great Art."

"Are there no boundaries at all?" Lucian looks at him closely.

"The way other people feel is irrelevant to me."

"You are just egocentric as hell," says Lou. "We can't see ourselves as separate from the whole human race just because we call ourselves artists. There are places where we just…*shouldn't* go. Out of respect for each other. Out of love at the end of the day."

"Art's like a force of nature, it goes where it wants to go. At the end of the day? You sound like a fucking Daily Mail reader."

Frankie lifts her head up from the cushion.

"That sounds like a rapists charter. I want to do it, so I'll go ahead and do it and bugger the consequences."

"And bugger the unfortunate victim too," says Gabe.

"It's not Art, it's just…masturbation." Vicky tries again. "There *are* images we shouldn't expose, Gabe. Places we should tiptoe away from, not because we're bourgeois or fascist, but because we know we're all connected and we have a responsibility not to emotionally abuse each other. Robin Prynn's just trying to make money from the freak show fans and the collectors."

"Connected, my arse. We're all separate freaks fighting for survival, that's all Connection's a cosy myth."

Gabe begins to sing in a voice so tuneful that Lucian wonders whether he had ever been a choir boy. He should have, he is so beautiful.

"Some of them want to use you...some of them want to get used by you...some of them want to abuse you...some of them want to be abused..."

The electric fan hums in the darkness, cooling the night. The foil containers, holding the last spoonfuls of sticky rice, gleam in a ramshackle pile. There is still wine left, and Lucian fills up the glasses.

Vicky hasn't given up yet. *"Listen*! What if it was *your* mother's blood hanging on that wall Gabe? What if it were someone you love?"

"Love? Love's just the infantile terror of people who are scared to death of life, *Vicky*. It's a pre-programmed chemical response. Love's a nice word for control and utter selfishness."

Lucian sighs, secretly he's had hopes they might be partners one day.

"You're a cold-hearted bastard, Gabe."

"Am I? Because I don't agree with you?"

Lou takes over tipsily.

"Gabe, you are from a different planet, man. Somewhere undiscovered...way beyond the ice-rings of Jupiter..."

"Yeah, they have discovered that planet, Lou," says Frankie, cackling, "It's called

Planet Masculinus. It's peopled entirely by men like Gabe and Robin Prynn. They spend their time painting and hunting and drawing up plans for weapons, which they test on women and children. The women and children are kept in special cages in the desert and used as models regularly."

Frankie is wagging her finger. Gabe's eyes have narrowed.

"And they all live in pubs, and communicate by fighting and

114

playing football."

"Competition is their God and love is the Devil."

The girls are laughing helplessly and falling off the cushions.

"Yeah Frankie, I believe you're right!"

"Read about that planet too!"

"*Read* about it? *I* went there for my holiday last year, by mistake. Bloody travel agent!"

Gabe speaks very quietly. "Listen to yourselves. Women never admit to their own cruelty. Any of you ever had an abortion? Because it just made sense?"

He knows at least two of them have.

"Oh shut up Gabe, you Dalek," says Vicky, and Lou puts an arm round Frankie.

They get up with exasperated sighs and leave, banging the door behind them. There is only a musky smell and a new silence.

"*Women get on my nerves,*" Gabe shouts after them. "Why do they have to *personalise* everything? Why can't they just think?"

Lucian takes a deep breath while he pours Gabe some more wine and lies back against the cushion. It smells of patchouli. Gabe is looking at him intently.

"*The years to come seemed waste of breath, a waste of breath the years behind.*"

"What are you talking about Gabe?"

"The end of the Irish Airman. People look up at him and think he's Captain Fantastic, guarding the skies, caring about their puny little lives, but all the time he really doesn't give a shit about any of them. He's just there where he's been told to be; hanging in the sky."

"Do you like him?"

"It's just a fucking poem Lucy, don't try to analyse me, it's not that easy."

They sit there in silence, cross-legged on either side of the low table. The music has changed to a ballad, haunting and soft.

"You seem…stressed out lately, Gabe."

"Yeah."

"You're working too hard."

115

"Art's all I have. If I didn't have Art I wouldn't exist."

Lucian is fighting a temptation to joke; the wine he has drunk works in his favour, slowing his thoughts, and stilling the glib words that his lips are trying to form. He nods instead.

"Sounds like a lifeline?"

Lucian allows his tone to rise slightly at the end, lending his words the mere hint of a question.

"Maybe I should cut the fucking lifeline."

Gabe is making snipping gestures in the air with his fingers.

Lucian is bored now; he is thinking that he likes to be happy. He likes to laugh and drink and make love; he should go to bed and leave Gabe to his tedious misery. He puts down his glass and starts to get up, but Gabe raises his hand.

"I thought I'd killed someone once."

"*What?*"

"Bastard was tormenting me."

"My God, you never told me this before. What happened?"

"He stamped on my blazer."

"Your *blazer?*"

A car drives past painting chequered light across the ceiling.

"I beat him up. I smashed his face against the rail. I kicked him to the ground."

"Bloody hell. Was he all right?"

"Yeah."

Gabe cackles like a parrot. It's eerie.

"He liked me after that. Wanted to be my friend again, but I wouldn't have it."

"Why?"

"Z. The last letter, the end of the alphabet soup. You can't be friends with someone you tried to kill, can you? It's about not crossing a line, Lucy. People need barriers, don't they? You all said so. Bradley crossed the line. He had to be pushed back."

Gabe begins to sing to the tune of *Margery Daw*: 'pushed back...into a sack...hard luck Brad...ley...'

There are giant scarecrow arms waving wildly on the wall. Gabe is painting on a wide, invisible canvas.

'Bars, barriers, boundaries, bars barriers, boundaries…'
It becomes a mantra.

Lucian is sweating. He gets onto his knees, but Gabe grips his arm tightly to stop him standing up.

"Are they prisons or incubators, Lucy? Tell me?"

He looks about ten years old.; Lucian wants to hold him.

"Come on, Gabe. All kids have fights."

"Not all kids are murderers though, are they?"

"You're not a murderer either; you said the other kid was perfectly OK. You stood up for yourself, that's all. There's nothing wrong with that."

Gabe is on the verge of tears. His hand is shaking.

Lucian shuffles round the table on his knees and stretches out his arms. As the two men embrace, their cheeks pressed together, Lucian can taste Gabe's tears. He kisses him, tasting red wine and smoke.

Gabe pushes him gently back, holding Lucian at arms length and tracing the outline of his face with a finger, like a blind man committing someone to memory.

Lucian sits back on his heels, and watches Gabe move unsteadily towards the door, wanting him, but afraid to speak.

Gabe's heart is fluttering inside his chest like a trapped and terrified starling. His bedroom, at the other end of the corridor, seems impossibly distant.

The air feels solid, and Gabe's legs are heavy as if he is walking through deep waters. He can hear himself breathe, a rasping sound grazing the silence. A casual observer would think he was merely drunk, but a crack has opened up in Gabe's world now, and he is teetering on the edge of space.

It seems as if hours pass before he finds himself naked in bed, with no awareness of how he got there. His life has become a series of frames, spliced together by a careless editor in a cutting room, and now he is melting, sliding, dripping away, while sudden red images of twisted and broken bodies come to pinch and pluck at his brain.

Drenched in sweat, he hangs on to the side of his bed, feeling himself floating high above the floor, too nauseous to reach out a hand to turn on the bedside lamp. The orange ray of streetlight that pierces his curtains is dangerous and evil.

Time has lost meaning; there is only an electrified present, and Gabe tosses and turns like a man on a rack, until the images fade and the blood tide dims and recedes.

When dawn comes, there is one tiny, clear image left glowing in the darkness and Gabe stares at the helpless man writhing on a wooden cross, until a profound sense of comprehension settles on him like the comfort of soft rain after a drought, driving out the fear.

He is the man on the cross. He is Christ, about to be crucified again. That was why Lucian had kissed him; it was the Judas kiss. The girls are stupid sheep gathered round the Lamb. The wine, the last supper, the treacherous embrace, he understands it all. He must be very careful, they won't crucify him again. Oh no, once was enough.

This time he'll make a very strong shield, to guard himself from Judas and the foolish sheep. Titanium. He'll make himself a titanium shield and go about his father's business in safety.

Focusing all his energy into a point of light, Gabe paints around himself, making sure there are no gaps. He's exhausted from the mental effort, but he's breathing more
easily now, and the sweating has stopped. His body is ice cold, but he feels pure and strong inside. He has conquered the forces of darkness, for a while. Of course, Lucifer is still out there, waiting for him.

Smiling, he gets out of bed and dresses in last night's clothes.

"I am ri...sen, I am ri...sen," he sings to himself, to the tune of *Bread of Heaven.* He steps towards the bathroom softly, like a cat, stopping to listen every so often, his head on one side.

EIGHTEEN

George is sitting on the edge of his bed, looking at the greenish brown dried mud between his toes. He woke up with memories of last night curling themselves around his brain like determined tendrils. Leena's bright dress, Soph's phone call, Jamie's mocking smile, cow dust time; that's all he wants to remember.

His heart is starting to hammer. There's a jaggedness behind his eyes as he tries to forget the rest of the previous night by looking around his room, thinking he needs coffee, he needs biscuits, he needs to shower.

Sun is pouring through the open curtains, lapping at his feet. There are rippling clouds this morning; he can see a bright blue sky meeting the green lawn where he'd sat with Leena before it got dark, before the pub, before the wine, before the strawberry mousse, before the brandy. He feels sick.

A woodpigeon is calling to him personally...*George you fool...George you fool...George you fool...*

He stands up in self defence, and his skull cracks open down the middle. The island is there in his window, refusing to fade away.

The last time he had drunken sex with someone he barely knew, it was under a pile of coats at a student party. She got pregnant and he worked nights in a warehouse for a year to pay back her parents for the abortion they never dreamed would cost so much. The look in her eyes when he took her home from the clinic in the taxi, made him swear he would never do anything so stupid again, and now he has. Beer and wine and brandy. Stupid, stupid, stupid. He splashes water on his eyes; it feels too cold. There is something pig-like about his face in the mirror this morning.

A rap on the door makes him jump.

"Morning George! Open the door. It's mountain rescue!"

He turns the shower on full and steps in quickly; perhaps she'll go away. He doesn't want to see her, ever, ever again. He has bruises on both his knees and a bloody graze on one elbow.

"*Come on, George!* Open the door. I braved the smell of fried eggs to bring you this coffee. I've a terrible hangover, and it's getting cold."

She'll never go away. George climbs out of the shower and wraps a towel around his waist. Before he gets to the door, he re-wraps it to cover his nipples, preferring to expose his knees.

Leena's brought a tray with coffee, orange juice, wholemeal toast, almond croissants, pale butter and cherry jam. She looks at his towel.

"Mmm. A sarong would suit you. George. Have you ever been to Thailand?"

She puts the tray on the bed and sits down; he stands as far away from her as he can, leaning against the wall. She is wearing sun glasses and a plain white shirt with narrow black trousers that stop just above her ankle. She's pinned up her hair, and looks as neat and fresh as Audrey Hepburn.

"Coffee, Sir? Shall I pour?"

"Leena, what was that all about?"

"Last night?"

"Of course, last night! What the hell else would I be talking about?"

He takes a cup of coffee from her, and dips in a croissant. It's warm and sweet and dissolves in his mouth, easing the pain in his head. He feels as if he doesn't deserve it, and puts it down again.

"You look really upset George."

"I am upset. It was- *what the hell happened*?"

She smiles, and looks at him at him over the top of her glasses. She is spreading butter and cherry jam on her toast.

"Dear me! Has it been that long?"

"I'm serious Leena. You know what I mean."

"Tomfoolery? Gypsy magic?"

"Hah. More like a gypsy curse."

She looks hurt, but he doesn't care; she started it. He finishes the croissant and takes another; she crunches her toast.

"I take it Sir wasn't satisfied?"

"Do you ever take anything seriously?"

She frowns and takes off her sunglasses, throwing them on to the bed. She's angry now. Her eyes are impossible; no one has eyes that blue; they're sapphire.

"Well, let me think. Poverty. Child abuse. Oppression. Disease. Only things that matter, George."

"Thanks very much. *Sex* used to matter in my day. And what about Soph?"

A flock of birds flies by, arrow-shaped, purposeful. The swallows will be leaving
soon. A few of them will make it to Africa, more will be torn apart by cats, or bigger birds, or storms at sea.

"Stop being tragic. You told me you and Sophia have given up sex."

"I'm not being *tragic.*"

"Yes you are. Listen. We both had far too much to drink. We talked, we laughed, we had sex – briefly, but pleasantly I thought. That's all. We didn't ram-raid *Sainsburys*, or start a fight with a policeman. No animals were harmed during the making of the programme. Grow up Georgie."

"Grow up! I suppose you think it's sophisticated to get drunk, take off your clothes and dive into a scummy hotel lake? Something mature about having sex with someone you don't even know?"

Leena is standing now. She's holding her room key like a revolver, and pointing it at George.

"I didn't ask you to dance."

"What if you're pregnant?"

Leena moves towards the door, kicking aside Georges' jeans and shirt, which are still in a tangled, damp embrace on the floor by the bed.

"I'm *not* pregnant, George, I'm sterile, as a matter of fact, barren as a witch's cat. And before you ask, I'm not HIV positive, neither do I have genital herpes or any other sexually transmitted disease. Do you?"

"No, I bloody well don't! I don't have casual sex!"

She stares at him and he stares back.

"Then you have a doppelganger who does."

"Very *funny*."

Outside, a mower has started to roar. Footsteps pass the door, and the babble of another language. They are glaring at each other. He won't give in first. Neither will she.

George's stomach quivers. Leena's left eyelid twitches. He's lost control over the outside edges of his mouth. He looks over at the window, but it's too late now.

He's rocking and gasping for breath and wailing with laughter. Tears are running down Leenas' cheeks and her shoulders are shaking. She gurgles and hoots and
clutches her stomach with both hands.

Their laughter meets and dances, curling and rising and twisting like brilliant smoke, filling the room with sound, falling back and bursting out again and again until finally they are quiet, panting for breath, their eyes shining.

Leena reaches for the door handle, and George's towel falls to the floor.

"Shit."

"Be careful, George. For someone who doesn't have sex, that could look like an invitation."

She waves and leaves the door wide open. Jamie is coming down the corridor, and George dives to shut it before he passes.

NINETEEN

It always feels cold in Jennifer's gleaming bathroom, where Jez is scrubbing his nails by the sink. She had the floor and the walls tiled in black and white; it's like being inside an enormous dice.

"Hi big bro, can I just…?"

She is pushing him out of the way, and checking her makeup in the large silver mirror, frowning as she tweaks tufts of her glossy, cropped hair.

"Lunch date Jen?"

"With Brendan McFall, self-important, council big cheese, sad, lecherous man."

"He sounds awful. What on earth are you going out with him for?"

"It's work actually, but he's the sort of man who likes to take full advantage of his expense account, so it has to be lunch. He wants an eviction order for the local travellers; he's quite determined to move them all off Heron marsh. God knows why. They've been there for absolute years and they don't do any harm at all, as far as I can see. We need the work though. Council contracts are hard to come by and we can't afford to risk it."

"Can he get them evicted?"

"I'm afraid he can, quite easily. It's just a question of finding a few petty infringements of conditions. Too many dogs, someone's Granny's moved in without permission, that sort of thing. Travellers have fewer rights than prisoners, George must be absolutely furious."

"George?"

"Sophia's husband. He works up there. Social worker. Remember? The other night? Are you blushing little brother?"

Jennifer is talking and putting on cherry coloured lipstick at the same time.

"Of course I'm not blushing. What's George like?"

"I don't know them very well, they're Phylls' friends. He's nice enough, I think. He's big and cuddly-looking. He's quite attractive actually, if you like the rugby type. Phyll says they don't get on too well; it's always a bit fraught when they're both together. They had a baby that died, or something. The son's rather an oddball."

"She told me. She seemed quite worried about him."

"He's very artistic and *spectacularly* handsome, but he's ice cold. He's got eyes like Antarctica. Sophia's uptight all the time and pretends not to be. She's got this big fake smile that never quite reaches her eyes."

"She used to have this lovely quiet spirit. She reminded me of a diver on the edge of a springboard when she was eighteen. We read '*Lord of The Rings*' together the summer before she left for university, and she painted these beautiful fantasy watercolours of shining mountains and dark forests and jewel coloured dragons…"

"How sweet."

Jez doesn't reply, and Jennifer sighs and sits down on the edge of the bath.

"You seemed pretty excited about running into her again."

"Well, you know, coincidence and all that. It took me by surprise."

Jez dries his hands on a red towel, and turns to face Jennifer. He is wearing his psychotherapy face, polite but giving nothing away.

"I seem to remember she broke your little heart, *Jamie-o.*"

Jennifer has always been able to get under his skin.

"At least I had a heart to break, *Jenny.*"

"Well there hasn't been much sign of it since has there? Is it still in recovery somewhere? You only ever date crazy women who get better and leave you for someone real."

"Whereas you, on the other hand, reign supreme in the Queendom of The Ice Bear, occasionally allowing the unwary trapper to buy you dinner, or take you to Tobago."

"Oh, that was so mean, J. I'll tell Dad."

"See if I care."

They both laugh, and Jez folds his arms and leans against the wall.

"You're right Jen."

"About the crazy women?"

"No. Well, yes, I suppose that's probably true as well, but as far as Soph is concerned, you're right. I've never forgotten her. I was so excited to see her again."

"That was obvious."

"Was it?"

"You looked like a kid at Christmas. Your eyes were actually shining."

"Could have been the wine."

"No it couldn't. I was thinking you used to look like that years ago when we were kids before…you know, before she…"

"Before Mum left? Did I?"

"Mmm."

"Oh Jen, are you crying?"

"Shit. *No*. Bloody hormones. Bloody middle age."

Jez is picking paint flecks from around the edges of his fingernails.

"You were the one who came home from school first and found all her stuff gone, as well as the bloody dog. It took me years to forgive her for that."

Jennifer shakes her head at her reflection in the mirror. "I never forgave her never, even when she tried to make up for it all. If only she hadn't taken Patchy."

The sun is catching highlights in Jennifer's hair. Jez is thinking how much like their mother she looks now her jaw is softening, and the lines around her eyes lie deep in the skin like carvings on a tree. She won't want to hear that.

"You're right. She didn't have to do that, taking the dog but leaving the children was cruel. When I started going out with Soph, it felt a bit like having Mum back. She was soft and warm and she smelled so nice. I used to sit next to Soph in the cinema getting high just smelling her perfume and holding her hand.

L'Aimant, she used to wear; I asked her what it was called once. She must have thought I was going to buy some for her, but I used to go into *Boots* and spray my hand with the tester, when no-one was looking."

"*Coty.* Same as Mum."

"Was it? Good heavens, I never realised."

"I used to hate smelling it on your jacket when you'd been out with her. I didn't realise you were weird enough to spray it on yourself."

"I'm sorry."

"For what? Being weird?"

Jennifer is rubbing cream on her hands and squaring her shoulders.

"No, I'm sorry it hurt you, but…it was a fucked up time for both of us, I suppose."

Jennifer tugs down her skirt as she walks, her heels clacking on the hard floor.

At the door she pauses, and looks back.

"Well you seemed pretty OK, with your beautiful girlfriend, and your brilliant 'A' levels and your cosy little job with Dad."

"I was, for a while. Dad seemed to be taking it on the chin, and I suppose I thought that was the manly thing to do, but then something happened and I realised I wasn't OK. Delayed reaction, I suppose. I completely fell to bits."

Jennifer is on the landing looking at her watch, torn between her need to leave and curiosity.

"*Did you*? You're telling me you had a nervous breakdown in a social unit the size of a tube compartment, and I didn't know anything about it. What the hell happened? Tell me quickly, I've got to go."

"Well…you see, one evening I made love to Soph…"

"Is that all?"

"It was after we'd been to the swimming pool. She looked fantastic. She was wearing this orange bikini…"

"Very daring for those days. I wouldn't have put her down as an exhibitionist."

126

"She wasn't. She was beautiful, but never vain. She had real class. We went back to her parents place, and they were out. She seemed keen…"

"Spare me the details, please. Will you get a move on? I'm going to be late for Brendan McFart."

"Jen, the thing was…well, I never got in touch with her again afterwards, you see. I still don't really know why. I wanted to see her again more than anything else in the world, I'd fallen in love with her. I wanted to tell her and I felt so horribly guilty, but I just *could* not pick up the phone. When I left her that evening I said 'Thanks' as if she'd bought me a drink, or lent me a record or something, and that was it. Thanks."

"You *prick,* James. Have you any idea what that feels like for a young girl?"

"I didn't know what was happening to me Jen. I stayed in bed for two days and told Dad I had flu, but really I couldn't get up. I couldn't stop crying. I was so bewildered…"

"It wouldn't have been anything to do with punishing Sophia for Mum's betrayal, I suppose, Mr great psychoanalyst of the bleeding obvious?"

"I never…"

He is talking to thin air. Jennifer is running downstairs and across the expensive lavender carpet in the hall.

"thought of it like that, Jen."

"And you never said a word to me did you? As far as I'm concerned, families stink. Or would you be happier if I said they're all bloody dysfunctional!"

She leaves her final words in the hall for him to trip over, and bangs the front door behind her.

His phone rings and automatically his hand moves to his pocket and his thumb flips it up. He knows how to save his thoughts for later.

"Hallo?"

Sophia had meant to thank him for the package and leave it at that. It's unsettling how strangers become friends and then lovers and then strangers again all in the space of one lifetime. She has no idea what sort of a man has emerged from that foggy time when they fumbled with each other long ago, like blind creatures mating.

He sounds pleased to hear from her. When she rings George these days, he speaks to her less warmly than he does to his secretary. Sophia is startled by the pleasure in Jez's voice and it causes an odd tremor in her own, as she attempts a polite thank you.

"You sound upset Soph."

"Me? No, I'm fine."

"You don't sound very fine."

"I am very fine…oh hell!"

She bursts into tears. He'll think she's crazy. He's qualified, he'll know she's crazy. He is supposed to be on holiday, poor man, having a rest from mad women's tears.

He waits while she blows her nose.

"Would you like me to come and see you, Soph, or would you prefer to be alone?"

"Come," she says, and after a few seconds, "now."

The normal rules of conversation don't seem to apply with him.

"I'll be there in half an hour."

She puts the phone down, feeling suddenly sick and stays kneeling on the hall carpet. She always seems to be here these days, as if she's moved down a notch in life to pet, or baby status. Her life is shifting and changing like a sand picture.

She smoothes down the old shirt she is wearing, wondering whether to change before he arrives. She should at least wash her face. She must look a hundred years old. She crouches slightly, and looks out at the empty road through the glass panel in the door. That holiday with George started all this; she's been restless ever since. Holidays explode the myth that all we need is a good holiday.

Jez has a way of making her talk. His presence is light as a feather. Or a kiss. Unsettled by the thought, she pushes it out of her mind, and runs upstairs to wash.

Jez is looking at his watch and has taken his sister's place on the cold, hard edge of the bath. Taking a small, silver file from Jennifer's shelf, he smoothes away the rough edges of his nails. His hands are planning on holding Sophia's hands, but he doesn't know it yet.

He jumps up quickly, grabbing jacket and keys and wallet from the half decorated kitchen as he passes. He talked Jen out of more of the clinical look and she's let him have in way in here, although she is not too pleased by the deep rose and creamy yellow walls. She says it reminds her of a 1950's cinema, but he thinks it is the softness that unsettles her. He's found the palest blue tiles for the floor if she'll cough up for them. He hopes so; she needs to be more tender.

Sophia has changed into a deep pink linen shirt that she usually keeps for work, and is looking out of her front window. She can see Amelia vacuuming her front room in the house opposite. She's wobbling; who else would vacuum in high heels? Sophia thinks of her own carpets. There is a housework mountain she should be tackling, not standing here in one of her good shirts, waiting for a man she doesn't know any more. George will be very annoyed with her when he comes back; he hates mess.

Sophia is about to reach for the phone to put Jez off, but she can hear a car rounding the bend, and she knows it will be him, and it is too late.

Can she trust him? She saw a therapist when Grace died, in the beginning, when she could hardly walk, brought to her knees at intervals by the savage attacks of grief that shook her, like a wild dog mastering its prey. The woman had a round, innocent face, and talked about stages of grief and healing as if Sophia and Grace were cardboard dolls. When Sophia wouldn't stop crying, she looked nervous and suggested anti depressants. Phyll made her stop going, and took her out swimming and walking and drinking while George looked after Gabe, until her tears finally dried and the fear lay down and slept.

Over the road, Amelia has stopped, and Sophia can see a tall figure standing behind her, his face bending into her neck. Amelia turns slowly and pulls the man's head down towards her own and Sophia spins away from the window breathing fast, as if the kiss were being offered to her own mouth. Bloody Brendan. He is a devious man. Lisa is going to get hurt again. Sophia breathes into her hands, she feels faint.

She is wiping off her lipstick when the doorbell rings, and she opens it with a tissue in one hand.

"Are you all right Soph?"

"Yes, yes, I'm fine. I was just a bit, you know…"

"Sure, sure."

"I'm fine now."

"Good, good."

Sophia feels cheated. She'd thought Jez was never awkward these days. Perhaps they should go out somewhere. He's saying something and she hasn't heard a word. She has got to try to focus. She drifts off these days, as if everyone has started to speak Russian.

"*Sorry*, I wasn't…?"

"I was wondering whether you'd like to drive down to the coast for lunch? Soph? The air will be fresher there. Not so humid, you know, cooler."

She is not looking at him.

"OK, Jez. Good idea. We could walk up to the end of the pier and get fish and chips. Do you remember the little café?"

"Yes, I do. Do you remember the tattoo parlour? I wanted to get one done and impress you with my steely courage, but you wouldn't let me."

"Well you wanted to get my name on your bicep and I thought…"

"What?"

"Well, I thought it would be really naff…"

He laughs, but she catches a flash of something in his eyes. It looks like disappointment. The past is full of unseen potholes.

"…and I thought your mother wouldn't appreciate it. She could barely cope with your hair…"

"She wouldn't have seen it. She'd left by then."

"Left? *Really*? I had no idea. I remember her as always being there, in your kitchen…"

"Perhaps that's why she left. Change of scene."

He sounds bitter; perhaps he is human after all.

"Why on earth didn't you *tell* me? I can't believe you kept something like that to yourself."

"I don't know, Soph. I think I was in denial."

"What does that mean?"

"Pretending it hadn't happened."

She doesn't reply.

They go out to his car, and she whistles. She hadn't taken much notice of it in the dark the other night. It's a Mercedes sports with red paintwork and cream seats. She relaxes into the soft leather.

"It's a bit different from my father's old van."

"You couldn't see the floor, only cans of paint and bits of old paper."

"I remember. You had to bail out water once as we were driving to- where? Glastonbury?"

"I don't know, could have been. I remember my purple suede boots were ruined."

"Oh, dear. I owe you a new pair."

"I'm past the purple boots stage, thanks all the same."

"Slippers?"

"Not quite there yet, either."

He glances down at her legs, and she crosses her ankles and tucks her feet away out of sight.

Jez parks on the promenade, and they stroll towards the pier.

They are chatting more easily now, relaxing in the sea air that carries the sad cries of gulls and the smell of hot fat. Sophia stops to tip a pebble out of her sandal, and Jez looks out towards the glinting sea. He puts a hand on the small of her back, drawing her towards the warm metal rail to stand beside him.

"Look at that, Soph. Isn't it beautiful?"

There is a dark grey cloud hanging over the ocean, with an invisible sun shining behind it, fringing the edges with pure gold light. Rays reach out towards the edges of the sky.

They turn towards each other. A too long look can start a fight,

131

or an affair she thinks, too late. Their lips are already touching. His breath is warm on her face.

The sunlight catches the tops of the waves, sparking a thousand camera flashes. Sophia tastes the salty air in Jez's mouth, and she feels the tide turn.

TWENTY

Garage music is pumping from next door, and their front door slams loudly, waking Lucian up. His bed is soft and his limbs feel pleasantly heavy. Stretching out his arms and legs crabwise, he yawns widely, like a happy puppy. He is remembering the smoky red wine taste of Gabe's mouth, and the hard feel of his body.

The house is in silence, though the traffic outside suggests it is closer to mid morning than daybreak. Lucian dresses quickly in t shirt and shorts, and walks down the landing on bare feet, glancing across at Gabe's closed door as he passes. There is no sound from inside.

In the sitting room, he pulls up the sash window, grimacing at the mess of bottles and the crumpled cartons and the smell of wine and stale cigarettes. He looks down at the street. Courtenay is sitting on his front step, smoking.

"Yo, Lucy! Ever heard of the a.m. time of the day, man?"

"Did she throw you out again Courtenay?"

"Girls are trouble, Lucian. I'm going to come and cuddle up to you tonight instead, my friend."

"I don't think so Courtenay. I don't want Letitias' nails in my eyes. And what have you been giving Gabe lately? He can't handle your Jamaican special harvest."

Courtenay sucks his teeth.

Lucian withdraws from the window and starts to clear up. He carries the bottles and cartons into the kitchen, and dumps them into the bin.

"Shit."

Lucian's bare feet are sticking to the floor, which is filmed with grease and spilled wine. He fills a bucket with hot water and lavender scented cleaner and grabs the mop, rubbing and rinsing

133

and squeezing and backing into a corner by the garden door. He steps outside onto the step to finish the last square, and looks down at the floor; he enjoys cleaning. Freed from their veil of dirt, the tiles stand out proudly blue and cream. He smiles at them as if they were children, scrubbed and ready for school.

A magpie calls his attention back to the rambling garden. Its blue-black wings and white tail feathers make an Edwardian hat for the wooden shed that sits, half covered in honeysuckle and ivy, at the top of what once was a lawn. There are bushy green shrubs with dog roses climbing around and through the branches in a pretty embroidery, a gnarled old apple tree still humbly offering ripe fruit, and along the grass below the high brick wall, a row of bouncy dahlias wave in the breeze, enthusiastic as carnival queens. There is a pergola that could be repaired with a few nails, and some timber and Lucian decides on a quick trip to the giant DIY store that covers the next corner like an aerodrome. He has a fleeting Lady Chatterly fantasy of bedecking Gabe with a daisy chain under the tree, and decides to buy shears as well to create a grassy bed, just in case this is a beginning.

Lucian whistles on his way up the road, and passers-by smile at him, enjoying his enjoyment. He rocks his shoulders and bounces on the balls of his feet like a fourteen year old walking home from school. He buys tools and some wood and a bunch of flowers, and on the way home stops to get fresh olive bread from *Picky's* the smart new delicatessen at the top of their road. He buys sweet yellow cheese, and dates stuffed with walnuts from the Turkish shop that fights for space with the flashy video arcade, full of skinny, dull-skinned boys with names like *Tig* and *Jazzy B*.

Courtenay is still lounging on his step, but not so feisty now. The beer has soured his earlier good humour.

Lucian grins at him. "Not back inside yet, neighbour friend?"

"Fuck off, batty b'woy."

Courtenays' lips are reaching for the can of special brew as urgently as a baby smelling a nipple. Lucian tutts and steps round him, holding his packages high in the air as if Courtenay were a muddy puddle. The hall is dim, but there is a spill of light from upstairs.

"Gabe! Are you up at last you lazy sod?"

Gabe's bedroom door is ajar. Lucian walks into the kitchen, already sharing brunch with him in his imagination, telling him about his plans for the garden. Gabe is sitting there at the old scrubbed wooden table where they have breakfast on Sundays, his head bent.

"Hi Gabe. I was hoping you'd be up."

Gabe looks across at him. Lucian's smile withers away and dies in seconds, like a seedling on a frosty night. Gabe is staring at a point on the wall. There is no breakfast, nothing at all on the table. When he sees Gabes' eyes, Lucian's skin tingles. His eyes are as empty as long dead shells.

"Gabe, hi."

Lucian keeps his voice soft and makes no further move towards the table, hoping he's wrong and this is one of Gabe's tedious jokes. He's a very good actor. Last Christmas he told Vicky that Frankie had cancer, and carried the pretence on until Vicky was weeping hysterically. Perhaps he's just pretending to be a zombie.

"Why?"

"Very funny. Do you want some breakfast?"

"You will not betray me again."

"Ok, ok. Hangover, is it?"

Gabe is looking down at the table in front of him. His pale hands are laying flat, long fingers extended. His long curly dark hair shadows his expression. A slackness is sitting around his mouth, as if the elastic has worn. He seems to be having trouble forming his words.

"You sank some wine last night, didn't you?"

Lucian doesn't dare say 'we'. 'We' might remind him of the kiss, and something tells him to be very cautious. '*Let this just be a really bad hangover*', he is praying silently. *Please, please, please, make this stop.*'

"It won't happen again."

Gabe's voice is low and sad.

"Never again? I've heard it all before, Gabe. Not till the next time, anyway."

"I'm going to my father's house."

"What? Going home, you mean? But it's the exhibition…"

The fridge hums, the clock ticks. Beyond the garden, a dog barks hysterically and a man roars in anger.

"How about going to the pub instead? Hair of the dog?"

Lucian plunges on, trying to laugh. It sounds hollow and false.

"Dog," echoes Gabe, "lying dog."

"What?"

Gabe looks at Lucian suspiciously, his eyes falling on the package Lucian is still holding under one arm. Lucian sees Gabe's look and moves swiftly over to the table. With mounting despair, he sees Gabe flinch away from him and shield his head with one arm. Lucian puts the package down, opens the bag and begins pulling things out, explaining rapidly. Gabe is definitely not joking this time.

"I thought I'd do some gardening Gabe, look, I got shears for the pruning, a decent hammer, nails and some wood to repair that pergola, it's in quite good condition really…"

His voice tails away; Gabe is staring at the tools. They seem to hold some special meaning for him.

"It's ok. Don't worry, I'll put them away."

Lucian begins to pick everything up quickly, dropping the nails all over the floor in his haste. They clink and bounce against the tiles.

"Sorry, sorry Gabe, listen, do you want…?"

But Gabe has got up from his chair, and is edging round the table with his eyes on Lucian as if he were holding a gun.

"Gabe, *please* …"

Lucian stretches out a hand to him, not knowing who needs comfort more but Gabe has already fled. The bang of the front door echoes through the house, shaking the window frames and rattling the cups on the draining board.

TWENTY-ONE

George neglected to sign up for a workshop in advance, and has dived into the nearest room where there are a few chairs left. His apology for arriving late was met with a friendly "Glad you could make it," from Lloyd the trainer, causing some of Georges' colleagues to snigger and shuffle their feet. George doesn't reply, disappointing the ones who were hoping for a little banter. George is beset by a sense of dread, for some reason, not unlike the feeling he had, he is thinking, each time Soph was pregnant.

He is in no mood for this workshop, and is frowning as he tries to make himself comfortable on the hard grey chair, one of a circle of twelve. His body is aching almost everywhere.

The workshop list had been sent to him at home two months ago, after he'd failed to respond to the second e-mail.

"Look at all this so called personal development rubbish," he'd complained to Sophia, " *'The Creative Use of Anger', 'Dynamics of Sexuality', 'Bereavement: Lost and Found'*...What *good* is all this? Peering into things, stirring up the pond. Don't they realise that real people just...get on with it?" Sophia said she thought it sounded pretty good, and he was lucky, her training days were never interesting, and George said it was all new age crap, and he was being force-fed like a Belgian goose, and Sophia gave up and went quiet. Another row they could have had.

Now George is in *'Lost and Found'* with Lloyd, who is sitting in the circle with them, stressing his equality, and smiling at anyone who catches his eye. He is wearing Levis and black hi-tops and a pale blue shirt. He probably likes this weather, George is thinking, his smile is Californian. George broods on the fee he is likely to be pocketing for today's work.

Lloyd clears his throat. "Let's begin. OK. I'd like us to go around the circle and introduce ourselves in turn. Leave out your work roles this morning, we're going to get into our feelings and there's no status in that world, right? I'd like to hear just your first name and a symbol for where you're at this morning. Just make it the first thing that pops into your head. Whatever. This isn't about getting it right and we're going to keep it totally confidential, so go for it. Who'd care to begin?"

The circle immediately freezes. There are coughs and the movement of chairs. One man lets out a breath in a long, popping sigh and George thinks he'll be damned if he'll be the one who cracks first. He never gives in to peer pressure. One of the women will start, because they always do; they can't bear the silence and anyway they love all the feelings stuff.

"My name is Kathryn, and, erm, this sounds really silly, but I'm thinking of a rabbit in a hutch…"

Lloyd smiles and nods as admiringly, as if she's just quoted Hegel, and turns his friendly gaze to the chair on her left. Now there isn't even a choice of turn, George thinks grumpily. There are three more before him.

He has decided to go home at lunchtime. He wants to be back at Heronmarsh, with its scrubby ground and forlorn caravans and taciturn people; where all you have to do to avoid the mess is to watch where you're putting your feet.

"I'm Dave. I'll have to pass on the symbol thing. My mind's completely blank I'm afraid."

Lloyd admires Dave's honesty no less than he had admired Kathryn's symbol. George scowls. He knows Dave is lying.

"Hi. I'm Sylvia. I'm thinking of- I don't know why Lloyd- a water dispenser, you know, an office one, and it's half empty, and the man is coming in to fill it." She beams at Lloyd. "Perhaps you're the man with the refill I need?"

"Fabulous, Sylvia, and…?"

"Jamie. Pork chops and chips. I'm starving."

Jamie thinks he's being clever, but even George winces at his revealing words.

Lloyd turns to face George, his face expressing interest and welcome, his legs uncrossed, his arms unfolded. He is leaning slightly forward in his chair and George is tempted to pass like

Dave did out of petulance, but in fact, there is an image flickering in his mind, and it won't go away. It's an ancient Chinese ginger jar, once beautiful, now cracked and mended with glue. It's coloured the traditional blue, and shows the lovers on the bridge in the ancient willow pattern. Too dangerous to use, too precious to throw away, it's been put away safely away on a shelf. Some pieces are missing in the swell of the belly, and George sees his fingers moving to the empty space and feeling sharp edges there. He decides to tell Lloyd.

"George. A jar. A willow pattern jar, with a crack in it."

"That sounds just like you George. An old crack pot."

Everyone laughs with Jamie, except Lloyd, who nods and then picks up his notes and begins to talk about bereavement. Fierce words drift past George, like sharks in an aquarium. *Shock...Anger...Grief...Hurt...* Does Lloyd really know anything that isn't in a manual?

He sighs loudly and Dave and Jamie turn to look at him, smirking, waiting for him to say something sarcastic. Lloyd falters in his smooth delivery, but George keeps his face impassive, looking straight ahead, like a schoolboy playing the innocent in class. He could start to hum, he thinks, or let off a stink bomb as he did in Second year chemistry. He hated that too. He doesn't like formulas for anything, he's not a formulas man. He doesn't want to hear about stages of bereavement or post-traumatic stress. He already knows about grief. It hurts for ever. That's all.

Lloyd regains his stride like a competent skater, and George half-folds his arms, cupping his left cheek in his left hand. His skin feels rough. He didn't shave again this morning. He must look like a tramp sitting here in his ill-fitting suit and he wonders how long it will be before they get rid of him. His face doesn't fit any more, and appearances are all that matter now. It's the dross decade. The Age of Crappius Superficialus.

Lloyd's voice is soothing, and George has fallen into reverie. He has his back to the window and the warm sun is reaching in and stroking the back of his neck and the tops of his shoulders.

He slips off his shoes and wiggles his toes in his socks. Lloyd will like that.

There's a rustling of paper, as Lloyd passes round notes. George doesn't take them.

"And now, if I could ask all you guys to get as comfortable as you can? Close your eyes and take some good deep breaths…"

George's colleagues close their eyes like mechanical dolls, but he stares defiantly back at Lloyd who smiles gently at him, like a woman.

"If you're willing. No pressure."

Clever, thinks George. Give somebody a choice and they'll do what you want them to anyway. He closes his eyes and breathes. Breathes angrily, forcing the air in and out of his stiff chest and reluctant lungs.

"Try to let go of any tension in your body…"

Let go. His whole bloody life has been about letting things go…innocence, hope, freedom, ideals, sex smoking, sugar, sweets…He'd let Soph go if he didn't think she was too feeble to survive by herself. He remembers her after Grace died, hanging round his neck like a drowning woman, her eyes full of tears. She couldn't be trusted with Gabe. She never heard him cry.

Damn Grace, he thinks suddenly. If she hadn't died, maybe they'd have stood a chance. She broke them both into a million pieces, and they're mended with a glue that isn't very strong.

"Let go of any anxious thoughts you have, take a mini holiday from those worries…"

As if it were so simple to jet off and leave his worries on a distant shore, where they'd stand wiping their eyes, and begging him to come home soon. Bye Gabe, Bye Brendan, Bye Sophia, Bye Leena. But Leena won't go. She's hanging around in his mind, despite Lloyd's banishment; how typical of her. Her eyes are laughing and her face is dripping with lake water and her dark hair is sticking wetly to her brown shoulders, like seaweed. Mermaids' purses. Again, her arms are reaching out for him. She's a siren. A witch. A lorelei. Was it was a set-up? Do the travellers want to blackmail him for something? She is one of

140

them after all.; blood is thicker than water. Oh God, he must be going mad. He *is* a crackpot. It's not funny.

His skin is prickling and he feels sweaty. Perhaps he's having a heart attack. Not enough oxygen getting to his brain.

"Now allow your mind to go to someone or something precious you have lost in your life…"

He can see his mothers' bright button eyes. She is the only woman he has ever known whose lips were hard. She used to kiss him like a woodpecker, tapping on a tree. George shifts in his chair, and then from behind a locked door in his mind comes Grace as a pretty toddler. Grace whose face lit up when he came home from work. Grace, who staggered down the hall on bandy legs, her fat little arms offering him a great basket of love and pleasure. Grace, who woke him in the morning by pattering her fingers on his eyelids and planting butterfly kisses on his nose.

There are tears in his eyes. Damn you, Lloyd, for a sadistic bastard. He doesn't *want* to think about Grace. She only exists in his mind as an ache that is his constant companion. If he pictures her at all it's when she was close to death, her child's eyes still searching his face, but with all the joy gone out of them and only a sad resignation there. Now this other image has come like a knife. It's Grace full of life, Grace full of strength. *Fuck you Lloyd. Are you trying to kill me*?

George presses his lips together. There's a home movie playing in his head, and he can see her sitting in the bath, splatting her hands down on the surface of the water, making him wet. He hadn't cared at all, kneeling there beside her. Grace had his heart; she never gave it back. Instinctively, like someone in pain, he takes deep breaths.

Jamie nudges him, thinking that he's fallen asleep.

There's a rattling of coffee spoons outside the door. The trolley's arrived, and Lloyd glances up at the clock on the wall.

"Please say a gentle goodbye to whoever or whatever it was that you lost, and imagine that now you find something in its place…"

Goodbye? He'll never say goodbye. George can see a little white coffin disappearing behind a brown curtain, in a fusty old chapel. There's a vicar with a fatuous smile, and all their friends are crying. He opens his eyes and shakes his head and rubs his face like someone waking from a nightmare. Enough. Enough. Enough.

From next door, there is a hum of relieved conversation. Their session has finished. Lloyd invites comments, but there are none. Sylvia is blowing her nose, Dave looks angry and Jamie is unusually quiet.

George follows the smokers outside and heads down towards the lake by himself. The air feels fresh against his skin, after the clammy heat of the workshop room. He leans against a solid oak tree, some distance from the water's edge, and looks out over the lake. A breeze is scooping up the water into scummy green ruffles. How could he have gone in there? How could she?

"George!"

He freezes, his back pressed into the tree. Leena is calling his name from a distance. He watches her sprinting across the grass towards him, her hair flying out behind her, her knees rising and falling as she runs. Leena isn't like anybody else in the world; the sight of her running towards him makes him hold his breath. As she comes closer, she slows down, and in the end approaches him walking. She is laughing and puffing and patting her chest.

"Why do I imagine I'm six years old again, when I see a big patch of green grass?"

She bends forward, her hands gripping her knees. She runs, thinks George. She probably runs marathons. Her hair sweeps against the ground, picking up grass. She straightens up slowly, and stretches her arms up to the sky, flexing her long bare fingers.

"That's better. My back gets stiff these days. She is looking directly at him and George's belly flips over like a frog surprised in a garden pond. "Perhaps I should grow up?"

She smells of oranges and wood smoke. There is the mere hint of a question in her voice. He can't look away from her sparkling eyes. They're like the flower lights Soph bought for Grace's first Christmas.

George wants to say "No, don't ever grow up," but it comes out as "Perhaps we both should," and sounds stiff and thick with disapproval.

He wants to take his words back; re-call them like faulty products. She takes a step back and he feels as if he has failed a simple test.

"Hey, George, you look awful. What's up?"

"No, nothing. Just, you know, tired. Everything, it's…"

"Are you in *Lost and Found*?"

"That's got nothing to do with anything. These training sessions bore me. I've heard it all before. It's bullshit."

"I'm in *Dynamics of Sexuality*. It's great fun."

"I'm sure it is," he says primly. "Your sort of thing, I suppose. Anyway, I've decided to go back early. To work, I mean. Skip the last day here"

"Lloyd will think you've chickened out, but actually I think we might both have to go. That's what I came over to say."

"Oh God, what's happened now?"

George can feel his blood pressure rising. He's sure he can. His neck seems to be swelling.

"Keep calm George, you'll give yourself a heart attack one of these days. Nothing much has happened yet."

"What is it, for God's sake?"

"Watch your temper, George. I won't stand for it. My grandmother rang me to tell me there was some sort of '*anti gypsy*' protest in the town, and it was pretty violent. No-one's mentioned it up here, but it was on the news apparently, and she's unhappy about Brendan's site inspection too. She said he was snooping around and waving his little black book and leader of the council pen."

"Oh *God*. I told you he said he was going to. Why did that have to happen as well while we're away?"

He glares at Leena, as if she were somehow responsible for it all.

"Don't shoot the messenger, George."

She turns to walk away. He puts a hand out in case she starts to run again; her bare arms are soft as velvet.

"Stop. Sorry, sorry. I just wasn't expecting there to be a problem, that's all."

"Well there is."

"You know me, Leena. Hot head in a crisis."

"What *crisis,* George? Nothing's happened yet. A few yobs in the market place? So what? Brendan might be showing support for a change. You always over react."

"I think you under react. I'll bet Amelia's got at him."

"Who's the hell's Amelia?"

"She's a neighbour of ours. I told Brendan not to take her seriously. She's always desperately wanted Heronmarsh for her apartheid bloody Brownie pack."

"Do you think we should both go back?"

"Suppose so," he says childishly, kicking at a tuft of grass. Seeds fly everywhere and Leena sneezes.

"Try and head Brendan off at the pass?"

"The only pass he's interested in making is probably the one he's making at Amelia."

Leena reaches up suddenly, taking him by surprise and he flinches. She brushes her finger tips across his cheek. Her eyes crinkle up at the corners.

"I think the party's over George."

George has heard the click of a closing door. Ironic that Brendan's adultery has put paid to his own. Adultery? Is that what he did with Leena? It felt less mature than that.

"Shall we go?"

She almost extends her arm to him, but thinks better of it, and plunges her hands in to the pockets of her shorts. He trudges back across the grass behind her, a thwarted child trailing behind a purposeful mother. Anyone seeing him would suppose him to be deep in thought, but the emptiness has come again; it's never too far away. The cold grey fingers that sleep inside him are stretching up towards his throat. One day they'll choke the life out of him, he thinks.

He feels himself stiffening, his shoulders beginning to ache. Once he was a warrior, he thinks, fighting poverty, fighting injustice, fighting bigotry. There was a point to him. He was full of fire. He was bloody Batman. 'Fire's out now, Georgie,' he thinks, watching a wisp of smoke from the golden fields beyond the hotel gardens escaping upwards into the strong blue sky. His chest aches. Is his heart really wearing out? Maybe it is.

Leena has stopped and is waiting for him to catch up.

"What did you say George?"

"Sorry. Just mumbling. First sign of madness."

He looks away.

"You look really depressed."

"Depressed, am I? I thought I'd just got old and tired."

There is an odd relief in accepting his depression. Sophia doesn't allow him to be depressed. For her, he's had to pretend to be strong all these years and it's nearly killed him. He can't do it any more. His eyes meet Leena's and he feels an anxious flutter under his diaphragm, and wonders again about the state of his heart. This time she does hold out her arm and he takes it.

They walk slowly back to the hotel, keeping step until they get close to the building, when each lets the other go.

TWENTY-TWO

"Who slammed the fucking door? I've an evil headache. What on earth are these nails doing all over the floor?"

Lucian is still sitting at the kitchen table. Frankie saw the look on his face moments after she spoke, and wishes for the thousandth time she were more sensitive. She dumps her books down on the unusually clean floor and sits down next to him.

"Hey, Luce, what's up?"

"It's Gabe."

"Oh."

She stiffens and withdraws a little. She doesn't like Gabe, and she hasn't forgiven him for his cruel remarks the night before.

"I think he's really lost it this time Frankie. He's having some sort of weird breakdown."

"Oh come on, Gabe's pretty nuts anyway. He's never been exactly normal, has he?"

"Well that noise was him leaving. He's just run out of the house. Literally."

"That's a first. I've never seen him run anywhere before. He thinks he's too cool to move quickly. Why?"

"I've no idea, something to do with these tools I bought, I think. I'd decided to have a go at the garden…"

They both glance towards the open door. A shaft of sunlight is striking the head of the new hammer, making it shine.

"I went off to the garden centre to get them while I was still in the mood, and when I got back, he was just sort of sitting here…"

"So what? Gabe's a lazy bastard. He's always loafing around the place."

"But he had this really *terrible* look on his face, Frankie. It was like…have you ever seen an animal die? You know the way their

146

eyes fade and fade until they can't see any more? He looked like that."

"No I haven't seen an animal die. I wouldn't just stand there, would I? I'd call the fucking RSPCA or something. Oh, come off it, Lucian. You're exaggerating, as usual, aren't you?"

"I'm *not* Frankie. When I got out the tools to show him, he just freaked. He looked at me as if I'd pulled out a fucking pistol. He kind of *edged* round the table, and when he got to the door he just ran out, like, I don't know, like somebody running away from an armed gang."

"Well, where's he gone?"

"God knows, Frankie, he wasn't going to tell me, was he?"

"Keep your hair on Lucian. It's not my fault, is it? I could have told you your precious Gabe's mentally unstable."

They both fall silent, over-burdened and resentful of each other. Frankie picks grease from the table with a ragged thumbnail while Lucian lights a cigarette and stares out at the garden. When Vicky and Lou come up the passageway, laughing uproariously, they stop on the threshold, the atmosphere in the usually uncomplicated kitchen an invisible barrier to casual entry.

"Christ, you two, who died?" asks Lou walking sideways over to the table like an uncertain gate-crasher, closely followed by Vicky, who sits down next to her, closing the circle.

"Why are you smoking in here? I thought we agreed?"

"It's bloody Gabe," says Frankie, "cracked up completely at last, surprise, surprise."

Lucian glares at her and goes over it all again, whispering in case he comes back unexpectedly and overhears.

Shadows gather in the kitchen as the sun goes in. A breeze has got up, making the back door bang. Every time it does, one or another of them jumps, but nobody gets up to close it. There is goose flesh on Vicky's arms, although the kitchen is warm.

"I think he should be in hospital."

"A mental hospital, Frankie? *Jesus.*" Lucian is horrified. "He's just stressed out, that's all. We've got to support him, not have him put away, for God's Sake."

147

Vicky nods. "If he gets taken in they'll lock him up and then stuff him full of pills. He might never paint again."

"Well if he doesn't get seen to he might do himself in, and then he definitely won't ever paint again. Plenty of artists have taken the one way train before him," says Frankie, not very kindly. Everyone knows she just wants him out of the way.

"Let's just wait for a couple of days. Keep an eye on him, yeah?"

Lucian feels as if he's pleading for Gabe's life.

"You keep an eye on him. He's your fucking *friend.*" Frankie spits out the word as if it's a pip. "I don't want to go anywhere near him. Fucking freak. He's always got to be the centre of attention in this house."

"I will. I'll…take a walk up to the studio now and see if he's gone there…"

Lucian is grabbing his sun- glasses and looking in the cupboard for chocolate. His stomach is growling with hunger and fear.

"Just *go,* will you Luce? You're not going on a bloody picnic."

A life class had already started when Gabe had arrived earlier and he'd slipped in unnoticed. When Lucian gets there, he positions himself where he can see him. The vast studio is quiet and peaceful. There is a soft noise of brushes and charcoal and breathing and a stifled sneeze from someone whose hay fever is lingering this summer.

In the centre, a spotlight shines upon a naked woman in a classic reclining pose. Her legs are crossed at the ankle and her body twisted to one side, one arm lying along the back of an ancient, purple couch.

Her flesh droops and sags into soft rolls and creases, and her face is grooved with age and experience. She looks like somebody's grandmother. The students are grouped around her in a semi circle, their eyes flickering up and down.

There is a smell of paint and turpentine. The old wooden floor is a marvellous mosaic of dotted colour, flicked from the brushes held by a thousand students over the many decades of its use. A moving patchwork of blue and white sky appears through the lofty glass roof.

This is Gabe's sanctuary. The odour soothes him as completely as a mother's smell soothes a baby. *'I have a shield'*, the words keep repeating themselves in his head like a tape on a loop, *'I have a titanium shield, I am safe, I have a titanium shield, I am saved, I have a titanium shield, I am safe, I have a titanium shield, I am saved.....*

His mouth moves but he doesn't make any sound; the students who notice assume he is listening to an ipod. No one notices his crumpled t-shirt and jeans, or his knotted hair. Gabe often turns up without having been to bed.

Inside him, the fear is shrinking back to a manageable size, and is coiled there. He settles himself more comfortably on his wooden stool and looks around, smiling emptily at his peers. Only Lucian catches his eye. Gabe is grinning with blank eyes, he looks like a life sized clockwork toy.

Lucian is thinking about the night before, and blaming himself. He'd meant to comfort Gabe. He really shouldn't have kissed him; he should have had more sense. He bites the stem of his brush hard, and flakes of black paint stick to the end of his tongue. He picks them off, and wipes his hand on his thigh, still watching Gabe from the corner of his eye. The skin of his face is taut with tension; an observer would probably pick out Lucian first, as the disturbed student in the room.

Gabe has been sketching the life model in soft charcoal, with swift, sure strokes. Now he shifts uncomfortably in his chair, Lucian's smile has unnerved him.

'So I'm being watched', he thinks, the dark terror stirring in his bowels like a nest of waking rats fatally linked by their tails. His heart is beating fast. Even here, in his own house, they've come for him. There's no hiding place anywhere, after all.

There is a sudden noise in the corridor outside, and the model's eyes flicker towards the door. That is enough for Gabe. He has seen the evil in her look and now he knows she's one of them. Two faces have appeared on his paper. One is calm and sweet, the other twisted and cunning. All the moisture has drained from his mouth and Gabe swallows hard, trying to think before they destroy his mind.

'I have a shield', he mutters aloud, 'Titanium. There's nothing stronger.'

The face on his sheet laughs at him shrilly: *'Titania, Titania, Queen of the Fairies!'*
It mocks him without mercy.

He leaps to his feet, an explosion of energy in his head, and stares, wild-eyed at the model. His stool falls one way, and his easel the other. All around the room, faces are looking at him, annoyed, puzzled, anxious.

The model grabs her wrap, and darts behind the solid old couch. Charcoal crunches underfoot as Gabe lunges towards her, his hands outstretched and reaching.

There is a piercing wail as Doug, the tutor, presses his panic alarm. Gabe trips over the leg of his easel and falls crashing to the floor as two burly security guards run in. One dives on him, expertly straddling his back and pinning him to the ground. The other stands guard. Lucian runs over, gabbling in his panic: "It's all right, it's all right. He's not well, for God's Sake. Give him some space, will you? He can't breathe!"

Gabe has found himself face down on the wooden floor. It's over. They've got him now. There's nothing more he can do. He begins to sob piteously, like a cornered child.

"It's not fair. I didn't do anything. It's not fair, they were trying to get me."

His shoulders are shaking beneath the weight of the hefty guard.

The other students begin to gather round the trio, who are locked together in an improbable tableau. No one knows the next move. Some kneel down, others move back. There is a buzz of inquiry and some nervous laughter.

Doug steps through the crowd and takes Lucian by the arm, drawing him to one side. Gabes' heart rending sobs are filling the air, making all present feel guilty, as if they should have done better, somehow.

"Lucian, what's the matter with Gabriel? Is he on drugs? Is he high?"

Doug's voice is sharp. Concern for Gabe is mixed with some anxiety that his protégée is going to let him down before the exhibition and rob him of his own moment of glory. Gabe is the most talented student he's ever had.; this was going to be Doug's own afternoon in the sun.

"No, no, I don't think so. He's not well, Doug, there's been too much pressure. Look, make them let Gabe go. He's in pain, can't you see?"

Lucian glares at Doug, accusingly. Perhaps all this is his fault.

Doug nods. "OK, Dave, thank you. You can leave it to me now."

Dave gets to his feet with relief, feeling increasingly foolish at pinning a sobbing man to the ground. The model walks over.

"Poor little sod. Looks like he needs his Mum. State of him! Lots of TLC required, I should think."

Doug frowns. Lucian nods eagerly, relieved that at last Gabe's mental state is out in the open. It's no longer all his responsibility.

"Right," Doug takes charge, "back to work everyone, please. This isn't a circus. Gabriel will be fine. He's probably just stressed out, that's all completely exhausted. There's nothing to worry about folks."

There are dubious looks. Gabe is curled up in a foetal position, moaning softly, his hands covering his head.

"Come on, move it."

Doug claps his hands sharply. Christ, what's the matter with the boy? He's probably too talented for his own good. He's gone over the edge into chaos. Some of them can handle it, some of them can't. For himself, he'd never been brave enough to find out. Which is why he's a sodding lecturer, he reflects, and not a working artist. As he looks at Gabe lying on the studio floor, he is honest enough to know that he made the right decision.

The other students are beginning to move back to their places.

"You all right Molly?" asks Doug.

"Yes love, don't you worry about me." There isn't much in life she hasn't seen before.

"Then let's go, people, let's *go.* "

Doug turns back to Gabe. Lucian is kneeling on the floor beside him, gently stroking his head.

"It's ok, Gabe," he's saying with tears in his eyes, "try not to worry, everything will be ok."

Doug wonders enviously whether they are lovers.

"Right, Lucian," he says crouching down, "do you have Gabriel's parents telephone number?" Lucian nods. "Then I'll order a taxi, and we'll get him to your place. We can ring them from there and call a doctor. I don't think there's any need for an ambulance."

Lucian turns back to Gabe. He's afraid.

"Gabe, shall we go home and call your mother? Ask her to come?"

He is half hoping Gabe will say no. That he'll suddenly snap together and be well again, but Gabe nods. He sits up but his eyes are still tightly closed. He knows they've taken him prisoner, but they haven't crucified him yet. Lucian is talking about his mother, but it could be a trick. They might bring him someone else. He wants his mother. He needs her to tell him about the lovely colours. The deep blue of a summer sky, a bright red pillar box, the spreading green of a Spring meadow, glossy black tar on a freshly laid road...

Gabe is totally silent while they take him home and cover him with blankets and ring for the doctor.

TWENTY-THREE

Leena is handing in her keys to the blonde girl on Reception who is never friendly, despite their previous late night meeting, when she feels a warm hand on her back. She turns quickly and Jamie steps on her foot. Her shoulder bangs against his chest and she stares at him, disappointed. She had wanted it to be George's hand against her spine, George's breath on the back of her neck.

"Gosh, I'm sorry, Leena. I didn't mean to startle you. Guilty conscience?"

She is annoyed with him, more for not being George than for hurting her foot and she doesn't reply.

"Are you off already? Where's old George? I thought you two were thick as thieves."

She hears a public school laugh in him she's never noticed before.

"Whoops, I shouldn't have said that, should I? Not with your heritage! No offence!"

Now there is a silence so stinging, that even the receptionist looks up, frowning.

Leena looks at Jamie. Her eyes are blue searchlights, the mocking laughter in his eyes fades and he looks contrite.

"Leena I'm sorry. I though I was being funny. Don't be cross."

She counts on her fingers: one…two…three.

"I am Romany. We are continually stereotyped as thieves. It's not funny."

He backs away apologising and agreeing. When he bangs into the revolving doors on the way out, she is glad. She sits down on one of the couches.

His remarks had hurt her unexpectedly, like a bedroom wasp in early Spring. The insults always come like that, out of the blue. *'Leena, Leena, toilet cleaner…'* She remembers a circle of little girls dancing around her at school, their grinning pink faces bobbing up and down, their shiny shoes skipping sideways, not allowing her out of the ring. She knew she should never have told them her father was a gypsy, but it was too late to take it back. *'My mother said, clap, I never should, clap, Play with the gypsies in the wood, clap'* Standing in the middle of that ring she'd felt loneliness as white and wide as a Colorado winter.

Another day, she'd asked Rose why people were so mean to them. Rose said that dogs hate cats because they envy the cat's freedom to live without a master. Leena didn't believe her; she knew dogs love their masters. She began to feel a pulling in different directions, as if one day she might tear in two.

She takes out her phone from her bag, a sudden impulse prompting her to ring George, wanting to feel his breath close to her ear, and when the message light flashes before she's had a chance to dial, she imagines by a strange synchronicity he is trying to contact her.

But it isn't George, it's a text from Nick: *Ru home sweetheart? Hope u not drowned! Champagne in my fridge, come over drink with me.* She strokes the screen with a forefinger, and smiles. Nick is as uncomplicated as Spring rain, as light and sweet as candy floss.

He'd found her on Hampstead Heath ten years ago, in the very early morning. He had come to practise Tai Chi, she was sitting on a bench where she'd been all night, wondering how it was possible to go on living without Ravi. Not how it was possible to live her life, that was simple enough. She had her own flat and a career and some good friends, but how to walk without him, how to eat, how to sleep, how to breathe, without him. Ravi had flowed in her and through her like a great river, his current sweeping her away into blue green depths until she lost sight of the banks completely. It felt like glory; he was her blood, her molecules, her DNA. When he left her, quite casually, for a blonde, blue-eyed sliver of light in Gucci and Prada, Leena felt as empty as a threshed field.

Nick had bowed to the first rays of the sun rising over the

heath, and strolled over to sit beside her. She had let him buy her coffee because it was easier than refusing, she let him teach her Tai Chi because she no longer cared at all about what she did, and it filled in the time that burned in her lungs. Later she slept with him because he'd saved her life and because he wanted nothing from her, no promises, no future, no filling in of the past. He is dear to her, and a wonderful lover, but even so she texts back: *No, No and no thanks.*

Sitting on top of a London bus, he reads it and nods, sensing a change.

Ten minutes later, she is in her car, turning off the winding road that leads from the hotel to the motorway that will take toward home. The road is clear, and she turns on the radio. She enjoys driving. She speeds up when George comes into her mind, turning up the volume, and pushing him out of her thoughts again. She promised herself after Ravi, there wouldn't be any more complications in her life, and George is definitely complicated.

A male tenor begins *Una Furtiva Lagrima,* and she sings with him in flawless Italian as the flat miles pass and the sun sinks lower in the sky. It is late afternoon when she turns off the motorway at last, and takes the road that bypasses the town centre and leads straight to the site. The shadows are lengthening under a Jaffa orange sunset and Leena slows down and wriggles her shoulders, looking forward to a drink in Rose's cool caravan. Her mother never knew how many times she'd skipped school when she was a child and spent the day there instead, listening to Rose telling her the old Romany stories. They formed the basis of her dissertation years later, but at the time there was just a warm comfort in them, like soup, or wearing gloves. She remembers her favourite story: *The Fox and The Dog.* It ended up '*I may be hungry, but I'll be free.*' Well she's still free, and she's not hungry either, unlike George. He's the one who's starving.

A small figure is trotting along the grass verge, and Leena slows down and opens her window.

"Hi Keely. Do you want a lift ?"

She beams. "Not half. I'm hot as fuck."

"Get in then and I'll take you home. I'm going to see Gran."

"She's been fretting, you know. She thinks we're all going to get chucked off Heron marsh any day now."

"Why's that?"

"Oh, some council bloke came snooping around, or something She says he's seen things."

"Like what?"

"Dunno. I'm not bothered anyway."

"But it's your home, Keely. You've lived there all your life. Wouldn't you care at all.?"

"Not really. Home's up here." Keely taps her forehead. "Heronmarsh aint exactly paradise is it? There's always somewhere. Anyway, if they move us on they'll stop bugging me about school."

"Haven't you been going?"

"Nope. I told Mrs Hughes I'm not going again neither until they stop picking on me. Do you think I like being picked on all day?"

"No I don't." Leena turns off the music. "Mrs Hughes?"

"She's my Art teacher. She's nice actually, she really likes my paintings. But I'm still not going."

Leena is quiet for the rest of the drive. Keely said George's wife is *nice*. She wishes Keely had said she's a bitch. She must be very nice indeed if Keely has taken to her so strongly.

She turns into the entrance to the site and parks her car, and walks thoughtfully over to Rose's pitch which is surrounded by a low white fence. Her grandmother opens the door before Leena has had a chance to knock, and stands aside to let her in. Leena can see an old woman looking out, she doesn't think Rose would survive a move now, at her age.

"Tea or lemonade?"

"Lemonade please."

As she pours a glass, Leena sees her swollen joints and the slight tremor in her hands.

"What have you been up to, Gran? Keely tells me you've been fretting."

Rose is cross. "What have the council been up to, you mean."

"Sorry. Yes I do mean the council. What's actually happened? "

"That McFall man came up here snooping all around and writing his notes down. And he's carrying on with that red headed one who organised the petition."

"What petition are you talking about?"

"She was all around the town, asking people to sign a petition to get rid of us. There was a whole bunch of them, handing out leaflets saying we're unsanitary and we're the cause of all the crime for miles around here."

"That's terrible. And illegal. What were the police doing?"

"They only turned up when the fighting started. Guess who they arrested?"

"That's completely unjust."

"Justice? What's justice got to do with it? Grow up girl! Did the Gestapo worry about justice?"

"Keep calm Gran, you'll have a stroke. Look, George and I are back now and we'll smooth the right feathers. And then there's meetings, appeals if it comes to that…"

"George and I, is it now?"

Rose has always been able to see straight through her.

"Well, I'm not really sure…"

"Will you open your door Leena? That's the question."

"I don't know. I'm perfectly happy as I am. "

Rose cackles and shakes her head but at least she's calmer now.

"Will you come and live with me, Gran?"

She laughs again. "Buy a canary if you're lonely, darling."

Leena walks off slowly into the gathering darkness. Tiredness has come over her, and her legs are leaden; she yawns and shivers. A wind has got up, rustling the newly withering leaves on the trees; she can smell Autumn in the air. She bows her head and folds her arms across her chest. It'll be time to get out winter clothes soon, light a fire and stay at home in the evenings. She's looking forward to it. She must be getting old.

George is in the office looking at a letter stamped '**Confidential**', and rubbing his chin. He doesn't go into the main office very often and his pigeonhole is stuffed with a pile of out of date minutes and leaflets, but this letter is dated the day before, and exactly what he has been dreading. *Bringing to your attention… consulted lawyers…council are taking steps to terminate licence…serious infringements of conditions…dangerous dogs…fires…livestock…extra persons staying in one of the trailers….*blah, blah, blah.

It's all bollocks and all because bloody Brendan wants to get his end away with bloody Amelia. They're a perfect match, George thinks savagely, crumpling up the paper as if he could crush them both. He snatches up the phone, knocking over the secretary's mug, which announces: **I'd rather be walking my dog.** Celia answers, and George hears Brendan whisper an excuse.

"I'm afraid he's in a meeting just now, Mr Hughes."

"Put him on Celia," George is snarling like a Sunday editor, "I can hear him perfectly well."

When George hears Brendan laugh as he takes the phone, he knows he is lost. It is the laugh of a man in love, the laugh of a man sleeping with the woman he has hunted and captured; triumphant, self satisfied, inviolate.

"You caught me out, George, you swine."

"Yes I did. What on earth's going on, Brendan?"

"Not much. I'm not too busy as it happens."

"Don't play innocent. You know exactly what I mean. I've got the letter in my hand."

"Ah yes. You're talking about the licence."

"Yes, of *course* the bloody licence. Is Amelia running the council now? Is this a little present for her? Wouldn't flowers and chocolates have done the job?"

Brendan is laughing even more heartily. "She's a demanding woman, George."

George is sweating. He grabs a pale blue tissue with a picture of a duck with an umbrella on it, and wipes his forehead.

"I cannot believe you are prepared to turn people off land they have lived on for fifty fucking years, just for the sake of shagging

Amelia. She's not even nice. She's an awful woman, frankly. What's on earth's the matter with you?"

Brendan's voice is soft and he has become Irish. "Sure it's nothing to do with me personally, George. It's the general public who aren't happy. They're not happy at all. There's been letters, a petition even, would you believe it?"

"Set up by your new friend and the cause of that outrageous so called demonstration by the town scum."

"Actually, I would have expected you to be a little more vigilant up there, George. Is it my fault if the tinkers have breached the conditions? There's no excuse for that now, is there?"

"They're bullshit and you know it. Don't think we won't fight this."

"Rules are rules, George. What can I do? I'm only a humble public servant. Just a slave to the people. My hands are tied."

"Tied by Amelia's kinky handcuffs, no doubt."

"How did you know about them?"

Brendan giggles like a girl, and George reaches the end of his tether.

"Oh- *just fuck off!*"

He slams the phone down and jams himself into the orange office chair. Air escapes from the vinyl seat with a small sigh. He wants a mug that says: **I wish I were dead.**

Without thinking, he reaches for the packet of cigarettes that is laying on the secretary's desk and lights one up for the first time in over twenty years.

TWENTY-FOUR

Late holidaymakers who can't afford peak season prices shuffle unaware and solemn eyed past Jez and Sophia as they embrace on the tawdry promenade. His hands are warm on the small of her back; she is startled by the erection nosing her hip bone, but she stands her ground, only swaying slightly. She smiles at the memory of the youthful curiosity that prompted her to reach for that part of him all those years ago and then recoil in shock. It's funny, until she remembers what happened next, and the humiliation of waiting for the phone call from him that he never made.

She jerks away again now, and takes a step backwards. He is breathing fast, lips still parted, and nostrils slightly flared but she folds her arms across her chest like a pantomime dame. The sea whispers and shushes and laps at the pebbles on the shore.

"I don't think that was *such* a marvellous idea." She speaks in her iciest tone, the one she reserves for crushing the adolescent male ego. "I thought you'd grown up."
She sounds silly, she knows she does.

If Jez is hurt, it doesn't show on his face. He is used to anger, his patients are often furious with him. He turns back to the sea, and looks out towards the horizon again. The waves are rising and falling, each one carried forward by its own music. Sophia glares at his profile, watching a muscle twitch below his left eye.

"So why did you drop me like that Jez? Didn't you know how much you hurt me? It was cruel and selfish."

"I'm so sorry Soph."

He turns towards her and his eyes seek out hers. She looks away, the eye thing is dangerous, her blood is still singing. He reaches out a hand, palm upwards, but she clenches her fists into her thighs, and he lets it fall back again.

She's not looking at him, shamed by the tears in her eyes, and the constancy of his gaze and the feeling inside her, damp as a dog's nose.

"I felt…you know it wasn't just a case of a bruised ego Jez, if that's what you're thinking. For years afterwards, I felt I was…invisible. Literally. *I* knew I was there, but I thought nobody really saw me…"

Her eyes are on his face now, and he is nodding at her as if what she is saying makes perfect sense, when she knows it's all just mad rubbish. "I didn't really want to teach when I left university, I wanted to paint. I only became a teacher so I could have my name on a register. So every day at least thirty people would know I was there…"

"It was reassuring."

"No. It wasn't *reassuring*. It was *necessary*."

He's nodding again. Will his neck wear out one day? He nods so much. Nod, nod, nod. I see, I see, I see. Perhaps psychotherapists insure their necks, like concert pianists insure their fingers. Does he really see? Or is he just a good nodder?

The smell of candy floss and popcorn is making her nauseous.

" That's why I married George, because he saw me. Or I thought he did, in those days."

The wind is ruffling Jez's hair. Women flash him glances as they pass, but he doesn't seem to notice. All his female patients must be in love with him she thinks, stroking his forbidden body in their sleep, in their dreams. She is grateful for the grit the wind has blown into her eyes. It allows her to let the tears fall.

"But George doesn't see me now. He looked away when Grace died, and he never looked back again. He didn't really trust me with Gabe, you know. Perhaps it was something in my eyes. Or maybe he looked at me and saw her. I don't know. Whatever it was, I disappeared again."

"Are you crying Soph?"

"No."

They carry on walking along the promenade, towards the pier.

"You never stopped being real to me."

"A real idiot."

"No. A real woman."

"I wasn't a woman. I was just a girl. Are you trying to be charming? Because it won't work."

"I never do that. It's just the truth."

"I won't forgive you."

He nods, accepting her harshness meekly.

She feels as if she can't breathe. Her chest is tight. Is this asthma? Her shirt is clammy against her skin and her foot hurts. That blister still hasn't healed. She stops and takes off her shoes, and they walk on in silence. The backdrop of their youth has barely changed, and in spite of her determination to be cold as stone, she exclaims and turns towards him.

"Oh look! *Madame Mandala* is still here."

They are passing a dilapidated yellow hut with a figure of a woman gazing into a crystal ball crudely painted onto a board outside.

"She must be a hundred and four by now."

"She told us we'd marry and have two children and be very happy. She must have said the same thing to every young couple."

"I believed her. I remember going home that day and telling Jen I was going to marry you. I was so happy. She told me nobody sane would ever marry me. Perhaps she had more psychic powers than our Madam M."

Sophia is staring at him, her eyes bewildered. "But if you felt like that, then why the hell didn't you get in touch after we…after…you know."

He clears his throat. "Jen says I was unconsciously punishing you for my mother's betrayal."

She frowns at him, her lips tight. "Why on earth did you tell Jennifer? She's a solicitor. Aren't you supposed to be the clever dick shrink?"

"You don't like psychotherapists much, do you Soph?"

"I saw one after Grace died. I thought she was the most horrible and *stupid* woman I'd ever met."

"Some therapists are very cold. They like feelings to be safely inside someone else."

"Are you like that?"

"Not now. I think I used to be."

"You used to be a prick."

"I know."

"Shut up in your own little box, watching the world go by."

"I suppose I still am."

"What?"

"Living in a box. Watching the world."

"Well, why haven't you married? Had kids, like everybody else?"

Jez is silent, and she wants to hurt him more.

" Too scared to join in?"

He looks sad. "I think I've come to the conclusion over the years, that I'm a one woman man. The first cut is the deepest, and all that."

She half laughs. "Oh charming. You mean your relationship with me was so awful it put you off women for life? Thanks a lot."

"I mean I fell in love with you so deeply, that no one else has ever even came close."

Sophia looks away.

"You had a very peculiar way of showing it."

"I still love you."

Her heart is hammering and her mouth feels dry. What is all this talk of love? *Love? Now?* She won't let him get away with it.

"Prove it."

"All right. How can I prove it?"

She looks around, and nudges him hard in the ribs with her elbow, jerking her head at the red painted shack on his right that says: *Billybobs "Tattoos".*

"Go and get one now. Get a tattoo for me."

"All right."

"On your hand. Get a pink rose on the back of your hand."

She searches his face for any sign of hesitation. If he demurs for one single second, she is going straight back to the station and

163

taking the first train home.

He looks at his watch and she smiles triumphantly, waiting for him to tell her he doesn't have the time, but instead he says: "I'm not sure how long this will take, Soph. Why don't you wait for me in the café?"

She stands gawping, like a child at a zoo, while he crosses the boards in three strides and disappears through the flaky, bowing doorway. A discordant jangle brings a voice from the back, and Sophia pads over to listen, carrying her shoes and hovering outside like an anxious dog. She can hear a gruff voice coming from inside.

"Nah mate, roses are for girls. I couldn't do it to you."

"I must have a rose in pink. Now."

"How about a nice serpent?"

"No."

"Winged dragon?"

"No."

"Lion's head mate. Final offer."

"I'll pay you double. Whatever it costs. I'll pay you double if you do it now."

"Are you drunk, mate?"

"No I'm not."

"From the telly? Taking the piss?"

"No."

"Trading standards?"

"Certainly not. It's a test. For a lady."

"Oh. Oh *right*. Gotcha. OK then."

He seems to understand this perfectly, as if modern day knights ride into his dingy parlour every day on chivalrous quests. Sophia can hear the scrape of a chair being pulled up. She can bear it no longer and bursts in with another wild peal of bells.

"*Stop.* That's enough. He doesn't really want one. Sorry. It's my fault."

Jez looks anxious. He has already unbuttoned his cuff and half pulled up his sleeve, and is standing with his wrist raised, fingers drooping like a dog with a hurt paw.

Billybob laughs triumphantly, as if he has had a hand in all this. He claps Jez on the back.

"Passed it mate, dincha? The test. You passed it."

Jez looks at Sophia, who grabs his still resolutely extended hand as if she can't bear to see it any more. She pushes it down.

"Yes. Yes he did. Thank you Mr…thank you. Come on Jez. Let's go. I do believe you. Really."

As they leave, Jez looks back over his shoulder. Billybob is still smiling proudly, like a knight grandfather. He punches the air as he watches them leave and carry on walking up the pier.

Sophia lets Jez put his arm around her shoulders although it feels too hot and heavy,
the air is like thick butter even here on the pier today. They are passing the old amusement machines, the laughing policeman and the Grand National. A little boy is peeping through his fingers at the haunted graveyard as a green and brown lead monster rises up from a grave, its arms outstretched.

"Look at that. It reminds me of a picture Gabe drew when he was little. I think he used wax crayons. It was of himself, with a big smiley head and a very fat stomach, and inside the stomach, there was a monster with claws and fangs and arms reaching out, like that. He frightened himself, and then didn't want to see it any more. I had to throw it away when he wasn't looking."

"We all have our monsters inside."

"Do we? You don't think it was anything unusual?"

"Well- oh look, here we are. *Marina Café. Fine fresh fish!* I feel as if I'm in a time warp."

"Look at the prices though. Seven ninety five! We used to pay one and six."

"You've got a good memory."

"Steel trap, George says."

He looks away, uneasily, she thinks. They step inside and he heads for a seat near the window, which looks out over the restless sea. In spite of the greasy warmth, she shivers. Seagulls are swooping low, crying out a storm warning.

"Cold?" He is already looking round for another table.

165

"No, no not really. Actually I'm really worried about Gabe. That's partly why I rang you, and why I was upset. I need some advice; I wanted to ask Lucian, but Gabe came in before I got the chance..."

"Lucian?"

"Gabe's best friend."

"They're close?"

"Oh *yes*, terribly."

"Is Gabe gay?"

"No he isn't! Stop ticking boxes, Jez. You're not at work now. I'm just asking you as a ...friend."

"I'm sorry."

How could she have let him kiss her?

"I really don't want to hurt you, Soph. You said you were worried and I'm just trying to establish some background, that's all, so I can get the full picture."

The waitress is standing beside their table with a friendly smile and a cheap notebook and pencil.

"Drinks, Madam?"

She smells of batter. Jez orders a mineral water, and Sophia a large glass of wine. When it comes, she grips the stem of the glass tightly, and grimaces at the bitter taste.

"God, this wine is awful. Jez, I just need to know what's going on with Gabe. He's saying things that don't make any sense, and he's put the telephone down on me and when I took him out for lunch last week he told me some tale about being bullied at school that I didn't know anything about, and he seemed to blame me. He was in a rage, and then he just left, didn't say goodbye or anything..."

Her eyes are on his face; they are wide and terrified. The moments spent waiting for a professional opinion hold a particular horror for her, even now. *Afraid...doing all we can...so sorry...* The shaking of her hand is agitating the wine in her glass.

"Mmm. It sounds a bit adolescent. What was Gabe like as a teenager?"

166

"Well, not bad, actually. Stayed out late a few times, got his tongue pierced, got a tattoo, that sort of thing, but he was never aggressive, always polite…Oh! Do you think all this is some sort of delayed rebellion thing? I never thought of that."

"We all need to find out who we are."

"It's such a difficult time for them, isn't it? I absolutely dread teaching the older ones. They're so hard to manage. I never thought much about what Gabe was going through when he was that age. Typical isn't it? Teachers always neglect their own kids, don't they?"

She's feeling much more cheerful. The wine is tasting better.

"Do they?"

"We don't have recognised rituals here, do we? Well, unless you're Jewish I suppose, no lions to hunt, that sort of thing. I suppose we were too easy going with him…"

Jez takes a sip of his water. "Were you honest with him?"

"Honest? Oh, completely, yes. He always knew he could talk to us about anything, sex, drugs, girls, well, he was never really interested in girls…"

The waitress has come back with two plastic plates piled high with steaming fish and fat golden chips. Sophia smiles at her.

"This looks lovely. Thank you."

Why didn't she think of that before? Gabe is still young; once he gets over this angry phase, he'll be fine. She smiles at Jez, she could kiss him. Again. She is remembering the feel of his lips, the taste of his mouth. He is eating chips with his fingers.

"You never told him about his sister, did you? He thinks he's an only child, doesn't he?"

She wasn't expecting that and Sophia begins to breathe faster. She feels slightly dizzy.

"So what?" she manages defiantly. She knew all along she couldn't trust him.

"Well, he's your second child, not your first, he's the younger, not the elder and he's not really the only one. He's lost a sister who everyone pretends never existed, so his maps are fake. He doesn't really know who he is, does he?"

She looks mutinous. "What difference could that possibly make? Grace had died before he was even a year old. He never really knew her at all, he never mentioned her when he could talk, he always completely accepted that he was an only child. In fact, he used to say he liked it. Two and two don't always make five, Jez. Typical shrink pitch."

He looks annoyed now. "*Look*, I'm not trying to hurt you. I wouldn't be saying this if I didn't think it was important. You asked me what I thought, and I think there may be an earlier problem. Babies absorb far more than most people realise; it's usually more comfortable for everyone else to imagine that they don't. I'm not going to lie to you Soph."

"You wouldn't dream of it, would you, Mr High and Mighty Freeman?"

She reaches for her glass. Her knuckles are white and he is afraid the stem will snap.

"Would you prefer me to lie?"

She looks at the wall above his head. There is a picture of the sea hanging there, as if someone had deemed the surrounding ocean not quite good enough.

"We did it for Gabe's benefit," she says without expression, "we thought it would be better for him. We all had to move on and put Grace's death behind us."

"Better for Gabe, Soph?" Jez is asking as gently as he can, but it's still too rough, "or less painful for you?"

Her shoulders are shaking. The waitress is watching from behind the counter, her thoughts written all over her face; *All men are bastards...She should leave the bloke...*

The food is congealing now on the plastic flowered plates and Sophia watches a fisherman on the pier reel in his line. He tosses a gleaming silver fish on to the planks, and it lands there with a dull thud. Perhaps he missed the bucket, or perhaps he didn't care. Not that intention makes much difference to the fish, she thinks, as she watches it flapping and dying in the indifferent air. She can barely speak.

"I just never *thought* enough. How could I have done that to

Gabe?"

He covers her hands with his. They feel inadequate to warm her icy fingers.

"Listen to me Soph. We're all only human. We just do the best we can."

She jumps up, knocking over her chair, sick of his understanding, sick of his tolerance. She shouts into his face, finally startled out of its composure like a complacent midwife finding an unexpected twin.

"It wasn't fucking good enough though was it, you patronising prick?"

She runs out of the café, the door slamming shut behind her and the sound of her running feet echo through the wide open windows. Throwing a twenty- pound note down on the table, Jez runs after her watched by the waitress who frowns as she tucks it into the pocket of her apron.

Sophia is running as fast as she can. Her chest is burning in a way she hasn't felt since she was a child running to win, and the pain from her blister only spurs her on.

Candy colours flash past blurring into each other, pink, yellow, blue and green. She can hear Jez shouting her name but she doesn't slow and an old boy calls: *"Do you want the police, love?"*

She yells: *"Leave me the fuck alone!"*

Yells it out to the old boy, to Marina Café, to George, to Gabe, to Jez. She yells it to Dermott, to her mother, to Grace, to Amelia, to Madam Mandala, to Billybob and her whole damn, stupid hurting life.

Just before she reaches the end of the pier, she jumps down onto the sludge and shingle that forms an uninviting beach, and sprints towards the sea. Watched by a row of excited pensioners in deck chairs, she crashes into the grey water that rises past her ankles and up her calves and laps the edge of her skirt.

"For God's Sake Sophia, stop!"

She is shaking and laughing and crying and Jez's hand is on her shoulder. His own momentum carries him forward, pushing her down into the swirling water where the coldness takes her breath away.

"Oh Christ, Soph, sorry, sorry, sorry. Are you all right? Take my hand, look, here, come on, it'll be OK, don't worry, please don't worry, I'm so sorry."

His chest is broad and finally she lays her head against him and cries hot tears like a very small child. She can hear the fast beating of his heart.

Gently, he guides her out of the water and back towards the promenade, wiping at her face and hair with a handkerchief and murmuring to her as if she were a frightened horse she thinks, beginning to breathe more slowly.

The elderly audience look at each other and grin and roll their eyes and click their dentures, finally going back to their naps and their puzzles and their knitting. Her teeth are chattering and Jez takes off his shirt and puts it around her shoulders. She flinches away from him, not wanting to see his bare chest.

When they get back to his car, he wraps her in a soft tartan travel rug and leaves her in the front seat while he sprints back to the pavement stalls and buys hot coffee and two large t-shirts.

"*Garfield* or *Superman*, Soph?"

"*Garfield,* please. I don't feel very super."

The drive home is almost silent ,and the air is still humid. The darkening sky hangs in swags of grey: pewter, gunmetal and lead. At the last roundabout, a few fat drops of rain plop onto the windshield. It stops, and brings no relief from the heat. Jez drives fast and efficiently, maintaining a safe distance from the car in front, unlike George who speeds and brakes sharply and swears at other drivers, scaring them to death. She doesn't want to go home.

When they arrive, dusk is gathering. Soon the clocks will change and summer will be over. The windows of the house gape like empty eyes and there are no reflections. Everywhere is dull as ink.

As she steps over the threshold, the phone begins to ring, making them both jump. Sophia beckons Jez inside with one

170

hand, while she picks up the receiver with the other.

"Hallo? Yes. Speaking."

He sees the colour empty from her face for the second time today.

"Oh no! Is he all right? Yes, of course. I'll be there as soon as I can. Tell him I'm coming."

She puts the phone down and turns to Jez, panic shining like headlights in her eyes.

"It's Gabe. That was his tutor. He thinks Gabe's having some sort of breakdown.
He attacked the life model. I have to go for him."

Jez takes a deep breath; this is as bad as he feared it might be.

"Ok, Soph. I'll come with you if you want me to. Let's just sit down for a minute and think."

She nods stiffly and leads the way through to the sitting room, turning on lights as she goes. Her hands are beginning to shake again. Jez sits down in George's chair and Sophia glances nervously out at the dark, as if a stalker could be hiding there.

She goes across to draw the curtains and as she stands there in the window, looks directly into George's face. He is staring into the house with an irritated, puzzled expression on his face, clearly wondering why there is a stranger in a Superman
t shirt, sitting in his chair, and why Sophia is wrapped in a blanket.

TWENTY-FIVE

"Hallo. You must be Sophia's husband. Pleased to meet you, George, you must be wondering what on earth's going on."

George automatically extends his own hand, although he wants to shout at this smooth olive skinned man, with the bright enquiring eyes. What the hell is he doing in the house? Why is he wearing that t- shirt? It looks ridiculous, stretched over his belly. Why is Soph all wet? Are they having an affair? Has he interrupted some weird sex game? Surely they wouldn't dare to be so cool?

The pain in George's chest has come back. He tries taking some deep breaths.

"My name's James Freeman. I'm an old friend of Sophia's. We bumped into each other by accident the other night, at Phyllis's. I'm Jennifer's brother. I live in London."

Jez keeps on feeding information like chunks of meat to this bear like man, who is now glaring down at him.

George is holding on to his hand, feeling its despicable softness. He wants to crush it like a biscuit.

Sophia is talking too fast; her voice is beginning to tremble.

"George, thank goodness you've come back early. There's just been a call from Gabe's tutor. Gabe's in a really bad way and they think he's having a breakdown. I knew he wasn't all right. I tried to tell you, but you just wouldn't listen."

The words hit him hard as a fastball and Soph sits down suddenly, as if they have rebounded and winded her too. George lets go of Jez's hand, and stares. Expecting him to offer his wife comfort, Jez stands aside, clearing his path, but George stays where he is and bellows like a bull: *"For God's Sake Sophia, pull yourself together and tell me what's happened properly!"*

172

She sobs something incoherent, and George turns back to Jez. His entire head has become a throbbing pulse. Jez explains.

"Apparently, your son tried to attack the life model in the university studio today during a class, and then he collapsed. The tutor thinks it's probably stress connected with the exhibition, and he needs a complete break. He's waiting with him in Gabe's house until he can be brought home."

"Thank you," George snaps, looking murderously at Sophia, who is blowing her nose now and looking around for her handbag. Why must she always burst into tears? He could kill her. Smash her head in with that fucking ioniser that sits in the corner, purifying the air, she says. She lies. The air in this house is foetid, it's choking them all.

Jez starts moving towards the door.

"Jez thinks there's more to it," says Sophia, sitting very still.

"Really?" George says rudely, " Perhaps we'll be the best judges of that."

He is stung by her use of the diminutive.

"Jez is a psychotherapist, George," she says wearily, "he thinks this could all be about Grace, and everything. We've lied to Gabe." She starts to cry again. "And now it's too late. It's all a mess."

George is suddenly weak as water and he sits down heavily in his now vacant chair, all the fight gone out of him. He feels old and tired. Jez is the only one still standing.

"Look, could I make some tea? You two need to decide what to do. I'll drive you up there if it would help."

Sophia nods, and George manages a small smile, grateful now for some support. Sophia can direct her damn panic at this psycho-bloody-therapist, or whoever the hell he is. He can't imagine a professional man would dress like that. He gives up trying to talk to her and George and Sophia sit in silence like people on a bus until Jez comes in with the tea, and George notes with some relief that at least he doesn't seem to be familiar with their kitchen. He has found cups and saucers they never use, and is apologising for not being able to locate the sugar. That's because they don't have any. Sophia decided it's bad for them some time ago. It took him ages to get used to coffee without.

George addresses Jez directly, for the first time.

"So you really think Gabe may have felt …confused all his life?"

Sophia is starting to sniff again.

"Well, our sense of ourselves…"

Here we go, George thinks to himself, these people would rather die than give a straight answer. They're all terrified of being sued these days.

"Just tell me what *you* think, Ja…" He starts to say James then tries to turn it into Jez. The name comes out, ludicrously, as Jaz.

"Obviously, I've never met your son, so I can only guess," He starts too slowly, irritating George again, "but secrets can be quite damaging for a child."

"What do you mean, secrets?" George is glaring.

They hadn't kept a secret from Gabe. They just hadn't said anything about Grace and the years went by and obviously Gabe didn't ask, and then there didn't seem to be any point. Surely he would have asked if he'd remembered her at all?

George is rubbing his chest. He's had heartburn for the last two days. It's all those biscuits filled with cream and jelly and chocolate chips and fucking oats and nuts and lumps of sugar. He is never going to a conference again as long as he lives.

"Well, a secret splits up a family into the ones who know and the ones who don't. It hangs there in the atmosphere like a cloud., and children nearly always sense that's something's wrong. Unfortunately, they tend to assume that something's wrong with them. It can cause serious difficulties. Depression, low self esteem, identity problems, that sort of thing."

He looks apologetic, George thinks. It's dangerous playing the messenger. Hermes needed his winged sandals so he could piss off again quickly. *Your son's cracked up, and it's all your fault. Sorry. Bye.*

George rubs his hand across his beard. It rasps. He can't help thinking of Gabe as a little boy. He was so bright, and so earnest.

"I remember when Gabe was about six," he says slowly, "we were playing football in the garden together. When we stopped for a breather, he came up and asked me to bend down. I knelt beside him and he whispered in my ear: "Daddy, are we all happy?"

There is silence in the sitting room.

"What did you say George?" Jez asks quietly.

"I just laughed. I ruffled his hair and said of course we were. Then we carried on playing. I let him score, though."

Jez nods and Sophia is crying again. How predictable of them both, George thinks. He leans forward.

"I wish I'd told him the truth then. I could have said that sometimes we weren't, and told him why. He'd have understood, he was so bright. Much brighter than the other kids his age."

A sudden breeze rustles the leaves of the plants, stirring the silence in the sitting room. There is a smell of far away bonfire. Burned boats, thinks George, burned bridges.

After a while Jez says "We all do our best at the time. We're only human."

"Shut up Jez." That's Sophia.

"There's no need to be rude, Sophia. He's only trying to help."

George changes sides. He likes hearing that it's not all his fault. They sit on for a while, each of them lost in their own thoughts while the light fades and their faces pale into the indistinct images of strangers.

There's a light tapping on the glass as the first raindrops fall, and Sophia seems to drift over to the window in the gloom.

"There's going to be a proper storm soon."

She stretches up to close the fan light as a loud crack of thunder comes, and more rain.

George walks over to the garden doors and leans against the lintel, looking out. The leaves on the roses are bobbing and shivering under the downpour now, and there is a smell of damp earth. He flinches at a sudden movement, before he sees the black and white cat jumping down from the fence and fleeing across the lawn. He used to have nerves of steel, he was well known for it.

They always used to call on him at work when somebody was drunk, or difficult. Good old George; he'll sort them out. Now he's startling at shadows, in this case Tweedledum, Amelia's cat. His brother, Tweedledee, disappeared last year and she'd told everyone the gypsies had stolen him to skin and cook. "I think you'll find it's babies they steal Amelia," he'd said to her, "so you don't need to worry do you?" She'd looked really hurt then; he shouldn't have said that. His shoulders are aching and he rolls them around, hearing his neck bones crunch like icy grit.

"George! Come on! We've got to go, Jez is waiting."

He feels as if he's in a dream. Why is she shouting? If only he'd stayed on at the conference with Leena, drinking coffee and eating biscuits and listening to crap and holding her hand. Her hands are warm and strong, like a pair of healthy puppies. He doesn't see why Jez should be driving, or why Jez should be involved with his family at all, but he hasn't got the strength to argue, or to drive either. Strength is draining out of him drop by drop and soon he'll have none left at all. He locks the door and pockets the key, shuffling behind the two of them, like an old man in a rest home.

It's uncomfortable in Jez's car, squashed into the back with Soph. She is clutching at his hand. Her fingers are rigid; he can feel her nails digging into his palm and he resents her touch.

"Any port in a storm, eh Soph?"

She looks at him, horrified, about to cry again, and he says he's sorry and takes her hand further on to his lap. It's a small price to pay; he can't stand any more crying.

Jez drives swiftly through the dark streets, heading for the motorway. The silence in the car is broken by the swoosh and clunk of the windscreen wipers and the intermittent click of the indicators.

George glances across at the clock glowing luminous green on the dashboard and Jez turns on the radio murmuring something about traffic news. George suspects he can't stand the silence any longer. He doesn't know that Jez's days are filled with silence. Hostile silence, fearful silence, sexy silence, contented silence,

176

Jez can identify them all and mostly chooses to leave silence undisturbed.

When Jez pulls up at some traffic lights, George looks out at the shining street. A boy in a soaked white shirt is running along with a girl who is stumbling in high heels. They are eating chips and dodging in and out of doorways and laughing. George wants to be laughing and running and eating chips with a girl. He can almost taste the salt and the vinegar. He presses a sad hand against the window like the Queen waving at real people from the coronation coach. Soph is leaning forward, her lips next to Jez's ear. For a moment, George thinks she is kissing him until he realises she is giving him directions. He is surprised at how little he cares.

"Left at the superstore, then take the first right and right again…"

She is the only one who knows this area; he's never bothered to visit Gabe and his friends at their house. Does Gabe resent that? He's never said so. George's heart gives a painful squeeze, punishing him for this failure among the many.

Bad…squeeze…father…squeeze…bad…squeeze…

Rubbing seems to help and he rubs harder, wishing Soph would notice, but she doesn't.

Jez is slowing down.

"Er, it might be better if you two go in and I wait in the car. It's sometimes best to try to keep things as normal as possible. Strangers can seem alarming to someone who's …fragile."

"Normal!" snarls George. "There is absolutely nothing bloody normal about any of this."

"George!" snaps Sophia, "James is simply giving us his professional advice."

George wants to hit her again. Why has she dropped the pet name all of a sudden? He's ashamed of himself, he never used to feel this violent.

"Sorry. That makes sense. Thanks."

He has given up addressing Jez by name now, no longer knowing what to call him.

"It's a worrying time for you both," says Jez calmly.

177

George doesn't want to arrive. He wants to drive off in the opposite direction with Jez and talk about psychology and leave Soph to deal with everything. He wants to turn back and find the running couple and go to the pub with them. He wants to replay the video of his life and stop it just before he met Soph and spend the next thirty years as a backwoodsman, logging and drinking red-eye with taciturn men who talk about snow and guns and hunting bears. His mouth is dry and he licks his lips.

Soph is pointing and Jez is pulling over.

"That's the one, over there."

There is something about a silent house with all its windows lighted and the curtains open in the middle of the night that broadcasts emergency. Lucian is looking out of an upstairs window, peering up and down the road.

Sophia is pulling at the car door handle and scrambling out, her knees bent and her chin tucked in like somebody on an assault course. She runs across the pavement and is sprinting up the steps before George has straightened both his legs. He can see Lucian at the door and the well lit hallway behind him, stretching out for miles like a hospital corridor. Lucian bends his head towards Sophia and guides her in. She looks terrified, George thinks, her face a ghastly Halloween orange in the streetlight.

Time is frozen, the way it was on the night Grace died. George moves towards the steps in slow motion, despite the storm. His cheeks are wet and his body is made of cold water. *'I'm afraid...I'm sorry...we're doing all we can...'* He can see the doctor now, as young and tired and scared as he was himself.

At the bottom of the step, George pauses and renounces parenthood with the vehemence of a postulant renouncing the devil and all his works. Then he runs up the steps, two at a time and strides along the hall towards the sound of voices. The bright colours inside remind him of the old Rainbow theatre in its heyday. He used to go there with Soph, when they were young. When they were normal. When they hadn't begun to kill each other.

He stands breathless at the door to the living room, looking inside. Gabe is lying on a couch and Soph is kneeling beside him, brushing the hair from his face. Gabe's breathing is deep and even; George has never loved him more than this.

Lucian is waving a plastic bottle of tablets around and trying to tell Sophia that the doctor has given Gabe powerful sleeping pills and said he must see his GP as soon as possible. She's not listening and he gives up and comes across to George, followed by Doug who, to his credit, has stayed to the end. George nods at Lucian and pockets the bottle with one hand while he takes a cigarette with the other from the packet that Doug is holding towards him. He's a smoker again now, he supposes. He's an adulterer and a smoker and a useless fucking excuse for a parent.

Doug speaks in his customary drawl. "Terrible shame Mr Hughes. Gabe has such a marvellous talent. Had to happen just before the exhibition. Sure he'll be back on form in a week or two. The doc seemed to think so anyway."

George stares at Doug, filled with loathing for everyone present, this languid man, the scruffy doe eyed girls with their purple hair, clustering together in the corner like weeds and above all for Lucian, who's obviously been crying.

"Let's get him out to the car."

George wades across the room, picking Gabe up easily as if he were a baby again. Lucian opens the door for them, while Sophia is thanking everybody over and over again as if they were leaving a bloody party, George thinks. He cannot stand her any more.

Doug, attracted like a magpie to the gleaming car, goes outside to alert Jez and to find out who he is.

It takes some choreography to get Gabe and Sophia into the back of the car gently. George curses and hisses instructions and bangs his head on the roof. Sophia sits sideways so Gabe can lay along the seat with his head on her lap. He hardly stirs as his head lolls and his arms and legs are moved around. It reminds them both of the nights when he was a baby and they would try to get him home and into his bed without waking him up.

George feels as if he's had to be careful for a thousand years. At least he doesn't have to sit beside them, this is all beyond him.

He is bleak and empty watching the grey dawn break and morning drag itself out of bed. Traffic is building up on the roads now and some of the small cafes are putting out their boards. The storm has cleared and a fine rain is falling.

"Coffee anyone? George? Sophia? I could stop and get us some."

"Let's just get home Jez."

Sophia sounds irritated by the offer and George can't be bothered to answer. Jez must be tired though, he's thinking. He's been up all night and done all the driving. Well, screw him. He didn't have to involve himself. George's former gratitude has worn thin. Jez could have got coffee for himself. He didn't have to kow tow to bloody Soph; she always gets her own way.

Jez doesn't seem to mind about the coffee. He is knocking on the car window with the knuckles of his right hand, pointing something out to George.

"It looks as though there's some trouble over there."

"Where?"

George snaps out of his sullen reverie and looks out of the window. They are passing the entrance to Heronmarsh where there seems to be a crowd of people gathering. Is that a placard he can see? What the hell is going on now?

"This sort of thing will make it easy for the council to move them on, I'm afraid. Jennifer and Phyll won't have much work to do."

"How the hell do you know about the eviction?"

"I'm sorry, I assumed...

George turns to Sophia. She is looking uncomfortable.

"Don't tell me Brendan's using Phyll?"

"Brendan asked them to look into it, George. She told me to warn you when it started. I'm sorry, I *completely* forgot. I meant..."

"Pull over please. Let me out here. "

George looks into Sophias' eyes. They are grey holes. Grace is looking out of them. He has to get away from her, let her and her pet shrink sort out this whole mess with Gabe.

180

"Do you ever, ever think of anyone apart from yourself, Soph?"

He whispers as loudly and fiercely as he can without disturbing Gabe, then he gets out of the car and splashes through the puddles, disappearing into the middle of the small but growing crowd.

TWENTY-SIX

The rain is lashing against the windows of Brendan's office, sweeping away this summer's grime and dust. He is looking out, his hands in his trouser pockets, watching frowning figures scurry across the car park, brief cases and folders and carrier bags clutched to their chests like swimming pool floats. No one seems to have a coat, as if this summer has been so long, they've all forgotten the procedure for wet weather.

The light in the room is dim and the air smells musty. Brendan shivers. He's wearing a cream silk shirt that Lisa gave him years ago, in the days when they were still inclined to give each other gifts for no reason other than the offering of unexpected pleasure. He only ever wears it when he's having an affair. Regular sex makes him feel feminine and sensual, and the shirt seems to go with the fucking. Lisa probably thinks he's wearing it to please her.

He reaches for his jacket, hanging on the back of the chair. He'd taken it off as soon as he'd come in this morning, intending to get down to a day's hard work. The letters are piling up again. He's been out of the office too much lately, and Celia is annoyed, but the mood has left him after only an hour or two. He grins at her as she comes in backwards carrying a pile of envelopes and a cup of tea.

"No coffee today?"

"I am *not* going out again in this, thank you very much. I got wet enough coming in."

"Sorry Celia."

"And it wouldn't hurt you to say thank you for the tea."

"I know, I know. Thank you for the tea Celia. I really don't

182

appreciate you enough. Would you sort these letters for me?"

She puts both hands down firmly on his desk and stares into his eyes like a parent explaining the principles of homework to an avoidant child.

"Brendan. I am your secretary. A secretary is someone who helps someone else with their work, not someone who does it for them."

He tries to charm her, gazing up with wide green Irish eyes and murmuring, "Celia, Celia you know you're far better at the job than I am."

She stands up straight and folds her arms, a picture of plump admonishment in a grey Marks and Spencer suit.

"Unfortunately for me, I don't receive your salary, Brendan. Where did we go for our family holiday this year? I'll tell you, it was *Butlins,* as usual. I gathered from the communal postcard that you and your family were in Australia and Cairns."

He casts around for an excuse and finds only lame ones.

"I've been up to my eyes lately, Celia. The members are always breathing down my neck, and there's been so many meetings…"

She doesn't bite. "We know who you've been having meetings with, Brendan. It's the talk of the offices."

He pales. He feels a bit sick. He hadn't realised it had got around so fast. E-mails bouncing like squash balls, forwarded from in box to in box, no doubt, probably even cartoons. Some of the people here could teach the FBI a thing or two about surveillance.

"Celia, how can you even think such a …"

"If you must deceive a lovely woman like Lisa, that's up to you, but everyone's saying that the member making all the decisions at the moment has nothing to do with the council, if you get my drift."

"Whatever are you implying, Celia?"

Brendan is still smiling and his words are soft but his mouth has taken on the tension of someone posing for a mug shot, and his teeth look wolfish in this light.

"People are *saying,* Brendan, " Celia is speaking slowly to her avoidant child again, "that you are corrupt. People are *saying* that you are only interested in evicting those poor travellers because Millie Massie is telling you to do it."

"Millie?"

"I was at school with her, she shagged the Maths teacher. Never did her homework and got away with it every time. She didn't care who knew. Discretion is not her middle name, Brendan, when are you going to wake yourself up?"

Brendan gives a brave laugh, shifting position in his chair. He's turned on by the thought of Amelia in a gymslip with her legs wrapped around a tweedy panting figure in the back of a Station Wagon or a Citroen.

"Tittle tattle and nonsense, Celia. I don't believe it for a second. Mrs Massie is a most respectable woman and the only purpose of my very *occasional* meetings with her is to discuss certain perfectly legitimate community concerns she has. You know about government policy- I have to be accessible to the public, open all hours and all that."

"I'm afraid I know what's open all hours, Brendan, and it's not regulated by government policy. Everyone knows she organised that petition, and that *you* did the leaflets for her. You left the master on the photocopier."

"Ah. Well, actually that was just for my own reference, Celia. I have my spies too. I stay ahead of the game you know."

"It's not a game, though, is it? Those poor people are going to lose their homes because of her. Where are they supposed to go? Nobody wants them anywhere."

"They've broken the rules. No-one made them do that. Actions have consequences in this life, Celia."

He looks at her expression. He wishes he hadn't said that. Wishes it very much indeed because Celia is looking at him as if he is a dirty nappy.

"It won't be me who loses my job Brendan, poorly paid and humble though it is. I'm not having extra marital sex when I should be working."

"Is there someone you like Celia? Feel free. I won't tell if you don't."

"Just don't say I didn't warn you. You should take steps before it's too late. Corruption Brendan. It's an ugly word for an ugly act. Think about it."

"Ce-celia, you're breaking my heart...you're shaking my confidence dayleeeeee..."

He is singing to her departing shoulders. It's only when the door shuts behind her, he starts worrying. She's right, corruption is a very bad word. In local government terms it's worse than fucking donkeys or selling crack to children. He sips his tea nervously and looks over his shoulder at Tony Blair. Tony's eyes are cold and critical. Brendan plays a tune on the edge of his saucer with his teaspoon. It starts off as an upbeat Mac The Knife, but turns itself into the funeral march.

He should stop this affair. Stop it now, before it goes any further, it's dangerous this time. He's never mixed up sex and work before.

He glances across at the photograph of Lisa and the children on his desk. It was taken years ago on holiday, when the children were little and tanned and glowing with the kind of special beauty only children have. They're great miserable lumps now, and Lisa hates his guts, but he has no intention of going to live in a bed sit with alimony as a permanent and miserable flatmate.

Amelia thinks she has him wrapped around her little finger, but she hasn't. She's far too stupid to know that he's just playing along. She doesn't seem to understand ironic posturing.

George is right, she is pretty frightful. And she's expensive. Lisa and the kids won't have much of a holiday next year if he keeps on buying champagne and jewellery and paying for nights in five star hotels. It's not right. Actually, it's wrong. Morally wrong. He sits back and feels Tony's eyes mist over with joy at the return of the prodigal.

He is reaching for the phone when there is a sound of raised voices outside his door.

"Excuse me, I said Mr McFall is not available..."

"Oh Celia, it's only me, he won't mind..."

185

The door opens and Amelia is standing there, shaking her hair and giggling.

"Sorry Mr McFall. Am I disturbing you?"

She is unbuttoning her shiny white raincoat in slow motion, like a stripper.

"Well actually, yes you are Amelia but now you're here…"

He begins firmly. He is going to finish it here and now. Whatever has he been thinking of? Risking his marriage and his job? Planning to turn twenty five families off their home just for the pleasure of sliding between Amelia's bronzed and toned up thighs like a child playing on a mud slick?

She shrugs off her coat, first one shoulder and then the other, letting it fall behind her onto the floor. She smiles and sits down on the edge of the chair opposite his desk. She smells of apricot shower gel and toothpaste.

"I'm *so* sorry. How much am I disturbing you, Brendan?"

She is swaying slightly in her chair. He looks down at his desk and covers both ears with his hands to block out that voice. It's deep, with a little break on certain words. Judi Dench marries Sarah Cox. His skin is prickling. He can still hear her, she's a siren, she'll lure him to his death. He'll crash against the rocks.

"As much as you disturbed your poor Maths teacher, *Millie Massie*."

She is laughing. "I've always liked men in authority."

She really believes he's important. It's that, more than the thought of her body that turns him on. Lisa understands that he's always been a nobody.

She moves her chair away to accord him a better view of her golden legs, like a woman visiting a long term prisoner.

"I had to come in out of the rain. I got so wet Brendan."

She squeezes her thighs together. The swaying has turned into full scale wriggling.

His resolve is dissolving.

"How wet did you get Amelia?"

She gets up theatrically slowly and strolls around to his side of the desk.

186

"I'm afraid I'm absolutely soaked, darling."

A torrent of rain hurls itself against the windows, begging him to stop her now.

"I had to take off my underwear."

She lowers herself onto his lap, straddling his thighs and guides his fingers under the hem of her skirt and up the inside of her leg. She kisses his mouth slowly.

"See?"

Brendan groans as much at the tasteless soft porn dialogue as at his inability to resist her.

She undoes his zip and he is Dennis Hopper riding a Harley Davidson. He is born to be wild. Fuck Lisa and the kids. Fuck the fucking travellers. The rickety chair bumps up and down on the old wooden floorboards. He can't stop now. Fuck Amelia. Fuck her fuck her fuck her fuck her fuck her.

Through the red curtains of her hair, he can see that she has left the door ajar. He has the strange sensation that his head is operating completely independently from the rest of his body as it bucks and jerks and shivers.

There is a click and the door closes, but Brendan can't stop and Amelia doesn't care. She is bouncing up and down on his lap, thinking of her Brownies, her elves and her pixies and her sprites running about freely on Heronmarsh toasting marshmallows and building campfires and putting up their tents.

TWENTY-SEVEN

Sophia reaches out and smoothes Gabe's forehead until her hand falls back on her lap and she looks again at the clock on the wall. She can't believe Gabe meant to attack the model. People are paranoid these days, always looking over their shoulders for trouble. He's so gentle; it must have been a mistake.

Her eyes are stinging and her thoughts are slow and jumbled. Jez's face floats into her mind like a dream. *'I'll be at Jennifer's if you need me...'* Why should she need him? It's George she needs, and he's furious with her for forgetting to tell him about the site... Jez looked very sad when he left...he said he loved her on the pier...

The phone rings and she runs downstairs, trying to reach it before it disturbs Gabe. It's probably the doctor ringing back. She asked him to come urgently but he doesn't trust her. He treats her like a child trying to wangle a day off school, questions her with his fishy cold eyes. She should change doctors and lie about her age. Lawrence won't come out anyway, he'll say Gabe's problem is connected with her age in some mysterious medical way.

"Hallo?"

"It's me, dear."

"Mum, I thought you were the doctor."

"What do you mean, the doctor? You sound out of breath. Have you been running?"

Her mother is suspicious. She detects any change in Sophia's equilibrium like a human heart monitor. She is not electronically objective though, and prefers her daughter to be calm and still. They're like two people on a water- bed.

"Only downstairs. I've got Gabe at home. He's in bed actually, not very well. We had to go up and bring him home last night."

"Not *well?*" She sounds as suspicious as Lawrence.

"*No.* Not well. Actually, he collapsed at University. He seems to have had some sort of… turn."

She can't say breakdown. It's not true. No.

"Not eating, I expect, dear. None of them eat properly any more. Isn't his friend a vegetarian?"

She says it in the same tone she might say 'paedophile' or 'suicide bomber.'

"I don't think…it's more likely to be stress…" She wants to agree.

"Goodness me, stress! Whatever does Gabriel know about *stress*? It's a good job there isn't a war on, that's all I can say. Everyone has *stress* these days. You can't turn on the television without hearing somebody talking about *stress*…."

She's off. It's oddly comforting to Sophia, clouds of comforting, familiar, hot air but she breaks in, interrupting her.

"Mum, I've just met Jez again. Do you remember him?"

"How could I forget him Sophia? All those nights you spent crying in your bedroom when he dropped you. I hope you're not getting mixed up with him again. Little skinny thing he was, with all that hair…"

"Well now he's a grown up psychotherapist and he says Gabe is *–stressed* - because…"

"Psychotherapist, he calls himself, does he? Gracious, everyone knows they're all mad themselves, dear. I hope you told him…"

Sophia hears movement from upstairs.

"Got to go, I can hear Gabe. Goodbye Mum."

There is a groan and the sound of bedsprings as he turns over. That bed is ancient.   Something else she hasn't replaced. Why hasn't she looked after him properly? Adrenaline swooshes and rushes in her ears as she runs back up the stairs.

Gabe is coming back from the deep purple sleep where blue shapes swam. He is trying to force his eyelids open, but they keep slamming shut.

Sophia pulls the curtains apart, nearly tearing them from the rail. Pushing open the window, she breathes in the cool wet air streaming into the stuffy room. Gabe must shower, must eat, must change. She searches frantically through his wardrobe, the empty hangars jangling. There's hardly anything here.

He is watching her through half closed eyes. His thoughts are brushing past each other, drifting through his mind like clouds. He watches her hands smoothing out an old t shirt and jeans at the end of his bed. He knows every inch of those hands, knows them as well as he knows his own. They've held him, stroked him, washed him and hugged him a hundred thousand times. They're wrinkled now. Worn out. He doesn't want her hands to get old.

He croaks, suddenly desperate for water, "Can I have a drink?"

"Oh Gabe," she hugs him, wrinkling up her nose at the smell of him in spite of herself, "I'll get you some."

She runs back downstairs again, almost slipping on the bottom step, and fumbles in the cupboard for a glass. She can see her right hand shaking as she holds it under the cold tap, and she grabs it by the wrist with her left.

Upstairs, Gabe is rubbing his face trying to force his thoughts to gather together. He hugs the duvet to him, feeling the stiffness of his clothes, reaching back to the other end of a long, spinning tunnel. He feels light as a feather, as if his skin and bones are very thin.

Her tread is on the bottom stair. She is hurrying, clutching the glass of water in her hand. It's slopping over the sides, he can hear it. He seems to be able to hear the smallest sound.

As she passes the main bedroom, she stops to open the curtains in there, wanting the gloom to be gone from everywhere. The light shows up the bed, still unmade from the previous day. Was it only yesterday she went to the coast with Jez? And kissed him? Why was she kissing Jez when Gabe needed her?

She puts down the water and picks up the heavy framed photograph. One, two, three four. Herself, her mother, George and Grace, all of them unprepared for the wrecking ball moving towards them and picking up speed. She is going to tell Gabe. She is going to clear up this mess. She is going to say sorry.

She picks up the photograph and the water and walks back along the landing to his bedroom. He struggles to sit up as she

190

appears in the doorway, pushing himself up with both hands, sinking back onto the pillows. His arms feel weak.

She sits down on the edge of the bed and hands him the glass. He drinks all the water in one go.

"How are you feeling?"

"All right Mum."

He gives the automatic response, without reflection. Gabe is floating. He can't remember why he's here and not in the house.

Sophia is pink, nearly bursting with relief.

"*Gabe*," She sounds as if she's about to announce a big treat.

He feels so much older than her. For some reason she's cradling the old photograph, holding it up like a rally driver showing the plate. The icy trickle of fear is starting up again somewhere in the back of his head, inching through his brain. Something's coming. Something bad.

"There's something I've- *we've*- never explained to you."

She is pointing to the photo now, as if she's giving one of her lessons and he shrinks away from her into his pillows. His expression has changed from trusting to suspicious, but she doesn't see it.

"What is it?" Gabe is sharp.

His mind has started to race. The sky's grey, the wardrobe's open, he's wearing clothes in bed, the clock has stopped.

"This baby isn't actually you."

He hears her voice as if it's coming from downstairs, but she's still here. He watches her mouth opening and closing. There are lines at the corners of her lips.

"Our first child –your sister Grace- died when you were a baby Gabe, and this is actually her, not you. We thought it was better, well, we decided anyway, not to ever mention her to you, and well, you never asked, so we thought you didn't remember. Perhaps we were wrong. If we were, I'm sorry. I am so sorry Gabe."

The ice in his brain shatters into shards. Inside his head there are a million small cuts. *Baby. You. Her first. Wrong. Sorry.*

Someone was here before him. In this house. In her arms. This would have been her bedroom. He wants to look around but he keeps very still, fearing something will bleed if he moves. Decided not to mention it? As if her first baby just slipped her mind?

"Are you all right darling?"

She's peering at him with frightened rabbit eyes and he remembers the rules.

"I'm a bit…surprised."

He's a ventriloquist's dummy and she's pulling his string. Clack, clack, clack.

"Of course you are…"

"But I'm OK. Doesn't matter to me, does it?

He forces the words out of a face that has become liquid rubber. Second child.   Second thought. Second hand. Second best. Second prize. Bring on the under study, the star's been taken ill.

Reaching out for her hand, he pats it gently.

"I'm fine. Don't worry. I'm just thirsty. And hungry."

She lays the photo down on the bed, very gently, Gabe thinks, and reaches out for him.

"You are a wonderful son."

He can't breathe in the warmth and darkness of her arms. It used to be the safest place on earth. He feels sick; he could vomit on her chest.

"I could murder a burger and chips."

She releases him. She's smiling. Her cup runneth over, he is thinking.

"Shall I go and get you one? Or two? Would you like two? And fries? Milkshake?
You seem so much better darling, thank God. Look, we'll talk properly about it all when I come back. You can tell me what happened yesterday. I'm sure it was nothing really."

"Ok."

He smiles back at her with genuine amusement. Talk properly to her? He's never talked properly to her.

"I'll just get my coat. It's started to rain again. You just stay there and relax."

192

At the door she turns and looks at him.

"Promise me you'll be all right? I'll be half an hour at the most."

"Just go, Mum. I'm starving."

The front door clicks behind her, and Gabe reaches out for the photo. Thoughtfully, he traces the pattern of interwoven silver leaves and fruit with his fingertips before he gets out of bed. His legs are as weak as his arms and he has to hold on to the door handle with one hand while he slowly takes off his shirt with the other.

When Sophia comes back humming to herself, she is holding a large brown paper bag. The kitchen door is closed and the sight of it makes her stop short. Her heart shies away from her ribs, and cowers somewhere in her chest. Slowly, she puts down her package on the telephone table, leaving the front door open. Doors are kind, she is thinking, they shield us from things we don't want to see. The door to the lavatory, the door to the operating theatre, the door to the abattoir.

She needs to use both hands to push it open. Gabe is curled up there on the floor, gripping something to his chest. The oven door is gaping, and the heat is roaring. There is a smell that makes her retch.

She falls to her knees beside him, ignoring the glass that glitters on the tiles. His eyes are screwed shut and his mouth is twisted sideways. Staring at him, hardly breathing herself, she sees, but cannot believe, that Gabe has branded himself with the silver frame.

Sophia begins to babble: "*My God, my God, my God….*"

"Mrs Hughes?"

She turns on her knees. The ground glass is biting into her flesh, forcing back the scream that is waiting inside her. It's Dr Lawrence. He came out after all.

"What's happened here?"

"It's Gabe, he's had a breakdown, we brought him back from the university yesterday, I told him about Grace and he's done this, I left him, he said he was hungry…."

"Calm down, Mrs Hughes. Hysteria wont help."

The doctor is speaking into his phone. "*Yes*, it is an emergency. *Immediately*. Thank you."

She tries to explain it all to the ambulance men, but they are more concerned with morphine and oxygen and stretchers. She follows behind them, still talking, still trying to make them see how it all happened.

In the ambulance, she means to ring George but she dials Jez's number by mistake, and he is the one who comes to the hospital and talks to the doctors and waits with her.

TWENTY-EIGHT

"Stop pacing, George. You look like a caged lion."

Leena is watching him walk up and down in Rose's caravan, stopping every so often to pull aside the flowered curtains and peer out of the windows. He makes the floor shake.

The voices that have been shouting from the gate are taking on a regular, insistent rhythm.

"Those *arseholes* are beginning to chant. Listen to them. If Amelia's there, I swear I'm going to fucking well kill her."

"I'll thank you not to swear in my home."

Rose is sitting still in the corner like a child who's been told not to move. Leena reaches out to squeeze her hand. It feels like a sparrows leg.

"*Where are the police?*" George demands to know as if Rose and Leena are keeping it from him.

"Dealing with a more pressing matter, I expect. Like where to have lunch today."

He rounds on her angrily and she frowns back at him.

"How can you be so calm Leena?"

He's like a volcano, always erupting. She likes quiet men. Light hearted men, like Nick.

"Well *you* look as if you're about to have a coronary. How is that helpful?"

"I'm sorry. I need to get back and see how Gabe is and I can't leave here until the police show up and see off those fools."

He comes over and sits down next to her. When did she get to know his smell? She finds herself sniffing him, like an animal.

"Have you started smoking George?"

"Not really. I found one on the desk yesterday and just lit up without thinking. I was so angry after I spoke to Brendan. He's behaving like America."

"Your smoking isn't going to change his foreign policy."

"Obviously."

"Don't be tetchy. I'm on your side."

"Then I smoked last night as well, when we were picking up Gabe. I couldn't bear to see him in that awful place. He was so pale. I felt I'd completely let him down."

"It must have been an awful shock for you. And now this, on top of everything."

He turns and looks at Leena. His broad shoulders are drooping and his eyes are sad. She wants to gather him to her. Rose is saying something, but she can't take anything else in, only George and his drooping shoulders and his sad eyes.

A change is happening, without her willing it, like chocolate melting, or the opening of a wild orchid in an empty wood. She didn't know falling in love could feel as soft as this. Is he leaning towards her or does he only seem to sway, like a tall building looked at from below? Is it a trick of the light that touches him with silver?

There's a heavy thud on the side of the caravan and she jumps up, oddly relieved.

"They're in," says George, "it's Rentamob. Oh Christ, we're in trouble now."

Through the window they can see a brick on the grass nearby, then comes the sound of a car screeching to a halt, the tyres spinning on the wet grass. It pauses in the clearing by the gate. The driver is revving the engine while six burly men jump out into the rain, waving sticks, fence posts, pick axes.

They run about jerkily in all directions, like prehistoric predators searching for meat. The car tyres finally get a grip on the grass and the driver speeds off, as the men go for the caravans and trailers, staving in windows and windscreens and headlights. The wind is blowing fiercely through the trees, and shaking the leaves down.

"*Who the hell are they?*" There is more astonishment than fear in Leena's voice.

"The town scum bags. Brendan's stirred up their shitty little pond with his stupid irresponsible dick and they've all crawled

196

out in support of Amelia's closure campaign. Oh *fuck.* "

Children are crying and there are screams. The dogs are barking and growling and snapping, and the men are coming out of the trailers and the bushes with grim determination. The noise is hellish. Fists and bottles, chains and crowbars, crunch and crash and smash.

The mob at the gates are swarming in; a victorious football crowd. Grey men with tattoos and white women with pitted skin and bleached split hair are swaggering and chanting: *Close it down, close it down, close it down...Gippos out! Out! Out!...We don't want you here any more....'*

Women caught outside are running with children in their arms, pulling others by the hand, shouting at them to go faster, go faster, bad people are coming to get them.

Leena sees Keely's two year old brother wriggle out of her arms and run off in the opposite direction. A boy aims a kick at his head and the baby topples like a skittle. The boy spits on the toddler's face, again and again.

George roars and pushes open the door of the trailer. He jumps the steps and lands running on the grass. He grabs the boy's shoulder and spins him round, but the boy wrenches free and George falls heavily, hitting his head on the brick. Leena runs out after him and picks up the baby.

"It's ok, Leo, don't worry don't worry..." She soothes him over and over again rubbing his head and wiping his eyes until he puts his thumb in his mouth and is quiet, watching the world over her shoulder with huge eyes magnified by tears.

"Is George all right?"

Keely is standing close behind, pressing against her. Her clothes are soaked and Leena can feel her shivering. "He looks a funny colour."

George is still lying on the grass, his face streaked with mud. There is a sticky redness behind his head. Keely sounds calm but Leena can feel her heart hammering against her back.

"I don't know. He's breathing."

George's head is pressed into the ground, creasing up his cheek as if he's sleeping. Leena tells Keely to take the baby to Rose, and takes George's head onto her lap, wiping away the blood from the gash with the bottom of her shirt. When one of the invaders comes up close, the sheer fury in her voice and her blazing eyes stops him dead in his tracks. He jeers uncertainly and runs off in another direction.

The police are coming now. Sirens grow louder and louder until they are suddenly in the heart of the battle, their pitch and vibration screwing the emotional tension tighter still. Bricks are raining down on the lorries and caravans from the toilet block that is being reduced to rubble by men with pickaxes.

George comes round slowly, while grim figures in black visors and body shields march forwards, medieval knights to the joust. Silently, they form a solid square around their squad cars and vans, and each side begins to pace outwards purposefully, banging in unison on their shields. They provoke a further, wilder surge of anger. Men and boys dart in between them and attack the police vans, tipping one over with a raucous cheer.

"*Ouch*. What the hell's happening? Take it easy, Leena."

George is struggling to sit up.

"Be careful. You were out cold. Are you all right?"

"*Ow*. Bloody hell. I think so. You?"

"I'm so *angry* George, I'm shaking."

He tries to laugh and winces and clutches his ribs. "Good Leena, you're angry at last. It's not just me, then?"

"No." She looks into his eyes, seeing the years of pain and the passion there. "No George, it's not just you. Come on, let's get you inside. The police mean business now."

In the southern corner of the field a fire is burning and a megaphone issues a metallic warning: *'We are about to employ tear gas. Leave the area immediately.'*

There is no gap between the announcement and the swirls of toxic grey smoke, sailing through the air like malevolent fireworks. The angry shouting collapses into coughing and choking, and the ones that still can, run away.

Inside Leo is playing happily with two of Roses' coloured

198

scarves. She looks drawn, the lines on her brown skin running deep. Keely is staring out of the window, her face pale and her expression blank. Her hair hangs down her back in wet tails. Leena turns towards Rose.

"It'll be all right now Gran, the police have got control. The mob's going."

Rose is murmuring to the baby that this is his Romany fate this is his destiny.

"Sure. All right until the next time."

"There won't *be* a next time, Gran. Don't talk to Leo like that, you'll scare him to death, poor little thing. Listen, everybody knows now ,that Brendan's mistress is behind all this and he's not going to want that made public. He'll lose his job and his wife too if she's got any sense. We'll just tell him we'll tip off the papers if he doesn't stop all this nonsense."

"You'll only make it worse if you threaten him. It's far better to say nothing. We should just go quietly. We're not the sort of people who can ever win in this world."

"We?"

"You must know you'll never be one of *them*. They'll never accept you, don't kid yourself."

Rose jerks her thumb at George and Keely sniggers. The baby picks up the words: *one of dem...one of dem...one of dem...'*

"I'll never be a man, Gran? You're right about that."

"Don't play the innocent with me. You know very well what I mean."

Leena holds on to the table. She is feeling suddenly sick and she thinks she might faint.

"Listen." She spoke more loudly than she intended to and they all look at her, Rose, George, Keely and Leo, who holds out one of his scarves. "This is not about us and them. This is about love and hate. Isn't it?"

Rose looks away and Keely looks puzzled. George holds out a finger to the baby who takes it into his mouth and bites it hard.

"And all the shades of grey in between," he said.

TWENTY-NINE

Gabe is sitting in a small, cream painted office, wearing blue striped pyjamas and an expensive, new, white robe bought for him by Sophia. His jacket is unbuttoned, showing a large white dressing pad. Every so often the tips of his bandaged fingers pluck at the frayed edges.

Doctor Wiseman is writing on a pad balanced on his lap, his soft slender hands flexing and dipping as he covers the lines. He looks up and smiles at Gabe. His black- rimmed spectacles have travelled down his shiny nose, and balance there in limbo, waiting for the finger that will push them back up to the bridge. Gabe has watched him do this three times in the past ten minutes.

"Uh, would you care to tell me a little about yourself, Gabriel?"

Gabe looks at him. There are mauve smudges under his eyes.

"No, I wouldn't care to, Doctor. You're the wise man and I'm obviously crazy, so why don't you tell me about me?"

Doctor Wiseman laughs and uncrosses his legs.

"OK. I'll tell you as much as I know. Your name is Gabriel Hughes. You're twenty- two years old. You're a Caucasian male, in good physical health."

"You're not very observant, Doctor. I'm sitting here with a fucking great bandage on my chest, and my hands don't work."

"You were admitted last week because you had apparently attempted to brand yourself with a photograph. You suffered a first-degree burn, which is healing well, although I imagine it is still very painful and will need further grafts. Your fingers are badly blistered."

Gabe looks out of the window. There is a sculpture of a tree made out of copper in the courtyard. A sparrow bounces cheerfully on one of the stiff branches, its head darting from side to side like someone in a hurry, waiting to cross a busy road. When an old man in slippers shuffles up to one of the benches and sits down with an effortful grunt, it flies away twittering a song of condolence.

Gabe drums his fingers on the arm of his chair.

"Painful? Life's always painful. Look at him."

Doctor Wiseman follows his gaze. "He's had one of his hips replaced. Life is going to be a lot less painful for him when he gets out of here."

"Hooray. I'm happy for him."

"You don't sound very happy Gabe."

"I'm not. I don't give a shit, actually."

"About…?"

"About anything."

"Because…"

"Because nothing. Stay out of my head, doctor. You don't have a boarding card."

"OK. Here are some more facts about you. You're highly intelligent. A straight 'A' student in high school."

"We don't have high schools here. Learn the lingo doc, or they'll send you back to Martha's Vineyard, or wherever the hell you come from."

"New York, actually. You sound very angry."

"Don't you mean mad?"

Wiseman laughs. "This feels like a swordfight. Shall I go on?"

"People always do."

"Right. You're a gifted artist, and an exceptional student."

"More of a piss artist, I think."

"Pardon me?"

"Oh, you know us, Wiseman. The self deprecating English. We don't go around blowing our own trumpets, the way you Yankee Doodles do."

There is a squeaking noise and a rattling outside the door, followed by a sharp rap. Gabe jumps, and Wiseman shakes his head sadly.

"That's the damn tea trolley. I've asked them so many times not to interrupt an interview. Would you care for some tea, Gabriel?"

A nurse is standing there in the doorway, scrubbed red arms folded across her starched chest, thick legs in black shoes standing firm. *"You can give your fancy American orders doctor,'* she seems to be saying, *'but we know patients always need tea. Tea and biscuits.'*

"I loathe tea, doctor. Why don't you just write me a prescription for drugs and get it over with? You *are* going to order me a large chemical cocktail, I assume? No olives?"

Doctor Wiseman waves the nurse away without looking at her and she tuts loudly before she heaves her life saving trolley out of the doorway. They squeak and rumble off down the corridor in search of more co- operative staff and patients.

"You're frowning, doctor. Now you look mad."

Wiseman throws his arms wide, dropping his biro. It falls to the floor, bounces twice and rolls under Gabe's chair.

"I'm angry as hell, Gabe. I've told that nurse to cut it out a hundred times. Why won't she do as I ask, do you think?"

Gabe leans over, wincing as his newly healing skin rubs against the dressing. He picks up the biro with difficulty, and hands it back to Doctor Wiseman.

"She wants to take your power away because you're a head doctor. You're our worst nightmare. You creep inside our heads and snoop around, turning up all our dirty little secrets, flushing them away with your medicine, or zapping them dead with your electric prod. You don't need a gun to deal with us, just your little pen. This one appears to be nicked from a *Holiday Inn,* by the way."

"Thanks. At the risk of stating the obvious, I'd say you don't trust me."

"Why should I trust you? You steal pens, you have a nervous tic and you get angry with people who are just trying to do their jobs."

"Do you?"

"Steal pens? Certainly not. I wouldn't be seen dead in a *Holiday Inn.*

"Do you ever get angry with people?"

Gabe smiles and leans back in his chair like a satisfied diner. The front legs are off the floor, and he is rocking backwards and forwards.

"No. I never get angry. Ask my mother."

"I already did. She said the same thing. You only got involved in one fight as a kid, and she didn't even know anything about that until just lately."

Gabe thumps his chair squarely on the floor and leans forward, his hands gripping his thighs.

"Is it common practice to interrogate the parents of an adult?"

"You were in bad shape when you were admitted. It was important to get some detail."

"My mother knows fuck all about me."

"You sound angry Gabe. May I call you Gabe?"

"I'm not fucking angry. May I call you doc?"

"You look angry."

"Appearances are deceptive."

"You hurt yourself very badly. You branded yourself like an animal, Gabe. That seems like a very angry thing to do."

Wiseman is speaking gently, pouring his kind, objective words like tea.

"I hate myself. There you are doctor. Diagnosis: depressive disorder. Treatment: lots of drugs. Now for God's sake write the prescription and get off my fucking back."

"I don't think more drugs are the answer here. I think your psychotic episode was maybe prompted by your recreational drug use."

"You must have talked to Lucian as well. You won't give me any drugs. You won't give me tea. What kind of monster are you?"

Wiseman meets his eyes.

"Who's the real monster?"

"Well, if it's not you, I suppose it must be me. Crazy old drug taking me."

"You don't seem like a monster, Gabe. You seem like an

ordinary guy. A little angry…"

"*I am not an ordinary guy!* Didn't they tell you? I completely lost the plot. I tried to kill the life model…"

"Did you know her?"

" *NO!* I…"

Gabe is pulling threads from the bandage on his chest .

"Who do you really want to kill, Gabe?"

Words explode from Gabe's mouth like sudden vomit.

"*All right, you stupid, fucking, prying arsehole- I Want To Kill Her!*"

"Your mother."

"Yes, yes, yes. My…fucking…mother. Are you happy now?"

Gabe bursts into tears, his head bent to his chest, his hands tearing at the dressing.   He is gulping air as if there is not enough. "*I…Hate…Her.*"

Wiseman passes him a box of tissues and almost whispers, "Hate her because…?"

"She doesn't love me."

Gabes' shoulders are shaking. His hands have moved to his face, masking his eyes with his fingers.

Wiseman chooses his moment carefully to murmur, "How do you know she doesn't love you Gabe?"

A rumbling and a squeaking in the corridor announces the return of the tea trolley.   Wiseman glares at the door like a lioness in cub.

"Because she lied to me, and…" Gabe has dropped his arms to his sides and is sitting back in the chair. He blows his nose. His shoulders are drooping and his eyes are red "…she never, *ever* let me cry."

"Everyone needs to cry sometimes."

"She used to ask me how I was all the fucking time and I had to say I was OK."

"That sounds tough."

"If I didn't she'd get this awful look on her face. It was like…oh, I can't explain.   I'm obviously crazy as a coot. Can I have the drugs?"

"Can you picture her face when she gets that look?"

"Yes."

"What do you see Gabe?"

"I see fear."

"She got very scared if you didn't pretend to be ok?"

"I suppose so. Yeah."

"And the time you had the fight? You weren't ok that day."

"No. No, I wasn't. I'd been bullied for months. I just snapped I suppose, I couldn't take any more of it. I lashed out at this other kid on the bus and I broke his tooth. I was so angry, and then I felt proud of myself, and after that I was scared shitless…"

Gabe is rubbing at the scar on his neck. It's silver against the skin of his neck.

"Did your mother find out?"

"No, I made up some story. Said I'd seen a dead cat or something, I think. It was always so easy to fool her."

"We believe what we want to believe as a rule."

Gabe is silent.

"Being bullied is a nightmare, and a first fight is usually pretty distressing. How did you handle all that with no support Gabe?"

Wiseman has put the tips of his fingers together and is bouncing them against his chin. He has become a member of a television panel, objectively avuncular.

Gabe is looking out of the window. Rain is falling on to the copper tree, making it shine. The old man on the bench gets up surprisingly quickly, and hobbles away towards the out patients café.

"Well, I don't know, I…"

His fingers are pattering at the scar, tapping out a rhythm.

"You hurt yourself Gabe."

There is a long silence.

"Just as you did last week."

"I'm not normal am I? Is it time for the drugs?"

Wiseman leans back and crosses his legs.

"You had no place to run to when you were a kid. We all survive disaster in different ways, and that was your way. Your

205

mother chose denial."

"She told you that too? You must be good. I suppose she was in shock, losing a child..."

"That would be a normal reaction."

"Normal. I hate that word, it feels like death. My bloody sister created a lot of problems."

"No she didn't."

"She didn't?"

"No. We create our own problems. Life is how we take it, that's all."

Gabe hears himself laughing without spite. He can't remember the last time he laughed like this. It sounds strange, perhaps it's a normal laugh. He looks across at Wiseman.

"A man goes to the doctor and he has a spoon sticking out of his arse. He says, 'Doctor, this medicine isn't working' and the doctor says: 'That's because you're taking it the wrong way.'

Wiseman grins, generously pretending he hasn't heard the joke a thousand times, thinks Gabe, but it doesn't matter. What matters to Gabe is that he can laugh despite having had a breakdown, and despite having a wound that hurts like hell and will leave him with scars for the rest of his life, and despite the shambles of his childhood, he can still laugh. He likes Wiseman.

"You know, there's a dream I have that comes back all the time Doctor. I've had it since I was a kid, but I've never told anyone about it before. It's a nightmare actually. Can you handle it?"

"Let's see."

"I'm in bed, and there's a war going on- explosions, bombs going off, that sort of thing. It's night time, but the sky's a bright orange colour and I'm excited at first, but then everything stops suddenly and I'm in this black room and there's total silence. I try to call for help but I can't make any noise and I'm absolutely terrified."

Wiseman nods and makes a note on his pad while Gabe sits back in his chair and looks out of the window at the shining tree.

THIRTY

.

George and Leena are sitting on an old wooden bench, in a corner of her garden. Honeysuckle and clematis scramble over high brick walls. A waterfall trickles and splashes into a deep green pool where flashes of orange break the surface and dive down again among the reeds and thick stems of kingcup and iris. The grass is green and long and threaded through with scarlet poppies and bright yellow buttercups. Daisies are everywhere, scattered like paper. Tall, slim Buddleia nod graciously at big buttery sunflowers, a swaying palette of lilac and lavender, creamy white and yellow. Butterflies are everywhere, dancing in the golden rays of the low sun.

George yawns and stretches out his legs on the yellow flagstones.

"It's cow dust time again."

She smiles, her eyes hidden behind sunglasses. "You remember that."

"Where did you hear it first?"

"I told you, in India. I went there with Nick."

"You didn't tell me about him."

"Why would I?"

"Well, who is he?"

"An old friend. A free spirit."

"Lucky man." George sighs. "Christ, Leena, what a summer. I feel as if I need another holiday. I can't believe it's only been a month since Soph and I were in Italy."

"How is she?"

"That's hard to say. I can't read her any more. I could once. Or I thought I could anyway. She's very thin. Pale. Anxious. Treating Gabe like a Ming vase, which he hates. She's never been able to see what she does to him. Anyway, she seems to talk to her old boyfriend now more than she does to me. She puts the phone down quickly when I come in, and looks guilty. I don't know why. I don't really care who she talks to."

"She had a terrible shock, you know. How's Gabe doing now?"

"Actually, he's not too bad. The chest wound's healing and there's some trick cyclist at the hospital he seems to have a lot of time for. An American. He's suggested long term psychotherapy."

"I'm glad. That sounds positive."

"Positively expensive. I suppose we'll have to fork out thousands of pounds so Gabe can explain at length to someone exactly what useless fucking parents we were, but still…if it works."

"That's the spirit, George. And you haven't been a useless parent. Look at my father. He didn't even stick around long enough to find out who I was, let alone pay my therapy bills."

George groans. "We probably all need bloody therapy. You, me, Soph. Perhaps we could get a group reduction with the ex-boyfriend. If he is still ex."

"Group reduction?"

"He's a shrink. Wanker. No, that's not fair, he's a nice chap actually. He's very calm. He drove us all the way to pick up Gabe that night, through that terrible storm."

"That was kind."

"It was kind. Goodness knows what he thought when I hared off to the site before we'd even got Gabe home. I was so angry with Soph, I couldn't even think straight."

"That was a terrible day. I've never been so frightened in my life."

"It was a miracle that no-one was killed. I'll never forgive bloody Brendan. He's always been a sod, but this time he seems to have lost his mind. If it wasn't for good old Celia threatening to shop him, I shudder to think what might have happened. Useful things, camera phones."

"Gran's taken it really badly. She hasn't got out of bed since. I'm beginning to wonder how long she'll be able to cope on her own. She couldn't bear to live in a house at her age."

"That's a pity. I'd ask her to live with us just to annoy Amelia. Well, you can tell her that there's no question of being moved off Heronmarsh, now. I made Brendan ring the Advertiser himself while I was there. He told them that the eviction plans were just a scurrilous rumour spread by racists. Quote Brendan: *'I can assure you that the council is firmly committed to the maintenance of Heronmarsh as a well kept and permanent site.'* When I waved the confidential letter he'd sent to me, he even said the council were going to put more resources in and that the travellers are an integral part of our community and our culture."

"That'll make them laugh. You must have scared him half to death."

"Brendan knows which side his bread's buttered. He's an idiot, but he's not stupid."

"And Amelia?"

"She is stupid, but she's got her pride. She won't hang on once she's been shown the door."

"Sensible woman. At least she knows where she stands."

George looks at her. Does she mean something by that? He feels lighter than he used to. As if he's dropped some ballast. He's hungry.

"Your garden feels like somewhere from forty years ago. Leena. We should be having a picnic on a blanket, with anchovy toast and seedcake and lemon barley water."

She smiles. "I could make you some sandwiches, if you're hungry?"

"I am- oh!"

"What is it?"

"I just remembered a dream I had about you. It was at the conference."

"Did you?"

"No, you wouldn't let me! Ha, ha. Remember that joke? From the same era as anchovy toast, I think." George looks at her and takes a risk. "But you did let me didn't you, Leena?"

There. He's brought it up at last; someone had to. She's been acting as if nothing had ever happened between the two of them.

Perhaps she thought it was nothing. He doesn't know much about the habits of single people these days. Perhaps they always fuck to finish off an evening.

Her face is still and he can't see her eyes. He wants to pluck off her sunglasses. For one unsettling moment he wonders whether he imagined the whole thing. Was it a drunken fantasy? Christ, she'll think he's a complete pervert.

"Take off the glasses Leena. Please. I can't tell what you're thinking."

She turns towards him. There are goose bumps on the tops of her brown arms. She's wearing a bright green vest and pink shorts.

"Tell me your dream, and I might."

"Ok. It was the picnic thing that reminded me. In my dream you and I were having a picnic, sitting on a very soft blanket, and you passed me a drink. I said I didn't take sugar, and you said that this was honey."

"Did you drink it?"

"Yes I did, I gulped it down straight away. I was so thirsty…"

She is crying. Tears are sliding down from under her glasses like sap glistening on a branch in spring. Why does he always make women miserable? He thought it was a nice dream. Oh God, he should probably go now. His chest is hurting.

"What the hell's the matter with you?"

She's taken off the glasses and she's looking at him. He wants to shield his eyes with his arm, like someone looking at an eclipse. She is saying something, but he can't seem to make sense of it.

"I'm in love with you."

"With who?"

"With *you,* George, for God's sake!"

His mouth is grinning so widely that his face hurts. She is twinkling at him like Father Christmas. Her eyes are as tender as they were on the island, and the pain in his chest has gone.

She tosses her hair, and the springy curls quiver and dance.

"Look, I know it's wrong of me. You're married and I don't

want to hurt Sophia, especially now, but I had to tell you because it's true and because…"

He reaches for her face this time and his lips find hers. They are warm and soft and her mouth does taste of honey. His tongue gently touches behind her lips and brushes the roof of her mouth and the inside of her cheek, getting to know her there. When her breasts press against his chest he can feel her nipples harden, but she pulls away from him and stands up, smoothing down her shorts and rubbing her arms. He's never seen her uncomfortable before, it makes him want to kiss her again.

"I'm going inside to get a cardigan. I'll make the tea while I'm there."

"Can I help you?"

"No, you stay here. There's something else I have to do. It'll only take a minute, but I can't leave it any longer."

George watches her go into the house through the kitchen door. She looks like a young boy from behind. He feels much younger than he used to. He wants to find out everything there is to know about her.

She fills the kettle, and takes a teapot and mugs from the cupboard, and a cherry cake from a tin. He can see the flash of a knife as she cuts up bread and spreads butter.
It's been days since he's had a proper meal. Soph seems to have decided to give up eating altogether.

George goes into the house after Leena, but she's gone from the kitchen and he can hear her walking about upstairs. When the kettle boils he makes the tea and shouts at her to come down.

"In a minute. There's tomatoes and Camembert in the fridge, and some egg mayonnaise, I think. Take anything you like."

He enjoys the intimacy of looking into her fridge. There is milk and some home made hummus with chilli and a slice of lemon, chocolate cheesecake and sushi and cream. When he reaches into the salad drawer for the tomatoes, his fingers find a cold bottle of champagne and he pulls back his hands, suddenly afraid. Champagne means toasting something, and he doesn't know what's happened.

211

She was saying she loved him and then crying and now she's disappeared and abandoned the tea. Perhaps it's nothing to do with him, perhaps she meant she loved him in a general sort of way. Perhaps she tells lots of people she loves them. Perhaps the champagne's for old friend Nick.

"The tea's made!"

He hears himself sounding like Sophia calling to Gabe when he was a teenager.

"Just one more second."

George gives an exasperated sigh, and carries a loaded tray out into the garden. When he puts it down on Leena's garden table, the mugs rattle and the teaspoons quiver.

"Mind my china, please George!"

Leena is standing right behind him, and he jumps, she's not wearing any shoes.

She is waving something in front of him.

"What the hell's that?"

His first thought is that it is some sort of special spoon. He holds out his hand and she drops it into his palm. He sits down on the bench and looks at the stick with the bright blue line, and then up at her. She is speaking slowly and without any expression, as if she is reading the news to him.

"This was not a plan George, and I want you to understand that clearly. I have no idea how this happened. I was told it wasn't possible. I've never been pregnant before, and I don't know how I feel about it yet."

George is aware that his mouth is half open and his cheeks are wet. He pulls a crumpled tissue from his trouser pocket. He can't feel his feet, and for a moment he wonders whether he has had a stroke. Leena takes two steps towards him and kneels between his legs. She looks up at him with an elbow on each of his thighs.

"Oh Christ, George."

"Bloody hell."

They spoke at the same time, and they both laugh nervously. She dips her neck like someone awaiting execution, and he leans forward and crowns her with his arms.

Two blue black magpies have landed on the edge of the table. They are edging towards the middle, wondering whether they dare to take a peck at the abandoned cake.

"Look Leena." George raises her head and turns her face gently towards the birds. "There on the table. One for sorrow, two for joy."

"Are you superstitious, George?"

"No. Just observant."

"Three for a girl and four for a boy."

"There's only two. I suppose we'll just have to wait and see."

She gets up to sit beside him, and they watch the birds feasting on cherry cake and egg sandwiches while their tea gets cold and the sun goes down.

THIRTY-ONE

"So how are you doing now Soph? I can't believe it was only a month since we were having lunch here, before everything happened."

Phyll is nibbling on the end of a sesame bread stick.

"I'm ok, I think. I've landed in Kansas"

"Pardon me, Ma'am?"

"You know, the yellow brick road? Dorothy gets whirled around in the gale, clinging to her bed, and then she lands and she finds herself back in Kansas."

"Is that why you've got that awful, smelly dog? You've been possessed by the spirit of Dorothy?"

Sophia takes a gulp of her wine and reaches for the breadsticks.

"He's not awful, he's my best friend."

"Thanks."

"Don't be stupid, Phyll. I mean my best doggy friend. And he doesn't smell any more. I've had him professionally groomed."

"You know what they say. You can take Rover out of the site, but you can't take the site out of Rover."

"No-one says that, and he's called Custard. I had to take him, I had no choice. He just turned up in my garden asking for asylum. He said he was too frightened to go back there again. I did try to persuade him."

"Not hard enough. You should do what the government does. Tell him Heronmarsh is officially safe now, give him a bone token and send him packing. He's probably one of these economic opportunist strays."

"Well I love Custard, and I believe him. He wouldn't lie to me. Anyway, he's company now George has strayed too, he makes me feel safe at home."

"He doesn't sound too brave for a dog."

Sophia frowns at the end of her breadstick and breaks off a

piece, crumbling it over the flowered cloth. She hasn't really got used to George not being at home any more.

"He's better than nothing."

"I'm sorry Soph, I'm only teasing you. How are you coping without George there? Have you seen him since he left?"

"He's coming round tomorrow to see Gabe, and to pick up some more of his things. I keep expecting to feel distraught, or really angry with him but quite honestly, I don't Phyll. Do you think that's odd?"

"Are you still in shock?"

Sophia is swirling a finger round in her crumbs, making spirals.

"I don't think so. When he told me about Leena, I was more astonished than anything. He was embarrassed and sheepish and worried about me, and while we were talking, I remembered who George was. Who he is - he's a really decent man. Actually, I feel glad for him. Not exactly happy, but definitely glad."

A waitress brings minestrone soup, pale green and golden and orange. She stumbles against Sophia's shopping bags, and splashes the tablecloth. Phyll wipes her spoon and looks disapproving.

"The service in this place is no better than before. What about Leena then? Middle aged marauder, or genuine sweetheart?"

"She came to see me on her own, you know."

"You're joking! What a bloody nerve."

Phyll puts down her spoon, and Sophia picks hers up.

"I thought she was really brave. Gabe wouldn't have anything to do with her, but she and I spent a couple of hours talking together in the end. I've never met anyone who's so honest. I do like her, she's certainly no Amelia. And she seems to really love George. That seems odd."

It is strange to know that Leena is carrying George's baby. Sophia feels almost as if she is related to it herself. *Don't be a girl,* she keeps thinking, *please don't be a little girl.*

"My goodness, Soph, you're a saint in the making. I must phone the Pope and get you onto the beatification induction programme."

Sophia sucks up vermicelli. Her appetite seems to have come back, she's hungry all the time now.

"The food here's still good. Don't ring the Pope yet though, - their baby's a different kettle of fish. I've had some pretty evil thoughts about that. Last night I dreamed Leena had a miscarriage and I said to her 'There! Now we can be sisters."

"Are you envious?"

"Yeah. Not very nice, is it?"

"It's human. Forget the sainthood, though Soph. It's just as well, I don't think I could be best friends with a Saint. Not even a close acquaintance."

"You know Phyll, more than anything, I envy her those lazy, pregnant afternoons on the sofa, before her baby's born. She'll feel it kicking and playing inside her and she'll sing to it and dream about it's future and it'll all be perfect. I don't want another baby, but I want a dream to come true, Phyll."

"Reality ruins dreams, as you know."

"And trying to hold on to dreams ruins reality. God knows, I made that mistake with Gabe. At least this time he'll know that he's got a brother or a sister. A half one, anyway, perhaps it'll make up a bit."

She sighs and pushes her soup away, and Phyll leans over and squeezes her hand.   There's a white band on Sophia's finger where she's taken off her wedding ring.

"Do you want me to come and stay with you for a bit?"

"No thanks. I don't think Gabe would like it."

"How is he?"

"It's early days, but not too bad. The University are letting him take the rest of this year off, and then we'll see. He has to have skin grafts, and he's started his therapy. He trots off twice a week and he does seem to feel better when he comes home. He's been sketching Custard, actually. Nice ordinary pictures, not like that dark stuff he used to do."

"Are they healthier, do you think?"

"Yes I do. And something else has happened as well..." Sophia is rubbing the place where her ring used to be. "I went to the cemetery yesterday. I don't know why I did, really. I don't go there much, anymore. Only at Christmas and on her birthday. I just wanted a place to think. It's really quiet."

"On account of all the dead people hanging around."

Phyll always has to joke about death. It frightens her.

"Exactly. They don't make much noise, bless them. Anyway, when I got there the first thing I saw was this single rose lying by Grace's headstone. I was so *angry*. No-one ever goes there except me, it's *my* grave."

"Steady on there, Soph."

"You know what I mean. I knelt down and looked at it, thinking that somebody must have made a mistake, and I picked up the little card and it said…"

"What?"

"It said… ' *I miss you Grace, love from Daddy'*

"George actually went over there after all this time. Wow."

"I know. Amazing, isn't it?"

The waitress barges into the silence with two steaming pizzas, sea food for Phyll and vegetarian for Sophia, and puts them down in the wrong places.

"God, she can't even remember who ordered what."

Phyll is snappy, making a performance of switching round the plates.

"Are you crying Phyll?"

"Certainly not. I never cry. The clients don't like it, it makes them nervous as hell."

Phyll blows her nose on a serviette.

"What are you thinking then, Phyll?"

"Do you remember in the old days of long playing records and turntables, when a record would get stuck in a groove?"

"And the same piece of music would play over and over again?"

"Exactly. And finally somebody would nudge it, and everybody would shout *'Don't scratch it!'*

"Yes?"

"And then the music would carry on, and sometimes there was

217

a scratch and the record was completely ruined, and sometimes there wasn't and it was okay?"

"And your point is, O woman who never cries?"

"My point is, well, it seems to me that the three of you have all managed to jump out of that groove, and now the music's playing on."

"Phyll, how very poetic. Is Leena our nudger?"

"What about Jez?"

"What about him?"

Sophia is chewing a slice of pizza, the pale strands of mozzarella looping down to the plate. Jez is a dangerous area; she doesn't know how she feels about him. It's too soon.

"Don't look at me as if that pizza's not going to melt in your mouth, Soph. What is going on between you two? Trust me, I'm a solicitor."

"Nothing's going on."

"You're looking furtive again. Wait a minute. Show me that stuff in your bag."

Phyll is looking at Sophia's shopping; the bags are expensive and glossy.

"Just what have you been buying Soph?"

Sophia pushes the bags across with her foot.

"You should have been a detective Phyll, not a solicitor. Help yourself."

Phyll pulls them on to her lap and reaches into the purple and pink one, feeling around inside with a grin on her face. She bursts out laughing.

"Bloody hell, Soph. These aren't your normal style!"

"Put them away, Phyll. People are looking. Stop it."

Sophia is blushing while Phyll waves around a handful of black lace and cream silk. It looks ridiculous in here in the early afternoon.

"Very nice. What else did you get?" She pulls out two packages. *"Sans Merci!* Mmm, this stuff is fabulous. Can I have a squirt? It must have cost you a week's salary at least."

"I thought I'd spend it while I've got it. I'm going to give up teaching."

"Good for you. You've been tired of teaching for years. When's the big event?"

"Well I'll have to give a term's notice…"

"No! Going to bed with Jez. This is obviously not for Custard's benefit."

"It might be. I told you, I really love Custard."

"Your love can never be, Soph. Come on, out with it. When's the tryst ?"

Sophia glances down at her watch.

"Tonight! It's tonight, isn't it, you fox? You're not going to smell of chlorine this time, are you? And what's this? A packet of *Featherlite?*"

"Put them away or I'll actually murder you, Phyll. The waitress is coming."

"She won't be the only one if old Jez has sharpened up his lovin' technique during the lost years. He's had hundreds of girlfriends, you know. I asked Jen."

"Oh stop it Phyll. That's just crude. I'm not even sure… it's just that he's coming over for dinner tonight, and I thought I'd…"

"Be prepared?"

"Exactly."

"Amelia would be so proud of you."

The waitress clears away the plates and forgets to offer desert or coffee.

"That bloody girl is quite hopeless. Do you want to order anything else, Soph? Shall I call her back?"

"No, don't bother. My stomach feels a bit strange."

"Is that fear or excitement?"

"I don't know." Sophia laughs. "How funny. Jez said that. Do you remember that night at your place when we met each other again? It seems an age ago now, another life entirely"

"He said his stomach felt strange? What a cheek! Everyone loves my spaghetti usually."

"*No*, not his stomach. He was talking about fear and excitement. He said it's difficult to tell the difference sometimes."

"I suppose it doesn't really matter, as long as you keep moving."

Phyll is waving a hand in the air, and the waitress peers over.

"Unlike that useless waitress. Let me get us some Irish coffee, Soph. Stiffen the sinews, summon up the blood?"

"Why not?"

There is a new expression on her face that Phyll can't read. The whisky slides down Sophia's throat and coats her stomach slowly, filling her with warmth, and something that feels as if it might be hope.

THIRTY-TWO

Coloured water is splashing down into the sink, collecting in a swirling rainbow pool before green and yellow and red merge into earth tones, and vanish down the plug hole. Sophia puts the last pot up on the drainer.

Indigo, Titian, Viridian, Burnt Umber. When she was a child, she made these names into her charms, she used to imagine that colour surrounded her like open arms. She thought it would protect Gabe too, when he called out to her in the night, crying that there were monsters behind his door. She hadn't realised that some colours are too bright and too strong. *Vermillion, Red Madder, Azure.*

She'd found her old paints in the shed when she went up there again to look for an old tennis ball for Custard. She'd hurled them in there after her last failed attempt when George was away. She opened the box there in the garden, her eyes sucking in the bright squares and misshapen tubes, the smeared bottles and the stiff brushes put away unwashed.

She picked roses again, the last ones on the bush, and put them in the jug on the kitchen table. She painted all day, past lunchtime and into the early evening. The roses became trees with pink and gold leaves touching a storm grey sky and roots that knifed deep. into dark and rocky ground.

Gabe didn't comment when he came in, but Keely picked the painting up and took it over to the window when she called in again to try to entice Custard back home to Heronmarsh. Custard refused to move from his basket, as usual. Keely's been back twice since, but they both know Custard belongs to Sophia now.

Gabe seems to like Keely dropping in. The other day, Sophia heard them both laughing and she stopped to listen, as transported as she had been by Gabe's first words.

She is drying her brushes when George arrives. He is looking

221

sombre, and she expects bad news. Surely he doesn't want to come back, it's far too late for that now.

Last night's passion has left the memory of warm hand prints on her body, and this morning she is moving about the kitchen with sweet, stiff pleasure. She can smell Jez's cologne on her own neck.

"Get down you bloody thing!" George is pushing ineffectually at Custard, who is bouncing on his strong back legs and nosing George's trouser pocket.

"Down, Custard."

The dog slinks away to his basket, and lies down with his paws on his nose. Sophia is always surprised that he finds some authority in her.

"I don't know why you're keeping that bloody dog." George is brushing hair from his trousers.

"I like him. So does Gabe, actually."

George needn't think he can carry on telling her what to do.

"Well what about the cat?"

"She's indifferent. What's the matter George? You look upset."

He sits on the edge of the kitchen table, pushing her painting aside without looking at it, and kicks a rubber ball towards Custard who watches it roll by his nose.

"I saw Amelia as I was coming in, and I wanted to hit the wretched woman. She caused so much trouble. She actually waved to me, as if nothing had happened."

"Well, it was Brendan's fault, too. Anyway, I thought it was all sorted out now. Hasn't he promised to safeguard the site, and repair the all damage?"

George is kicking the table leg.

"Leena's grandmother's had a stroke, and it's touch and go. Leena's over at the hospital now, she thinks it's all the stress."

"Oh dear."

Something about his dejected posture irritates her.

"Leena's really upset. I've never, ever seen her like this before."

"I expect she is. Why wouldn't she be upset? Coffee?"

222

"Yes, please. I don't know what to do."

Sophia looks at him over her shoulder as she fills the kettle.

"You don't like women collapsing, do you George? We're supposed to be strong."

"Well, no, I suppose it makes me feel…" He is looking uncomfortable.

"Annoyed?"

She puts biscuits and sugar on the table, pushing them into the middle, away from Custard's dark eyes.

"Yes. Is that really awful?"

"Not really, it's hardly surprising. Your mother was always so feeble, she treated you like a husband. We could never go on holiday for longer than a fortnight in case she had a crisis, remember? You had to phone her every single night no matter where we were, or how inconvenient it was."

Sophia is surprised at herself. She seems to be able to say things to George now that she's only ever said to Phyll before.

George sighs. "I hated it. What are you doing with chocolate biscuits and sugar lumps? I thought you didn't buy them."

"Phyll was complaining and…I don't know. It doesn't seem to matter much any more. Have some."

"No thanks." George is patting his stomach. "I'm trying to get fit. Sleepless nights on the horizon."

"Rather you than me."

She smiles at him in case he thinks she sounds bitter, and pours out the coffee.   George is looking beyond her at the garden, big and restless and embarrassed.

"I'll do that fence for you at the weekend, Soph. I left it too long."

"You'll be a good dad. You are a good dad. I saw the rose you left for Grace."

He looks at her anxiously.

"It's *all right,* George. You don't have to be strong all the time. Your mother expected you to be Hercules, it wasn't fair of her."

"I suppose *your* mother thinks I'm a complete bastard now, leaving you like this?"

"I haven't told her yet, but I am going to have to do it soon. Gabe says he's going to tell her himself if I put it off much longer. He says he doesn't want any more secrets hanging around in this family. I can understand that, the last one nearly killed him."

"Do you want me to talk to her?"

"No. I want to make sure she understands that I'm not a victim in all of this. I want her to know that we're all just moving on with our lives. We're seizing the time, going with the flow. Not that she'll understand that, my mother doesn't believe in flow. She believes in…what's the opposite of flow?

George ponders. "Stagnation? Constipation? Stoppage? Blockage?"

They are both laughing when Gabe comes downstairs barefoot, and sits down next to George on the kitchen table. Custard rolls over on his back and waves his paws in the air, and Gabe rubs his pink, hairy belly with his toes.

Gabe raises an eyebrow. "Such hilarity in a poor broken home."

George looks over at Sophia but she shakes her head and says firmly: "Actually, this home isn't broken, Gabe. It's mended."